Jolene's Justice

Nighthawk Search and Rescue

Book 7

Amanda Zook

For more
information, address: amandazook@amandazook.com

First paperback edition September 2023

Cover design by Kari March Designs

Edited by Beth Lawton, VB Edits

http://www.amandazook.com

JOLENE'S JUSTICE

Contents

Warning: This book contains scenes of domestic violence against men.

Like most men, Finch kept his experiences with a past relationship hidden. The following are statistics about men in abusive relationships from The National Coalition Against Domestic Violence

- 11 per cent of men abused by female partners try to kill themselves, compared with 7.2 per cent of women who are abused by male partners.

- 1 in 4 men have been physically abused (slapped, pushed, shoved) by an intimate partner.

- 1 in 7 men have been severely physically abused (hit with a fist or hard object, kicked, slammed against something, choked, burned, etc.) by an intimate partner at some point in their lifetime.

- Nearly 1 in 10 men in the United States has experienced rape, physical violence, and/or stalking by an intimate partner and reported at least one measured impact related to experiencing these or other forms of violent behavior in the relationship (e.g., being fearful, concerned for safety, post-traumatic stress disorder (PTSD)

  symptoms, need for healthcare, injury, contacting a crisis hotline, need for housing services, need for victim's advocate services, need for legal services, missed at least one day of work or school).

- 1 in 18 men are severely injured by intimate partners in their lifetimes.

- Male rape victims and male victims of non-contact unwanted sexual experiences reported predominantly male perpetrators. Nearly half of stalking victimizations against males were also perpetrated by males. Perpetrators of other forms of violence against males were mostly female.

- From 1994 to 2011, the rate of serious violence (rape, sexual assault, robbery and aggravated assault) committed by an intimate partner declined 64% for males.

- During the most recent 10-year period (2002-11) for which data is available, nonfatal serious violence accounted for more than a third of intimate partner violence against males (39 percent).

- 13.4% of male high school students report being physically or sexually abused by a dating partner.

- 48.8% of men have experienced at least one psychologically aggressive behavior (being kept track of by demanding to know his whereabouts, insulted or humiliated, or felt threatened by partner's actions) by an intimate partner in their lifetime.

- 4 in 10 men have experienced at least one form of coercive control (isolation from friends and family, manipulation, blackmail, deprivation of liberty, threats, economic control and exploitation) by an intimate partner in their lifetime.

- Approximately 1 in 71 men in the United States reported being raped in his lifetime, which translates to almost 1.6 million men in the United States.

- 8% of men have experienced sexual violence other than rape (forced to penetrate someone, sexual coercion, unwanted sexual contact, and non-contact unwanted sexual experiences) by an intimate partner at some point in their lifetime.

- 1 out of every 19 U.S. men have been stalked in their lifetime to the extent that they felt very fearful or believed that they or someone close to them would be harmed or killed.

- Among male stalking victims, almost half (44.3%) reported being stalked by only male perpetrators while a similar proportion (46 .7%) reported being stalked by only female perpetrators. About 1 in 18 male stalking victims (5.5%) reported having been stalked by both male and female perpetrators in their life.

- 1 in 20 (5%) of male murder victims are killed by intimate partners.

- Between 1980 and 2008, in cases in which the victim/offender relationships were known, 7 .1% of men were killed by an intimate.

- The percentage of males killed by an intimate fell from 10.4% in 1980 to 4.9% in 2008, a 53% drop.

Domestic violence—whether against women or men—often goes unreported. Men in particular may decide not to report violence by an intimate partner to law enforcement for fear of being labeled the instigator or not believed. No instance of domestic violence is justified. Whether you're male or female, it's never your fault. If you are dealing with domestic violence, call the National Domestic Violence Hotline at **800-799-SAFE (7233)**.

If you or someone you know are dealing with issues stemming from toxic or abusive relationships, talking to a therapist can make a big difference in how you feel. Abuse in any form should not be tolerated, but therapy and reaching out to your support network can help you recognize this and develop an exit plan.

National Domestic
Violence Hotline
1-800-799-SAFE
(7233)
TTY 1-800-787-3224
Text
"START" to 88788

AMANDA ZOOK

Domestic Violence Support | The National Domestic Violence Hotline (thehotline.org)

Chapter 1

10 Years Ago

"**M**ARRIED!" JOLENE PRITCHETT'S VOICE was loud and full of confusion as she shouted, trying to make sense of the word. "Married?" With a focused look, she bore a hole into the man using the same steely gaze she employed in her kitchen. The man who was supposed to be her whole world.

But the real world was a bitch. And reality was her consort.

A harsh reality confronted her, like a bitch slap to the face. She could feel the foundation of her beliefs splintering under the weight of betrayal and a pair of sharp blue eyes.

The restaurant's kitchen had gone deathly quiet, the smells of freshly cooked food replaced by a heavy, almost oppressive atmosphere. The only sounds were the hiss of the frying pans, the whir of the dishwasher's spray arm, the roiling bubbles of the boiling pots, and the sizzle of meat that needed attention before it overcooked. They were the usual sounds of a professional kitchen that never failed to put a smile on her face. But now, an eerie stillness replaced the usual hustle and bustle of seven o'clock on a Thursday night.

It was as if she was deaf to it. The only noise that filled her ears was the roaring of her heart. A white noise that muted everything around her. Her head swam, and she steadied herself by placing her hand on the cool, metallic surface of the counter.

Her gaze bounced back and forth between the two people standing in front of her, their voices echoing in the stillness of the room. The woman smiled smugly in her Elie Tahari belted minidress. The Pepto Bismol pink sateen stood out harshly against the chrome and steel colors of Jolene's kitchen. As if to taunt her, the diamond on her left hand shone brightly under the bright lights. The jewels around her neck and in her ears jingled with every movement, the facets of the expensive stones glittering. The woman looked like she'd stepped out of the pages of the Saks Fifth Avenue catalog and probably shouldn't be so close to the sizzling food. Jolene hated her on sight.

The man next to her was just as refined in the bespoke suit she'd once found so appealing on him. His blue Prince of Wales ZEGNA wool suit was as equally out of place among the typical attire of white chef's coats and black server's uniforms.

Jolene's coat was a vibrant eggplant color, with sleek black piping and buttons. It went perfectly with her red hair and made her stand out as the head chef. It was her hair that the man in front of her always said attracted him to her first.

Jolene had met Harrison Walker Winston III—yes, that's how he always introduced himself—while in culinary school in Chicago. The Kendall College School of Culinary Arts had been a dream, and she'd been ecstatic to be attending. Just before graduation, Jolene and her friends had been letting off some steam at a bar in downtown Chicago. Harrison, who lived in New York City, had been attending meetings in the area and ended up at the same bar with his coworkers.

He eventually revealed that he had only asked her to dance because of her hair. He'd found himself drawn to her because of it. After dating intermittently for over a year, Jolene accepted the chance to move to NYC to begin her chef career and be in the same city as Harrison.

Noitiña, her NYC restaurant, had been Jolene's dream. As a child, she'd watched her parents work tirelessly in their neighborhood pub, the Dafty Neighbor. People from all over Chattooga County came to their pub to taste a bit of Scotland in small town Georgia. Gorden Pritchett emigrated to the US when he was a boy but never forgot his Scottish roots. The menu had the usual pub fare, but the Scottish dishes quickly became favorites. Jolene's father's mince and tatties dinner was one of the most requested meals. The ground beef and potatoes dish, a favorite in Scotland, was the perfect way to soothe the soul with its warm, inviting flavors.

Noitiña, Gaelic for dusk, had been born from Jolene's love and respect for her parents. She'd taken Gorden's old favorite Scottish recipes and given them a high cuisine twist. After a year, Noitiña had earned the highly coveted three-star rating in the Michelin Guide. It went on from there.

She owed her success to Harrison. Having fallen fast and hard for him, she'd trusted him with her body. How could she not trust him with her dream? Together, they'd opened the restaurant. She, as the talented chef. He, as the money. It was an agreement that had worked well for years.

The sudden loss of stability now as the rug was yanked out from under her was tremendous. Dizziness swamped her as she internally windmilled her arms to regain a stable footing. She felt a crushing pain in her chest, like a vise was squeezing her heart. A single word reverberated in her mind like a relentless torment.

Married.

The man she'd intended to spend the rest of her life with already had his forever. The man who was supposed to be her soulmate already had a perfect partner. And Jolene could feel the weight of her gaze, like daggers stabbing her from across the kitchen. Her *husband*—she could hardly believe that fact—stood next to her and shrugged.

Shrugged!

He'd lied to her. Five years of her life. Wasted.

Oh God! She was the other woman!

A weight dropped in her stomach that was as heavy as a stone. It churned, and a sour taste filled her mouth. The plummeting stone shattered into bile, thick and acidic. It roiled. A deep, burning sensation rose up in her gut. Jolene swallowed thickly, her throat burning with the taste of stomach acid.

She studied the man she'd trusted with everything. She searched his eyes, looking for the truth and praying this was all an elaborate joke. His dazzling blue eyes were now icy with indifference. His expression was wooden and emotionless.

His wife, however, wore an expression of smug, righteous superiority. Paris Winston sneered at Jolene with a condescending countenance. It was hard enough to stand her ground under the wife's condemnation—she hadn't knowingly done anything wrong, after all—but the venom that shot out of her mouth hit Jolene like a whip. Flaying her open until she had nothing left.

"My husband no longer has any use for his whore. Your time in his bed is over."

Chapter 2

Present Day

JOLENE COULDN'T BELIEVE SHE'D agreed to this. She must have been out of her mind. Truthfully, she hadn't been in her right mind. Between the shit going on at the bar, the stupid wrong number texts that kept spamming her phone, and the call about her father, she'd felt out of control. It was a feeling she hadn't had since Harrison's infidelity came to light.

She'd lost a lot that day. She refused to lose again.

But right now, she needed to focus on her father. Which meant putting up with Finch, another jackass liar. *Why did she always attract them?*

Her acceptance of his offer to fly her home came at a moment of weakness. Not being able to find a flight until the next day only made things worse. She needed to get to her father as quickly as possible. But why did it have to be *him*?

He'd been a perfect gentleman since he'd picked her up, just like always. He'd lugged her suitcase for her. He'd opened the door for her and had lent her a hand as she climbed in and out of his truck. All the tasks were carried out with a wide smile on his face. Finch was polite and well-mannered in every aspect of his life, except when it came to being honest about his own backstory.

But Jolene could see a hint of trepidation in his eyes as he helped her climb into the helicopter. An uncomfortable wariness had become a common theme in their relationship since she'd discovered the truth. Every day since that terrible night, their relationship had been filled with awkward silences and a lingering bitterness, mostly from her. When they were in the same room, the space was always filled with an uneasy silence, occasionally broken by stilted conversation. Not the easy rapport they had once shared.

She put on a facade of civility when their friends were around, despite the caustic animosity she felt that lay beneath. She kept her distance from him, managing to keep her resentment under control for the sake of their friends.

It was a different matter when they were alone, which she tried to avoid at all costs. She wasn't about to give him the opportunity to spew lies. Been there. Done that. Lost everything as a result.

The memory of the despair she felt when she'd discovered the extent of Harrison's lies and had lost everything as a result still haunted her. She wasn't about to put herself through that again. It was better . . . safer . . . to avoid.

Keeping her distance from Finch had been an act of self-preservation. She didn't trust easily, especially after Harrison. She had grown skeptical, and she guarded her heart closely. Finch had broken through her barriers with his charm and wit. She had been so close to being completely consumed by him until she'd learned the truth. With the harsh reality uncovered, she'd locked herself down tight and vowed she would never let another man in again.

She had to find a way to make the most of the difficult circumstance she was currently in. She needed Finch. He was her only hope to get to her father quickly. The call she'd received only a few hours ago had sent her into a whirlwind of emotions. Her father was in serious condition in the hospital after suffering a heart attack.

Since her mother had died eight years ago, her father lived alone. If it hadn't been for the neighbor . . . Jolene couldn't bear to imagine the awful scenarios that could have taken place.

The stubborn old goat refused to give up his house, which was in serious need of repairs and far too big for one person. The pub was another issue. He should have either sold it or found someone else to manage it when her mother died. But he argued that he could never watch strangers run the pub he'd put his blood, sweat, and Scottish stoicism into.

Gorden was a force to be reckoned with. He had a strength and determination that was undeniable.

But he wasn't getting any younger, and he sucked at the day-to-day stuff that came with owning a house. He had been poking around the weathered boards on his porch—handyman work was not his forte—when the heart attack occurred. The woman who lived next door had spotted him and called 911.

Jolene had no idea how serious his condition was, which was why she'd reluctantly agreed to allow Finch to fly her down to Georgia. It was the fastest way, and she wanted to be with her father just in case the worst happened.

Being confined inside a cockpit with the man who made her blood boil was not ideal. Yet she was grateful for the offer. His kindness was incongruous with what she knew about him. She couldn't reconcile the lies she'd uncovered with the incessant thoughtfulness he showed. The confusion made her uneasy, and she felt it was best to keep her distance.

She watched from her seat inside the helicopter as Finch carried out his preflight checks. His dedication was apparent as he conducted his last inspection of the aircraft, and Jolene couldn't help but admire his attention to detail. It was reassuring to know that he was taking their safety seriously.

A strong gust of wind blew through, tousling his hair. His short red curls were usually unkempt, a feature she had once found endearing. She was partial to a redheaded man. Finch's hair had a burnished copper hue that gleamed in the sun. Her own hair was more of a vivacious red, with subtle hints of gold. She and Finch together would have made beautiful redheaded babies.

Shit. Where had that thought come from? She needed to lock that way of thinking down quick. No matter how much she wanted to push his tousled curls off his forehead, she had to remember he wasn't the man she thought he was.

Still, she couldn't keep her eyes off him. When he made it to her side of the aircraft, he glanced up and caught her watching him. His hazel eyes that had once shone so brightly had lost some of their luster since she'd learned the truth. As did his smile. She felt a twinge of guilt, but then reminded herself that it was he who had been dishonest. Not her. The reminder caused her to blink and turn away from his gaze.

A chime on her phone drew her attention. She peered at the display, trying to make sense of the strange text message she had just received. She couldn't believe how many strange texts she was receiving from this wrong number.

THINK YOU'VE WON? THINK AGAIN.

The texts seemed a little strange, and she couldn't quite put her finger on why. There was a strange undercurrent to the texts that gave her pause. She shook her head, trying to clear her mind of the latest unusual message, and focused on her mental to-do list. Even though she had many concerns threatening to swamp her, she tried to push them aside and concentrate on the immediate problem. There were questions she had for her father's doctors. His condition was the top priority, and she couldn't help but worry about it.

A few minutes later, Finch climbed into his seat beside her. "Ready to go?" he asked. She nodded, unable to find her voice. Her usual banter had been replaced by awkward silences when she was around him. She was afraid of the venomous words that would spew out if she were to lose control. So she often said nothing at all, until her silence became a heavy presence in the room. Or, in this case, the cockpit.

Finch's hands moved swiftly as he flipped switches that created a symphony of clicks and hums without her knowing what they did. "Let's get this bird in the air," he said as the beast rumbled to life and the rotors overhead began to spin, the vibration shaking the seat beneath her.

He grabbed a headset that hung over his shoulder and put it on while pointing to the one on her side. She adjusted the thing over her head, and his voice came through like a subtle seduction caressing her ear. She loathed the way it still caused her skin to tingle with anticipation. "Can you hear me?"

"Yes," she answered, a slight tremor in her voice. She didn't mind flying. Usually, she was indifferent to it. But this was different. There wasn't much between her and the ground, which was steadily growing farther away as they rose into the air. In an airplane, she could ignore the fact that she was thousands of feet above ground. Especially since she couldn't see it from her preferred aisle seat.

"This isn't the Nighthawk's helicopter," she remarked, having expected to take the search and rescue group's helicopter, which was about twice the size of this one.

"No, it's not."

"Whose is it?"

"Mine."

His answer caught her off guard, and she snapped her head to look at him. It shocked her to discover he'd finally bought his own. He'd talked about it all the time. He'd been searching for a helicopter he could bring back to life and make his own. Jolene remembered the way his voice had risen with enthusiasm as he discussed his plans. It had been a dream of his for years.

Jolene felt a twinge of regret that she'd missed out on seeing that dream come to fruition.

"Oh. Is it new?" She looked around the cockpit. The four seats, two in front, two in back, were covered in a soft, buttery tan leather. The carpets on the floor were identical in color, the texture soft and plush and appeared brand new. The tan interior was punctuated by the bright, illuminated instrument panel. All the switches, dials, display screens, and other doohickeys she didn't know the names of gleamed as if new. She could detect a subtle yet distinctive new-car smell lingering in the air.

"I restored it. I had a lot of extra time on my hands over the last year."

"Oh." It was all she could manage to say. While she'd thrown herself into her bar, he'd apparently thrown himself into restoring a helicopter. To each their own.

Jolene's voice stammered as she searched for the right words to express her thoughts, and they came out of her mouth in halting syllables. "Well, congratulations. It's nice. I like the exterior color." The inanity of the statements made her cringe, even if it was true. The helicopter was a stunning Nordic blue, reminiscent of Finch's eyes in a certain light.

"Thank you. I'm glad you finally got to see it." Jolene brushed off the dig and turned her attention to the patchwork of farmland below, visible through the window.

They'd connected through their shared friends, and their chemistry had been palpable. Once Natalie, Jolene's best friend, had reunited with her high school crush, the men he worked with at his search and rescue training facility made Jolene's bar their go-to spot for post-training and post-mission meetups. Finch was a regular with the group, as he was Nighthawk Search and Rescue's pilot. He and the others were often heard talking about their latest mission at her bar.

But it was the times when he came in alone and the room filled with the warmth of his presence that she had truly enjoyed. They'd been on the brink of something special. Until she'd discovered the truth, and everything she'd thought she knew imploded.

"Did it need a lot of work?" she asked, attempting to ignore the knot in her stomach. She could do this. She was capable of having a straightforward conversation with him. They had been friends first. If she pushed the hurt deep down inside, she could go back to being his friend. *Right?*

"Not too long. Somewhere around eight months."

"Well, it's beautiful." She didn't know much about helicopters, but the construction of this one impressed her. She couldn't help but be in awe of the gleaming metal and bright paint job. "Do you think you'll use it for any of your Nighthawk missions?"

He shrugged. "Maybe. But probably more as a transport. Compared to the Twin Huey that Nighthawk uses, this isn't a powerhouse in terms of its SAR capabilities."

"That makes sense." Jolene searched her mind for something more to say but came up blank. She settled in for a long trip.

They stopped once to refuel and were back in the air in no time at all. Her thoughts shifted to her father, worried about his condition. Her mind whirred with too many thoughts. Like what would happen when he was released. Would he need to go to a separate facility? Would he need special equipment or a home health care worker if he was sent home? What would happen to the pub? The issues at her own bar were piling up, and she couldn't imagine having to tackle another one on top of it.

The rustling of plastic broke through her spiraling thoughts. Jolene glanced over to see Finch had opened a bag of gummy worms and was in the process of biting one in half.

"What are you? Five?" she teased.

Chapter 3

FINCH FROZE, A GUMMY worm hanging from his fingers halfway to his mouth. He'd heard those words countless times, but this time, they were spoken in a different, unfamiliar tone. But all he could hear was *her* in his head.

"What are you? Five? You are such a child," Angelica sneered. *"Why do I put up with you eating that crap? Grow up and be a man, for fuck's sake."*

"I like gummy worms. There's nothing wrong with eating what you like." He tried defending himself. He always *tried to defend himself. Often to no avail. She never wanted to hear his opinion. Hers was the only one that mattered in their relationship.*

"It's wrong if I say it's wrong," she bit out, smacking the bag of snacks out of his hand. A burst of colors flew out of the bag as the worms shot across the floor. She huffed in exasperation at the mess. "Now look what you did."

Typical Angelica. She never accepted the blame for anything. It was always his fault. Dinner went cold because she was texting a friend and hadn't bothered to let him know it was ready . . . his fault for not coming to the table quick enough.

He bent to pick up the mess, but she wasn't done with today's tirade. "God, you are useless. Can you do anything right? You are always making such a mess for me to clean up." He wanted to point out that he was the one cleaning up the mess but knew that would do no good. He was always the one to tackle the mess left behind after one of her outbursts. He worked steadily as she ranted and raved at him. Wearily, he slogged through the cleanup in silence while her voice rose and fell in a relentless stream of complaints. This time, at least, the waves of her anger were comparatively mild.

Jolene's faraway voice roused him from his musings. He glanced at her and saw her studying him with a questioning, furrowed brow. He was so deep in his thoughts he hadn't even registered that she had asked him something. "I'm sorry. What?" he asked, trying to push away the echoes of the memory that still lingered in his mind.

"Can I have one?" she repeated.

He stared at her in disbelief. "You want a gummy worm?"

"I'm partial to the bear variety of gummy, but in this case, I'll settle for a worm."

Jolene's smile, one he hadn't seen directed at him in a very long time, was a balm on his soul. He wanted to clutch his chest where he felt a pounding against his rib cage. It was like her smile had jump-started his heart. It had felt dead for so long that its revival was almost painful.

He shook off his asinine thoughts and held the bag out to her. She grabbed a red and yellow one and bit it perfectly in half until only the red end was left. "I don't know why I always ate them like this. Guess I felt the need to separate the colors."

He smiled at her musings. "I did the same thing."

"Did you do it to two of them and try to stick the remaining ends together to make a new color combination?"

He stared, slack-jawed. It was something that Angelica had constantly ridiculed him for, but Jolene was attempting to do just that with the red and a green halves. He cleared his throat, trying to compose himself, and then said, "Yeah. All the time."

"Look. Christmas," she said, holding up the newly formed gummy worm. Her playful smile was so infectious he couldn't help but return it. Her eyes twinkled with amusement, and when the two halves fell apart, the sound of her laughter was enough to make his heart skip a beat.

She popped the two pieces into her mouth and chewed. "As a chef, I really shouldn't be enjoying this snack so much."

"A little indulgence never hurt anybody." She sent him another smile, and the sight of it was so captivating its radiance washed over him.

"I guess," she acknowledged. "I still enjoy gummy bears more, though."

"But you get more gummy in a worm."

"But you get more bears in a bag," she countered.

"Guess it equals out then."

Her lips curved into a half smile as she softly replied, "Guess so."

The sharp, unexpected movement of the helicopter lurching caused her to jump in surprise and drew his attention back to his instrument panel. Beside him, Jolene drew in a sharp breath, and her hand flew to his arm. Her fingernails pressed into his skin as her grip tightened.

"It's okay," he calmly stated. "Just turbulence. We're heading into a storm."

"A storm?" she asked, her voice slightly quivering in uncertainty. "Isn't that dangerous?"

"Don't worry. I've got this. I've flown in much worse conditions." The cockpit darkened as they converged on the storm. He'd checked the weather radar when they'd stopped for fuel and noticed the storm cells. He was hoping to beat them to their destination, but it appeared they'd moved faster than anticipated. Still, they didn't have much farther to go, and he had flown in worse conditions. It was simpler to fly through a few gusts of wind and drops of rain than through an artillery barrage and bullets. War was thunderous, while the sound of wind and rain brought a feeling of serenity.

The cockpit was briefly illuminated by lightning as huge gusts of wind buffeted them. Finch expertly maneuvered them through the storm until all hell broke loose. With a sudden yaw to the right, the cockpit filled with the glow of a warning light. The aircraft shuddered as he lost tail rotor control. The control pedals were completely unresponsive.

"What's that?" Jolene asked in a frantic, high-pitched voice.

Finch immediately put the helicopter into autorotation, cutting power to the main rotor. With a heavy sigh, he slowly decreased the airspeed to perform an engine-off landing. Through the darkness caused by the storm, the soft glow of their intended landing strip lay ahead, manned by a buddy of his.

"Make sure your seat belt is fastened," he ordered. "I've lost tail rotor control." The fear in her gasp resonated within him, but he kept his face expressionless. "We're landing just ahead. I've got this, but it's going to get a little rough." As if to punctuate his words, another strong gust of wind rattled them.

"Are we gonna crash?"

His voice was steady and reassuring as her panic seemed to grow like a palpable presence. "No, Jolie." He tried for a gentle tone as he used the pet name he'd once given her. "Trust me, okay? We're gonna be fine."

He took a moment to contact his friend, announcing his emergency just in case the landing didn't go as he planned. He was well versed in emergency procedures, yet Jolene's presence made it more nerve-racking. She was precious cargo.

Her hands were shaking as he glanced to at her and he wished he was able to give her some comfort, but both of his hands were needed to manage their descent.

"We're almost there," he said, his teeth clenched as the wind pushed back. His grip was so tight that his knuckles turned starkly pale as he clamped down on the cyclic.

As they lined up with the runway, he made the necessary adjustments with precision to land them safely.

Beside him, Jolene's body tensed, and he could hear her panicked breathing, despising the fact that he had put her in this position.

With a bone-jarring jolt, they were down. Finch spun around to Jolene, his eyes quickly sweeping over her as he searched for any injuries. "Jolie, are you okay?"

Her head moved in a slow nod, but her body stayed still and tense. He fumbled with the buckle of his seat belt before unclasping it and pushing open his door. His buddy had just reached them, but Finch paid him no mind as he rushed to Jolene's side. The scent of rain still lingered in the air, mixed with the distant rumble of thunder as he yanked open her door.

Her hands were clamped so tightly over the edge of her seat that her knuckles had gone a stark white, and she sat there rigidly. Her grip on the leather was so tight that the crescent-shaped imprints of her nails were sure to stay. He reached across her and unlatched her belt, then cupped her face in his hands, turning her to look at him. "Jolie. You're okay. We're safe." As he spoke in a gentle voice, her eyes remained unfo-cused.

"Jolie," he said, his voice ragged with emotion, "please look at me."

She blinked slowly as he watched her regain her presence of mind. "Finch? Did we make it?" The tremor in her voice just about killed him.

A small lopsided smile tugged at the corners of his mouth. "Yeah. We're good. How about we get you out of the helo?"

"Okay," she said, far too docilely for his liking.

He gently removed her hands from her white-knuckled grip on her seat, then helped her swing her long legs out of the helicopter door. With an arm wrapped around her waist, he held her steady as she climbed down. She was a bit wobbly, but he held her up as they walked toward the small hangar building. His friend followed them through the door.

"Hey, Matt," Finch finally greeted. "Thanks for this."

"No problem. What happened, Bro?"

That was the question of the day, wasn't it? What did happen? He'd done a thorough check before take-off. Everything was in order; there were no signs of anything out of the ordinary. He wouldn't have dared put Jolene in danger like that if he felt any of the parts on his helicopter were damaged.

"Think it was the storm?"

"I don't know. The wind was pretty strong, but I'm not convinced that's what damaged the tail rotor."

"Want me to check her over?" Finch had served with Matt Blankenship and knew his ability to repair and diagnose aircraft mechanics was unparalleled.

"That'd be great. Thanks." He turned to Jolene, intending to introduce her to his friend. She swayed slightly, and he was quick to react, his arm still securely around her to keep her steady. "Jolene," he said softly. "This is my buddy, Matt. Matt, Jolene."

Matt held out his hand, and Jolene hesitated until a gentle squeeze of encouragement from Finch had her placing her hand in his. Matt smiled as he said, "Nice to meet you," and shook her hand gently.

Jolene's voice strengthened as she apologized. "I'm sorry. I'm not quite myself at the moment."

"Understandable."

"Why don't you have a seat?" Finch suggested. "I need to see to the helo, but I'll be back as quickly as I can. Matt can keep you company."

Matt held out a bottle of water to Jolene and indicated a chair next to a long metal table. "Absolutely. Go take care of your bird."

Since she was unsteady, Finch was hesitant to leave. He crouched down in front of where she sat and cupped her cheek. "You okay?"

She inhaled deeply, leaned into his palm, and smiled. "I'm good. I'm okay. Just a little shaky, but it will pass."

"Are you sure?"

"Yeah. Go take care of what you need to do. I'll be fine."

Unable to resist, he kissed her on the forehead, hearing her sharp intake of breath and feeling her tense beneath his touch. His lips lingered for a moment before he released her and stepped away, wishing he could kiss her more intimately.

Chapter 4

JOLENE DIDN'T LIKE THE feelings ricocheting through her. Her legs felt like rubber, a remnant from their close call. The adrenaline dump was a tangible thing as it slowly seeped from her body. It left her jittery and worn out.

Then there was Finch and the feelings he provoked. The warmth of his lips on her skin lingered, and she didn't know how to process the confusing mix of emotions.

He'd been amazing during the emergency. So calm and confident. He soothed her with gentle words while effortlessly dealing with the crisis. She knew he was skilled at flying. As a former member of the Air

Force, that was to be expected. And his skills had to be top-notch to work for the Nighthawks. She imagined there weren't many people with the skills to fly the way he did to save lives. It was incredible to think of the expertise needed to navigate a helicopter with precision in any kind of weather and terrain while making sure those on board were safe.

Throw in a malfunction, and his skills were even more astonishing. But it was the way he took care of her during and after the emergency that left her in a state of confusion. The sound of his voice, full of compassion and worry for her. The feel of his hands, gentle and comforting, as he supported her wobbly weight. His kiss . . . *Gah!* She had to stop letting him chip away at her defenses, making her feel vulnerable. She couldn't let herself be lulled into a sense of security by him . . . not again.

She closed her eyes, wishing things could be different.

Her eyes shot open. *No!* She would not allow herself to weaken. Fool her once and all. Harrison's lies had been bad enough. But Finch's . . . she hadn't seen coming.

She needed to focus on her reason for being here. Her father needed her. That was all that mattered. Finch and her pitiful, broken heart could go fly off a cliff.

While she waited, she made small talk with Finch's friend. She'd learned they'd served together. Matt had worked on the aircraft that Finch had flown.

"Maybe we should have waited for the storm to pass," Jolene mused, thinking that was what had caused the damage.

"Nah. That tiny storm wouldn't have stopped Finch. He was always the one who took on the riskier missions," Matt said. "It was like the more dangerous, the better. I always wondered what drove him to do that. Some days, I worried he had a death wish. But he always came back. Mission success."

"Hmm" was the only response she could give. She didn't know much about how his missions with the Nighthawks went. Did he still have that death wish? She hadn't heard the guys telling any crazy stories about him. Maybe he'd grown out of that daredevil mentality. Or was there more to it than she was seeing?

Ugh. Why did she care? She shouldn't. She didn't! She wanted to insist that she didn't care, but her wayward heart refused to let go completely. Her mind tried to deny it, but her heart was still heavy with longing. And it pissed her off.

"So he was a bit of a daredevil?"

"You could say that. Especially when we were back home. There were days he'd storm onto base looking for a challenge. I have no idea what lit the fuse on those days. He was one of the few pilots with a girl at home. His life seemed perfect." Matt's expression shifted. His smile disappeared and his brow creased, as if deep in thought. "But that one time I saw him with Angelica—"

"Ready to go?" Finch asked, interrupting what Matt was about to reveal. Jolene's heart was in her throat. Matt had inadvertently given her more information than she'd ever allowed Finch to provide her with.

That name again. She could still hear the weariness in Finch's voice when he spoke the name.

"Sure," she answered, rising on her still wobbly legs. Finch was by her side in an instant, placing a steadying hand on her arm.

"You okay?" he asked. The concern in his expression caused a confusing mix of warmth and anger.

She pulled away from him under the guise of throwing her water bottle into the trash can. "I'm fine," she muttered as the bottle hit the bottom of the can with a clang.

She turned just in time to see Finch mask a hurt expression. A sudden stab of guilt hit her for causing his pain but she quickly buried the emotion deep down. She had nothing to feel guilty about. She'd do well to remember that.

Finch thanked Matt as she made her way to the door, but then halted in her tracks when a realization hit her. "Um . . . Finch?" He turned to face her with a questioning brow. "How am I gonna get to the hospital?" In her haste, she had completely overlooked the issue of transportation. The airfield was tiny, and the only thing that could be seen was the vast openness of the land, without any car rental counters.

Finch grinned and held up a set of keys. "*We* are going to drive the car I rented." Jolene noticed the emphasis he'd placed on the first word, and it sent a ripple of stress through her. He couldn't seriously be thinking of accompanying her.

"Okay . . . um . . ." She racked her brain to try to figure a way out of this situation. "Well, if you can drop me off at the hospital, I'd appreciate it." She could call an Uber when she was ready to leave.

"I'm not going to leave you alone to deal with this, Jolene."

"No, really. I'll be okay. You don't need to come with me."

"Sorry. No can do. I promised Natalie."

"What?"

"Natalie made me swear that I wouldn't leave you alone. It was an easy vow to make, since I was gonna stick to your side like glue."

She couldn't believe this. This man couldn't stay with her. She didn't want him to. She'd managed to avoid most interactions with him for nearly a year. Just long enough for her to build up her walls. She was aware that spending too much time in his presence could cause her walls to start crumbling. There was no way she was taking that chance.

"No," she stated firmly. She crossed the room to where he stood, the keys still dangling from his fingers.

When she tried to snatch them from his hand, he swiftly moved them out of reach. "Yes."

"No." She lifted onto her toes, straining to reach the keys to no avail. She was of average height, but he clearly had the advantage, towering almost a foot above her. Losing her balance, she toppled into him, and he wrapped an arm around her waist, holding her close. She inhaled sharply as the musky scent of him filled her nostrils. A captivating aroma of the freshness of the outdoors and the sweetness of candy.

"Listen. Let's not waste time arguing about this. Let's get to the hospital so you can see your dad."

Jolene stepped out of his arms with an abruptness that left her feeling hollow. She gritted her teeth and willed the despondent feeling to disappear, letting anger take its place. "Fine," she agreed. She could argue about it again later.

She smiled and thanked Matt for his kindness as she stepped through the door, following Finch. The storm had passed, leaving a cool, damp evening in its wake, typical of early spring in northwest Georgia. Finch helped Jolene into the SUV he'd rented, and she noted he'd already transferred their luggage into the back.

Turning on the car, he programmed the address of the hospital into the navigation system, then set off. Jolene watched the trees blur past the window as they drove. The Chattahoochee National Forest stretched out before them, with the Appalachian Mountains rising in the distance. Her little hometown of Sunnyvale was nestled along the Chattooga River, about eighty miles outside of Atlanta.

Growing up in Sunnyvale had been idyllic; the population never exceeded five thousand, the streets were peaceful, and the people knew each other like family. Her ambition to be a big city chef made her leave behind the familiarity and security of home. Thinking of how that had turned out, she wondered if she never should have left. And on the heels of that came the question of why she never returned.

But when her life in New York City had crumbled, the weight of her failure was too much for her to bear among the people who had known her since she was a child. Instead, after spending some time licking her wounds in the house she'd grown up in, she chose to go somewhere unfamiliar, where the only other person she knew was an old acquaintance from college. She didn't regret the move. She loved Lake Haven. It had the same small-town vibe that Sunnyvale did. Most nights, Jolene's Bar was packed with her friends and neighbors, and the room was alive with music and laughter. The atmosphere catered to both families and the singles scene, offering good food and the occasional entertainment for everyone. She was proud of the life she had built there, even though recent events had left her feeling helpless.

A few orders she had sent to her suppliers were nowhere to be found, and upon further investigation, she discovered they had been canceled. That was just the tip of the iceberg of odd occurrences that had left her feeling baffled and frustrated. Fear and uncertainty swirled in her mind as she considered the potential repercussions if she couldn't fix the issues.

She had built strong relationships with most of her suppliers, so they worked together to fix the supply issue. She was grateful for the strong rapports she'd built in her network. Her reputation was well established in the area. But knowing all that didn't ease the anxiety she felt waiting for the other shoe to drop. She just hoped Ox and Nan could handle any complications that might arise while she was caring for her dad. She could always count on her head bartender and head server to have her back. Their loyalty was solid.

Her phone buzzed in her pocket. She pulled it out and checked the notifications. It was another wrong number text. They had been sporadic over the last few weeks. Always worded in a weird, non-threatening manner. This one was a little different.

ARE YOU PROUD OF YOURSELF? EVERYTHING YOU'VE BUILT CAN BE DESTROYED IN AN INSTANT.

She shivered. She hated the texts and tried to block them, figuring they were a wrong number, but they kept coming. Someone was unwavering in their goal of making another's life miserable. She wondered who the sender really meant to send the messages to and what that person had done to piss them off so badly.

She was so lost in her thoughts she almost didn't notice when Finch pulled into the parking lot of the hospital. As he made to get out of the SUV, she knew she had to try one more time to reason with him.

She lightly touched his arm to stop him. Their eyes connected as the last light of day shone in his hazel irises. "Go home, Finch. I'll be okay by myself." The words she spoke had a sharp edge, but they were necessary.

He gently laid his hand on top of hers. "Not going to happen. Aside from the fact that my helo needs repairs and I'm currently grounded, I wouldn't be a very good friend if I left you alone."

"Is that what we are? Friends?" She despised the way her voice sounded fragile and hesitant.

His expression softened as the orange light of the setting sun filled the sky. "I hope I can still count you as one of my friends."

She shifted her gaze away, not knowing how to respond. Her conflicted heart was torn in two. She wanted his friendship, and she didn't. She'd once wished for a lot more, yet she now held herself back from wanting anything.

He uttered, "I know I hurt you," with sorrow in his voice. "I wish you'd let me explain, but I understand your need for distance. Just know that I'll always be here for you in whatever role you need. At this moment, I'm here to be a supportive friend, so let's go find out how your dad is doing."

He was out of the car and hurrying to her side before she could respond. She still wanted to push him away, but the fear and worry overwhelmed her when he assisted her out of the car and she saw the hospital. He may have a point. She may need a friend to get through what lay ahead.

Chapter 5

Finch trailed behind Jolene as she entered the hospital, noticing the rigidness of her shoulders. He was aware that the tension was due to him, and he longed for things to be different. He hated that he'd hurt her. He'd wanted to take something for himself for once and hadn't thought about the ramifications of his actions.

Maybe he was as stupid as Angelica always said he was. Her voice screamed at him in his head, and he'd do anything to get her out of there. All the times she screeched at him. He was worthless. Useless. Immature. She'd call him pathetic, then proceed to list all the reasons she thought he was a poor excuse for a man.

She was appalled by his clothing and complained that she could never be seen in public with someone who dressed so terribly. His hair was too brassy and messy. She'd prefer a man who was more clean-cut with a "normal" hair color, not his garish copper curls. His job was shit, and it was clear to her he didn't care about her at all since he always left her to go fly his "little toys" in someone else's war. He'd earned his bachelor's degree, but that wasn't good enough. She berated him time and time again, questioning why he couldn't have become a doctor like so and so's husband. He was a well-respected man, while Angelica's husband was nothing. A loser.

At the beginning, when she'd exploded on him with harsh words, she'd apologize and plead for his forgiveness. She'd insist she'd only said those things because she loved him so much and she was just trying to help him and their relationship. As the years went on, the apologies became few and far between.

The times when he called her out on her actions, she'd accuse him of being too sensitive. Or she'd state that he'd never been in a real relationship before and didn't know what it was like. He was always left feeling off-center and questioning his own instincts.

Meeting Jolene had been like a breath of fresh air. She'd muzzled the overly critical voice in his head. He could breathe in her presence and not worry that she'd tell him he was doing it wrong. He had a burning desire to erase his past and focus on a brighter future, one that included Jolene at its core.

But then that past came roaring back into his life, ruining everything he'd been building. His stomach churned with regret, knowing that his dishonesty had been partly to blame for the fallout. But he'd honestly never thought it would be a problem. Jolene had stalked off, not wanting to hear a single word of explanation. He had looked for chances over the last year to be alone with her, but no matter what he did, something always got in the way. If he had been any other man, the weight of her rejection may have been too much for him to bear, and he would have given up on being forgiven. But he couldn't do it.

Maybe this situation was fate's way of stepping in, giving him the chance to be alone with her. The time wasn't right, of course. Her dad's health took precedence. But maybe once he was on the road to recovery, he'd get his moment.

His heart pounded with the hope he'd sequestered for over a year. *Please, God, let her open her heart enough to listen.*

As he followed Jolene through the hospital, he took a deep breath, pushing aside his optimistic thoughts in order to concentrate on her and her father's needs.

It struck him that she'd known exactly where she was going as she headed straight for the elevators. "Should we ask for directions to your dad's room?" he asked.

"No need," she replied, hitting the button for level five upon entering the elevator.

They didn't speak as the elevator rose. Finch took the time to study Jolene from head to toe. She stood with her shoulders against the back wall, the heels of her hands pressed into the railing on either side of her. Her chin was down, and she stared at the floor tiles. She was a walking example of how stress could manifest itself in a person's appearance. Her face was drawn and her brow furrowed as she struggled with whatever was going through her head. Her pale skin made her freckles stand out in stark contrast, and her eyes were ringed with shadows.

Looking back, he could recall the signs of stress and anxiety that had been etched in her features for weeks now. She was worried about her father. That was a given. But was there something else? He could imagine owning a restaurant was stressful, but she'd never seemed to struggle with it in the past. Something was weighing heavily on her.

Despite the lines of tension his fingers itched to smooth out, she was still stunning. With her jeans clinging to her curves and her lightweight plum-colored sweater, she had a relaxed yet sophisticated look. He found her brown leather boots, which covered the lower portion of her legs, extremely seductive.

The glimmer of her red hair was the eye-catching accent to her already remarkable beauty. As usual, she'd gathered the long wavy strands into a ponytail. Every time he saw her, he longed to loosen her hair tie and feel the silkiness of her hair as it cascaded around her shoulders. He hadn't gotten the opportunity to delve his fingers into those luscious locks before . . .

He knew it was unlikely he'd ever get to do what he desired, but he couldn't keep his fingers from twitching with anticipation.

The ding of the elevator brought him out of his musings before the doors slid open to an empty floor. Jolene's heels clicked against the floor as she strode toward the nurses' station. He thought she would stop at the desk, but instead, she kept walking, her footsteps echoing in the quiet hall until she reached room 514.

As they approached, he could hear voices from inside the room. "Please, Mr. Pritchett," an exasperated voice pleaded. "You need to follow doctor's orders and stay in bed."

"I've been doing just fine on my own for many years, lass," came the gruff voice of a man with a heavy Scottish accent.

"You've never had a heart attack before," the woman reasoned.

"How bad could it have been? I feel fine."

"That's the pain medication talking, Mr. Pritchett."

"Pfft. Yer bum's oot the windae," Jolene's dad said, his accent so thick Finch had trouble understanding.

He wasn't the only one. "What?" the nurse asked.

Jolene stepped through the door, saying, "He thinks you're talking nonsense."

"There's my bonnie lass." The moment his eyes fell on his daughter, the man's face lit up with pure joy. He shifted in the bed, attempting to sit up straighter, and the nurse quickly approached to help, but he waved her off. It was as if he was determined to project strength and hide any weakness from his daughter. Finch could respect that in a man, but he hated that he would hide things from Jolene.

"Hi, Da," Jolene greeted in a hushed tone, her voice carrying a soft and warm timber that filled the quiet room. She bent to hug her father, squeezing him gently, conscious of all the wires monitoring his heart. Straightening, she asked, "How are you feeling?" As she spoke, she sank into the chair beside his bed and reached out to touch her father's arm. With a nod, the nurse left the room and closed the door behind her. Finch hung back, giving them a little privacy.

As he leaned against the doorframe, Finch studied the man before him. The steady beeping of the heart monitor provided a constant soundtrack, while the sterile scent of hospital antiseptic overwhelmed the faint aroma of flowers on the windowsill. His leg was propped up on a pile of pillows, wrapped in a temporary cast.

"What happened to your leg?" Jolene asked.

"Broken. Fell when the attack happened."

"Da," she replied, the shock evident in her response. From where he stood, he observed Jolene as she scrutinized her father for any other missed injuries.

Jolene's eyes were a mirror image of Mr. Pritchett's, leaving no doubt of their relation. His glimmered with the same jade green light that shone in hers. Despite his age, his hair was still thick and full, though now more silver than red. His complexion may have been pale, but he had a robust and muscular physique. His energy and vitality were reminiscent of his daughter's, who had once been just as lively as he was now.

He couldn't help but notice that she had lost some of her spark recently, and he suspected that she was keeping something to herself. There had to be more she was struggling with than just their falling-out. She was too strong-willed to be brought down by the mistakes of a man. His desire to regain her trust once more may be futile, since he was no longer in her good graces, but he wouldn't give up.

"A'm fine," her father replied.

"Da," Jolene scolded. "You are allowed to feel less than fine. You just had a heart attack. Not to mention the broken leg. Are you in pain?"

"Dinnae fash yersel. Ah've got a gammie heart, but I'm not dying." Translating Mr. Pritchett's words once again proved to be a challenge for Finch.

"I am worried, Da. A heart attack is serious. What does the doctor say?" Jolene placed her hand on his arm, and the sight of it resting there was a small but tender moment. A gesture of comfort and connection. Through that touch alone, Finch could see the deep connection between the pair. Some of the tension left her shoulders when her dad covered her hand with his.

"A'm fine. The doctor wants to keep an eye on me for a few days. A'm a wee bit knackered. Nothing a few days of rest won't cure."

Jolene's skepticism was clear in her voice as she said, "I'll have to hear that from the doctor himself."

"Would I lie to you, my own bairn?"

"Lie? No. Fudge the truth to get your way? Absolutely."

"Haud yer wheesht. You don't know what you're talking about."

Jolene laughed. "If maw taught me anything, it was to never hold my tongue around you. She always called you out on your shit."

"Och, she taught you too well." While the two shared a private moment, Finch recollected that Jolene's mother had died before she arrived in Lake Haven. It was evident from the way they talked about her that they missed her greatly.

Mr. Pritchett's eyes narrowed as he studied his daughter. "Yer looking a bit peely wally. Are you okay?"

"I'm fine, Da. Just worried about you."

As he squinted, focusing intently on his daughter, the corners of his eyes crinkled with a mix of love and concern. His gaze was intense, as if he could see through Jolene's façade and uncover the truth behind her words. Finch straightened from his slouch against the doorframe, hoping Jolene would cave under her father's scrutiny. He wasn't the only one who was worried about her.

His movement drew her dad's attention away from his daughter. "Hullo. Whit's yer name?"

Jolene glanced at him over her shoulder from where she sat. "Da, this is my friend Finch."

"Finch?" Mr. Pritchett echoed with a slight questioning tilt of his head, his eyebrows raised in confusion.

Finch stepped up to his bedside and held out a hand. "Atticus Mobey, sir. It's a pleasure to meet you."

Mr. Pritchett studied him as he shook his hand. A slow smile spread before he said, "Atticus. *To Kill a Mockingbird*. I get it. Very clever."

"My master sergeant thought so," Finch responded.

"Army?"

"Air Force, sir."

"Ma name's Gorden. Gled tae meet ye. An airman, huh? Thank ye for your service."

"You're welcome."

"How do you know my Jolene?"

"He's a Nighthawk," Jolene said, simplifying their relationship for her father.

"One of those rescue guys you told me about?"

"Yeah. He works with Emma." Emma Watterson was one of their newest Nighthawks. Emma and Jolene's paths first crossed in college, but while Jolene honed her culinary skills, Emma opted for a career in the Coast Guard. It was only recently that he and his fellow Nighthawks learned the reason why she'd left the Coast Guard. Her tragic tale took a turn for the better when she was put in charge of training Marcus Rayne, the A-list actor who was producing a movie about the Nighthawks. Emma and Marcus were now blissfully in love and currently traveling the world for the movie's premiere.

"And how's our Emma girl doing?"

Despite Jolene's efforts to hide it with a smile, Finch could sense that she was missing her friend. "She's good. She and Marcus are promoting the new movie about the Nighthawks."

"That finally got made?"

"Yes. It comes out next month. We're all going to the premiere."

"That's pure barry. Cannae wait to see it."

Finch raised a brow and looked down at Jolene. "Pure barry?"

She translated. "He's saying it's fantastic." Then she looked back at her father sternly. "You're not going anywhere unless you start telling the truth about your health."

"Och, lassie. Right back at ye." With tense silence between them, the father-daughter duo locked eyes. As they stared each other down, the father's jaw clenched and the daughter's eyes narrowed. They were both unyielding, their stubbornness evident with each passing moment. As a fellow redhead, Finch knew firsthand about the tenacity that came with the stubborn gene. Maybe that was why he could never give up hope of gaining favor with Jolene again.

Jolene relented first, her shoulders sagging in defeat. "Really, Da. I'm fine. Just some issues at work. No big deal."

"Is that feckin' fandan bawbag still causing you trouble?" Gorden's eyes narrowed, and his lips tightened, his expression turning fierce. Gorden's tone betrayed his extreme dislike for whoever he was talking about.

Had he not been paying attention, Finch would have missed Jolene's reaction entirely. It was as if her entire being was holding its breath, every muscle in her body coiled tight. Curiosity piqued, he resolved to discover the identity of this enigmatic "bawbag" and the troubles they had brought upon Jolene.

"No, Da," she hissed in answer to her father's question. "Nothing like that." She sent a subtle sideways glance in Finch's direction, as if hoping he didn't notice her unease. "And we don't talk about that, remember?"

"Pshaw. You should talk about him. It wasn't fair what he did to you." Finch was intrigued, and he needed to know more. Had this guy hurt Jolene? Rage surged through him at the mere thought of some man laying hands on her. If that was the case, he'd do whatever it took to find the person who had wronged her and make him regret it.

Jolene's eyes briefly met Finch's, but then she turned away, as if silently conveying to her dad that she didn't want to discuss it in front of him. That was fine. He knew it would take time, but he was patient, and eventually, he'd get the story from her.

"Not here, Da. Please."

Gorden's mouth opened as if to say something, but then he shook his head, shifted in the bed, and remained silent. Her ramrod straight posture in her chair betrayed her tension.

A knock on the door preceded a doctor's entrance. Jolene greeted him with a barrage of inquiries as soon as he stepped into the room. She was clearly very worried about her father.

Giving them some space to talk about her father's diagnosis, Finch slipped out into the quiet hall. The hospital's unmistakable smell of disinfectant and the sound of beeping machines immediately took him back to a time when his father had his own health scare.

He'd taken leave and rushed back to Maryland to be by his side and support his mother. He had asked Angelica to come along, but she had refused, leaving him to confront the fear of losing a parent alone. The reason he refused to leave Jolene's side now was partly because of it. He knew how that fear could grip your heart and not let go. This was one of the few things he could control.

He'd had no control when it came to his marriage. Not that he wanted to be a controlling dick. He'd wanted an equal partnership. But Angelica had different ideas. From the very beginning, she had demanded dominion over him, to dictate his every move, and he had failed to realize it until it was too late.

Her response to his father's health scare—which ended up being appendicitis—had been eye opening. She hadn't wanted him to go. Had gone so far as to order him not to. It was one of the most violent fits she'd ever thrown. He ducked and weaved as she unleashed a barrage of objects in his direction. He'd been struck by a glass vase she'd launched at him. The vase shattered against his shoulder, sending fragments of glass flying in all directions and slicing up his shoulder. His primary concern had been getting to his parents, so he'd ignored the need for stitches.

The scar, jagged and red, served as a constant reminder of that day. The beginning of the end had arrived, and there had been no turning back.

He wished he had broken free from her grasp sooner. He had waited too long to begin divorce proceedings. He'd been weary from having put up with her shit for so long that he was content just to be separated from her. Not long after he'd met Jolene, he'd decided it was time to cut ties with Angelica officially, but things were moving slowly. She fought him, demanding more than he was willing to give her. The moment she'd crossed the line and ruined what he had been building with Jolene, he knew he had to be more assertive in their divorce proceedings.

He had clung to the final nail in his marriage's coffin, fearing the judgment that would come with the truth being exposed. The awards gala had been the breaking point for him. That night, he'd made the decision to let his lawyer use what they'd discovered against his wife, despite how it made him appear like a fool.

He peered through the narrow window in the door, fixated on Jolene's every move. He could hear the muffled sound of her voice but couldn't make out the words. The sound of her laughter floated through the door, and it made his heart skip a beat. As she laughed, her long auburn hair, which hung in a single tail down her back, swayed. He watched her chest rise and fall with each breath, completely captivated. As she sat in the chair, she appeared small and delicate and so alone. But she was anything but. She had a spine of steel that was enviable. As he watched her from afar, he felt a mix of emotions. Curiosity, longing, and guilt all rolled into one uncomfortable lump. He hated that she was in there alone. He wished he could be closer to her.

Looking at her, a sharp ache bloomed in his chest. What would she think about what he'd lived with for far too long? He wondered if her opinion of him would be negatively impacted. It would be worse if she only felt pity toward him.

He doubted she would react negatively, but the possibility still lingered in his mind. Anxiety filled him, making it difficult to breathe, like a weight crushing his chest.

Jolene must have exhausted her list of questions since the doctor was making his way to the door. She glanced over and spotted him through the window. When he realized he had been caught watching her, he couldn't look away from her piercing gaze. They locked eyes, and he could feel his heart racing. The intensity of their eye contact was electric. He longed to reach out and touch her, to feel the softness of her skin, but he remained rooted to the spot, unable to move. The connection they had formed in that moment felt too fragile.

Maybe it was time for him to stop worrying and waiting and start chasing his dreams.

Chapter 6

JOLENE HAD BOMBARDED THE doctor with questions the moment he'd walked through the door. She listened attentively until the doctor was ready to leave the room. That's when she noticed Finch peering at her through the door's tiny window. His expression left her feeling breathless and disoriented.

His piercing gaze and the intensity in his eyes made her feel as if she was drowning in a sea of emotions. The sound of her own heartbeat pounding in her ears drowned out the faint hum of the air conditioner. Her knees felt weak and her hands trembled as she struggled to catch her breath.

As she stared, her senses were overwhelmed. All she could think about was the way he looked at her, leaving her breathless and unable to focus on anything else.

It was almost as though she was the embodiment of all his wants. It was all right there in his eyes. As if he was trying to tell her he was done pussyfooting around and was determined to grab hold of her and never let go.

Her insides quaked. Did she want him to grab hold? Despite the events of a year ago, he remained a constant presence in her life. He never let their differences come between their friendship, and he was always there for her. Even now, he had given up a lot of time to be here for her. It revealed a lot about the kind of man he was.

Yet he'd lied to her. She had been under the impression that he was unattached until she found out otherwise. She'd felt played. The aftermath of that night had been devastating. The memories of which still haunted her.

The night had been absolutely perfect. A thrill of excitement and anticipation swept over her, knowing this was going to be a magical night. They'd been building up to it for weeks. With eagerness budding in her heart, Jolene knew that tonight was the night.

Brimming with a vast expanse of black and white tuxedos and sparkling evening gowns in every shade imaginable, the ballroom was a bustling hub of excitement. The air was thick with the sweet perfume of floral bouquets and the gentle aroma of cologne, while the soft hum of chatter and laughter filled the room, creating a symphony of sound that echoed off the walls. Plush carpeting underfoot offered a comforting sensation, as guests mingled and danced to the lively music playing in the background.

Jolene was in Finch's arms, exactly where she wanted to be as they danced. The energy of the music infected their friends, too, and soon they were all dancing around them. Natalie's and Annika's eyes were locked on their partners, lost in the love and the intimacy of the moment. As Jolene danced with Finch, she noticed her own smile reflected the happiness of those around her.

A flash of silver caught her eye, and she smiled. Marcus Rayne, the actor that had been training with the Nighthawks, was pulling Emma out onto the dance floor. Marcus had been gone for months, but before he left, he and Emma had been at the beginning of something special. A sense of relief and happiness washed over her when she saw her friend back with him. The months apart had not been easy for Emma, and Jolene hoped this moment was the start of something wonderful. Or was it the continuation? Whatever it was, Emma deserved to be happy.

Finch's hand stroking up her spine drew her attention back to him. His eyes, a mix of green and brown, took on a blue hue as he peered down at her. The gentle glow of the chandeliers illuminated the room with a soft, warm light, casting a romantic atmosphere that was almost fairy-tale-like. The soft lighting added a bit of sparkle to his eyes that made her smile.

With his hands on her back, he pulled her in closer to him. The softness of his tux jacket cushioned her cheek as she laid her head on his shoulder, swaying to the music. She closed her eyes and let herself be carried away by the rhythm of the dance, feeling the heat of his body and the hardness of his chest beneath her cheek. As he leaned in, she breathed in the scent of his cologne, a sweet and earthy fragrance.

She pushed her hands through the hair at his nape and felt more than heard the groan rumble up from his abdomen. "Wanna get out of here?" she asked.

He whispered, "Absolutely," with his lips gently brushing the top of her head.

With a big smile on her face, she lifted her head to look at him. His eyes were flooded with longing and a hint of something else. It almost looked like he was fretting over something. She had no idea what he could possibly be worried about. She was a sure thing.

"Give me a few minutes, then come up to my room?"

He nodded, and she reluctantly stepped out of his embrace, already longing for the warmth of his body. As she weaved her way through the throng of people, she couldn't help but steal one last glance over her shoulder at him.

She didn't bother saying good night to her friends, too excited for the evening ahead. She knew they would understand. Some of them were too lost in their own partners to care about social niceties.

Since Finch was sharing a room with Tin Man, they couldn't go there. Although she was rooming with Emma, she was confident that she could persuade her *best friend to find alternative accommodations. With the way she and Marcus were cozying up to each other, Jolene hoped Emma would end up with him for the night.*

Quickly, she threw Emma's belongings into her suitcase and wheeled it to the door. Hearing the click of the door lock, Jolene met Emma at the door, blocking her way into the room.

"Can you go stay with Maddie tonight?" she asked.

"What?"

"I . . . um . . ." Suddenly nervous, she couldn't find the words. She should have known her best friend would understand instantly. A wide grin spread across her face.

"Can I at least get my stuff first?" she asked, the grin turning into a knowing smirk. Jolene grabbed her suitcase and wheeled it through the door. "Ha. You were that sure I'd agree to this?"

Jolene reached out and brought Emma in for a hug. "That's because you love me."

With a wink, Emma grabbed the handle of her suitcase and started down the hall, throwing "have fun" over her shoulder.

As soon as the door clicked shut, Jolene's heart started pounding with nerves. She looked around the room for something to do. Something to distract herself as she waited for Finch. She could strip and wait naked on the bed. But then she realized she'd have to let him into the room and would rather not do that naked.

Spying the bucket sitting on the counter by the mini fridge, she grabbed it and lined it with the thin bag provided. Snatching her key card off the dresser, she left the room and hurried down the hall to the ice machine. She stopped when she heard raised voices.

"What the fuck do you think you're doing?" a shrill voice hissed.

"Angelica," a man said in a tone that conveyed resignation. Wait . . . that sounded like Finch.

Jolene took the few steps needed until she entered the elevator vestibule. Finch stood with a woman whose face was red with anger. Standing a few inches taller than her, the woman's dark brown hair and piercing brown gaze conveyed that Jolene's presence was not welcome.

"Is this her?" she ranted. "Is this the little whore you think you can cheat on me with?"

Every drop of blood from the top of her head down dropped into the pit that was once her stomach. Not again. This could not be happening again.

The woman's designer slacks sat snugly on her waist as she stood with her fists on her hips. Her top's scoop neck was obscenely low, revealing her cleavage as she bent at the waist to glare at Jolene. Jolene deliberately averted her gaze and turned to Finch. As soon as she saw his face, her heart shattered into a million pieces. A wave of nausea washed over her, and her stomach twisted uncomfortably.

Finch looked at Jolene with an expression of remorse and entreaty. At least he looked repentant for betraying her. Harrison never had.

The woman wasn't done spitting out her vitriol. "How could you, Atty? How could you do this to me? And with her?"

"Angelica," Finch implored in a tone that was far too patient for the situation. "Please keep your voice down."

If looks could kill, Finch would be lying dead at their feet. Jolene's hands shook, dislodging the lid of the ice bucket. The plastic disk dropped to the floor, drawing the woman's fury.

"You're nothing but a hussy, aren't you?" The woman's disdainful look traveled from her head to her stiletto heels, leaving her feeling exposed. "Slut."

That did it. She'd had enough of this woman calling her names. Her stubborn pride wouldn't let her just stand here and take the abuse from this stranger. Deliberately, she set the ice bucket down on the brass table across from the elevators.

Turning back to face the pair, she gave the woman a quick once-over of her own. "And who are you?"

"I'm his wife. That's all you need to know," the woman said, but her words were lost in the sudden buzzing that entered her ears at the mention of the word wife.

Jolene stumbled, feeling lightheaded and unsteady on her feet. She stumbled over to the wall, her body shaking and her breath coming in ragged gasps. Her fingers scraped against the texture of the wallpaper as she tried to steady herself.

God! This could not be happening again.

Finch made a move to go to her, drawing her attention. With one hand raised, she stopped him in his tracks and glared. The intensity of the sense of betrayal made her feel like she had been punched in the gut. A weight sat on her chest, making it hard to breathe.

How could she have been so stupid? Had she not learned a thing from her experience with Harrison? She'd spent so many years walling off her heart. Then Finch had walked into her bar. With one smile, her defenses weakened. Stupid.

Now she was right back where she'd started nine years ago when she'd fled the city after Harrison's duplicity.

The woman laughed. The sound pierced through the buzzing in her ears, causing Jolene to flinch. "I see he didn't tell you. Typical. He never could do anything right."

Jolene turned her gaze toward Finch. His desperate, imploring expression twisted at her heart. She shut that shit down. "Is it true?" she asked, her voice sounding surprisingly steady despite her inner turmoil.

His gaze dropped to the floor with unquestionable guilt.

"Oh God," she cried. She put her hand over her mouth, hoping to stifle the sobs that wanted to escape. Or the scream. At this point, it could go either way. She tried

to keep her composure, but the weight of her emotions was too much to bear.

"Jolie." Finch's whispered use of her nickname made her feel sick. "Let me explain."

She wanted to laugh. What was there to explain? He was married. The end. Oh God. She'd nearly slept with him. Another married man turning her into an adulterer.

Never again.

She threw her shoulders back and straightened her spine. She would not let this break her. "No. I don't want to hear it." With that, she turned around and fled down the hall to her room. She heard his voice calling her name, but she kept moving forward. She barely made it inside before the waterworks started.

Chapter 7

DURING THE CAR RIDE to Jolene's father's house, the only sounds were the hum of the engine and the occasional passing car. Jolene's eyes were glued to the window as they drove down Summervale's main thoroughfare. She tried to focus on the sights outside rather than Finch's presence beside her.

Nothing much had changed. The pizza joint they used to go to after school was still there, just as she remembered it. The neighborhood fitness center seemed to be thriving. Jolene had never been there because the large windows gave her the feeling of being trapped in a fishbowl. The thought of someone watching her struggle during her workout had always made her uncomfortable.

The real estate office was cluttered with posters of properties for sale. Jolene would stop to look at them whenever she was in town. It had been nice to dream about what her future house would look like. Although she loved her cottage in Lake Haven, it didn't quite match the dream she used to envision. There was no husband to welcome her home after a long night at the restaurant. No kids making her laugh with their silly antics. It was nice, but empty. Kind of like her.

They soon passed by the high school stadium where her first kiss had been bestowed upon her in eighth grade. Grady Smith had been the first guy to make her swoon and wouldn't be the last. She'd lived for that swoony feeling as she'd looked for "the one." Maybe that was her problem. Grady had made her feel special, and her heart had pounded in anticipation of that first kiss. That kiss had left her with a fluttery, happy feeling that swirled inside her for days. It didn't last long. He was the first person to break her heart.

When the guy she'd been crushing on for most of her senior year asked her to the senior prom, her stomach had filled with a swarm of butterflies. Turned out he'd only asked her because he thought she'd be an easy lay. She broke his nose when he'd gotten too handsy.

Then there was Harrison. He'd given her all the feels. The stomach flutters. The pounding heart. The intense anticipation of all the firsts. She'd experienced them all with him. She'd given him her virginity. She'd given him her heart. And he'd betrayed her in the worst way imaginable.

When Finch came along, she'd fought the feelings he'd awakened in her. But he'd broken through every barrier she'd erected without even trying. It wasn't just his kindness that made an impression on her, but also the way he made her feel like she mattered. He'd talked to her as an equal. He was funny and disgustingly charming, yet there was no macho posturing. His polite nature and empathetic attitude made him stand out.

It was as if he possessed an extraordinary ability, almost like a sixth sense, to make everyone feel heard and understood. The way he listened intently to others, with his eyes locked on theirs, was like watching a master at work. His gentle voice carried a soothing tone that calmed even the most anxious of souls. It was impossible not to feel at ease in his presence, as if he had a magical touch that could dispel any worries or fears.

It was those exceptional qualities that made him an expert at his job. On a few occasions, she'd observed him instructing his trainees on how to provide care and advocacy for victims.

Although he had a caring and compassionate personality, his wit was often wicked and irreverent. His sense of humor was infectious, and he had a way of making everyone in the group laugh. He had a talent for lightening the mood and making even the most serious situations a little less tense.

All of those attributes had been like a battering ram against her defenses. Once again, she had allowed herself to succumb to the swoony feelings, and it had cost her dearly. The weight of the broken trust hung heavily on her, and she struggled to see a way forward.

Finch's voice jolted her back to the present, interrupting her contemplation. "Are you hungry?"

Hunger pangs reminded her that she had neglected to eat throughout the day while worrying about her father. She suddenly felt famished. "I could eat."

"Great. Do you have a specific idea in mind, or do you want something quick?"

"We could go to my dad's pub. It's mostly bar food, but it's excellent."

"Sounds good. Just point me in the right direction."

Having lost track of their location while lost in thought, Jolene glanced out the window. "Take a right at the next intersection," she directed. She had driven this route so many times that she could do it with her eyes closed. She knew every turn and curve of the road. Every year, she'd known exactly where the potholes were and how to steer clear of them until the public works department filled them. And, like clockwork, they opened up in the exact same spots each spring.

Jolene directed Finch to the parking lot of the Dafty Neighbor. The familiar building still stood tall and proud, seemingly unchanged from the day she left home. The brick walls looked weathered and worn but sturdy as ever. The faded green paint on the front door brought back a flood of memories.

She was so deep in her observations that she didn't hear the sound of the SUV door opening until Finch offered her his hand to help her down. The sound of cars passing by on the busy street nearby mingled with the distant hum of a lawnmower. She inhaled deeply as she climbed out of the SUV, taking in the scent of freshly cut grass and the sweet aroma of the pine trees that surrounded the pub. The smells were as familiar to her as the building itself.

As she made her way closer to the door, she ran her hand along the exterior of the building. The rough texture of the brick under her fingertips. It was as if time had stood still and she was transported back to a simpler age. The memories of her childhood were etched into the very bricks themselves.

She hadn't been back in over a year, and each time she opened the door, it was like stepping into the past. The familiar creak of the old door. The hum of the neon signs hanging in the windows. The din of conversation. Even the sticky, rough-hewn boards under her feet. Nothing ever changed.

"Caio, bella." Jolene's attention shot to the bar, and the familiar face beaming at her brought a smile to her lips. "Aren't you a sight for sore eyes."

With his mouth near her ear, Finch spoke softly. "Your dad has an Italian bartender in a Scottish bar?" She grinned at him over her shoulder and shrugged. Her father and Dante were as different as could be, and the language barriers between them were highly entertaining. But they were the best of friends.

"Dante," she called, making her way to the end of the bar. The Dafty Neighbor's long-time bartender enveloped her in a huge hug, pulling her off her feet. Her laughter echoed through the room and her feet swung back and forth as he rocked. "Put me down, you big brute," she teased, slapping him on the shoulder.

"Did you see your dad?" he asked as he set her back on her feet, the concern in his eyes easy to see.

Dante De Lorenzo had been the bartender since the Dafty Neighbor had opened. His lankiness was accentuated by the way his clothes hung loosely on his frame. He appeared to have lost quite a bit of weight since she'd last seen him, and she worried his age was catching up to him. His presence filled the room. It was just as robust and powerful as it had always been.

"Yeah, we just came from the hospital."

"How was he?"

"Ornery. Denying he was in pain or even that the heart attack happened. Driving the nurses to drink."

The crinkles at the corners of Dante's eyes deepened as he chuckled. "Sounds like he's almost back to normal. The man is nothing if not difficult."

She let out a snort of laughter. "You mean he's a stubborn ass."

"You're damn right," he chuckled before his eyes narrowed and he scrutinized her face. "And how are you holding up?"

"I'm fine now that I've seen him."

He studied her as if ascertaining whether she was telling him the truth.

His gaze raked over her from head to toe as he held her at arm's length. She did the same with him. His dark hair was more gray than black but was still thick and full. The deep creases etched on his weathered face were a testament to the many years he had lived, each one marked by the joys and sorrows of life. As he smiled, the corners of his eyes crinkled like the edges of a well-thumbed book. The sound of his laughter was like music to her ears and never failed to cheer her up.

"Ah, bellissima as always."

She grinned and said, "Aw, bless your heart." His smooth talking and quick wit made him a natural charmer. And a perfect bartender.

"If only I was ten years younger."

Jolene scoffed. "Ten years? That would still make you old enough to be my grandfather."

"Haven't you heard? Age-gap romances are all the rage on that tickety-tockety app thing. We could make it work."

Jolene laughed. "What do you know about age-gap romances?"

"Just what Marjorie tells me about them during poker night."

Things never changed. Marjorie had been her mom's best friend. She, Dante, and her dad had been playing poker with each other every Monday night for as long as she could remember. Her mom used to be their fourth, but since she died, they'd had a revolving door of friends who'd taken her spot.

"What has that woman been filling your head with?"

"You could use an older man in your life. Your track record hasn't been so hot in that regard."

"That's not true," she complained.

"Grady Smith." Dante threw the name out at her, and she could feel the heat of a blush rise in her cheeks.

"Jesus, Dante. That was when I was in eighth grade."

He didn't let up. "You let that boy kiss you, and then what happened a week later?" he prompted.

A wave of embarrassment washed over her. It was like she was a pre-teen all over again.

"He was kissing Cynthia Maddox." She remembered how devastated she'd been. She'd gone to the same spot he'd first kissed her, hoping for some more lip lock action, only to find those lips on Cynthia Maddox. "In my defense, I was young and stupid."

"That may be, but everybody knew that boy was a player."

"Hey," a voice from the bar called out.

"You know it's true, Grady," Dante replied over his shoulder. Jolene peered around him and saw none other than Grady Smith, her first kiss, sitting at the bar. He looked older, of course, but still had that playful, mischievous glint in his eyes. His hair was thinning, and he tried to overcompensate with the facial hair. Despite that, he looked good.

He'd been an easy-going guy in high school. Dante was right. He had been a bit of a player. And he'd been unapologetic about it. She'd heard through the high school grapevine that he'd gotten married, but she couldn't remember to who.

Grady swiveled around to face her, assessing her with a secret glint in his eyes. It was the same look he'd given her after that kiss. What had she been thinking, letting him kiss her all those years ago? She rolled her eyes. Some things never changed.

"Hey, Jolene. You're lookin' mighty fine," he crooned with that sly smile. Finch stepped forward and positioned himself as a barrier between her and Grady's semi-lecherous gaze that came across as more silly than anything else. She suddenly remembered that he'd also been somewhat of a hothead as Grady stood and narrowed his eyes at Finch, ready to face the obvious challenge. "Who the fuck are you?"

"Someone you don't want to mess with."

"Is that so?" Grady's fists clenched, and Jolene felt Finch's body tense in anticipation. It was so subtle she was sure only she could detect it. Outwardly, he appeared at ease, yet he stood strong, ready to defend her honor. Jolene fought the need to roll her eyes again. She could fight her own battles, and Grady Smith wouldn't be much of a challenge for her.

"Jesus H. Christ, Grady," Dante cursed. "Sit the fuck down and drink your beer. Nobody wants to see you get your ass kicked. At least not tonight."

"I don't know, Dante. I'd consider paying an admittance fee to see that show," a woman's voice shouted from the other end of the bar.

"Shut up, Cynthia," Grady shot back.

Jolene stared at the woman, a little shocked. It was surreal to see so many people from her past all at once.

Grinning from ear to ear, Cynthia Maddox stuck out her tongue at Grady before heading over to Jolene. When the petite blond woman wrapped her in a hug, Jolene was stunned. They'd been friends in high school, as she was with most everyone in her class. That was small town life in general. Everyone knew everyone else, and you were all friendly, but not necessarily best friends. Jolene would call Cynthia a tertiary friend.

"It's good to see you, Jolene," she said, stepping back before Jolene could return the hug. "Sorry about the whole kiss thing in eighth grade. I was young and stupid, too."

Jolene chuckled. Despite the fact that they'd never talked about what happened, there was no animosity between them. "No worries. We both wised up eventually."

Cynthia winced. "Not exactly. I was stupid enough to marry the asshole."

Jolene noticed Finch's attention turned toward the glowering man, who was sitting on his stool, trying to be invisible. "You hit on another woman in front of your wife? What is wrong with you?"

Cynthia's laugh was so loud and distinctive that Jolene was sure it could be heard even from the other side of the pub. "Don't worry. I know he was only teasing. He's totally addicted to me."

Grady hooked an arm around Cynthia and pulled her to him. "You got that right, darlin'," he crooned before kissing her soundly on the lips. The absurdity of the situation was not lost on Jolene, and she burst out laughing.

"I'd say I'm sorry to hear that, but it looks like you're not," Jolene remarked.

Cynthia shrugged. "He's a changed man, even if he can still act like a dick on occasion."

"Fuck, Cynthia. Take it easy on my man," the guy sitting next to Grady said. "Can't you see he's nursing the burns he's gotten tonight? Give the man a little sympathy."

Cynthia glared at the guy. "It's my love language," she replied simply with a shrug. "Anyway," Cynthia continued. "Who's this handsome devil?" she asked as her gaze swept over Finch. The irrational jealousy hit Jolene like a bolt of lightning, catching her off guard. Finch wasn't hers. So why did she feel like laying claim to him right here in front of everyone?

Lost in her confounded thoughts, she didn't answer right away, and Finch filled in the awkward silence. He held out a hand to Cynthia. "Hi. I'm Finch."

Grady snorted. "Stupid name," he mumbled, making his friend snigger. Jolene ignored them, her gaze entirely fixed on Cynthia's hand in Finch's. A hand she was holding for far too long. As she watched, Cynthia stepped in closer to Finch and peered up at him. *Was she batting her eyes?*

"Hi Finch. I'm Cynthia. That's an interesting name."

"Thanks," Finch answered, appearing a little bewildered by Cynthia's weird attention. "It's a nickname."

"Stupid nickname," Grady muttered. Jolene rolled her eyes and noticed Cynthia do the same.

"Ignore him," she said, covering their clasped hands with her other one. "I think it's a great nickname."

"Um . . ."

"I'm Dante De Lorenzo." Dante saved Finch from the awkwardness of having to formulate a response by smoothly interjecting. Cynthia had no choice but to release Finch so he could shake Dante's proffered hand. Her pout was so absurdly over-the-top that it was impossible not to laugh.

"Atticus Mobey," Finch replied, his eyes meeting Dante's with a grateful nod as he shook his hand.

Dante smiled and tipped his head. "Ah. Now I understand the nickname."

"Still a stupid nickname," grumbled Grady, receiving a smack on the back of the head from Cynthia. Beside her, Finch flinched like he was the one who'd been slapped. A curious glance in his direction revealed a tension in his jaw.

"Shut up, Grady." Cynthia's order drew her attention to the feuding couple and away from Finch's strange reaction.

"So, how do you know our Jolene?" Dante asked.

"Since I couldn't get an immediate flight, Finch was kind enough to fly me down so I could get to Dad faster."

"Well, then. I guess we owe you a debt of gratitude," proclaimed Dante.

"You some kind of hotshot top gun pilot or something?" Grady asked, an unmistakable note of derision in his tone.

"That's hot," Cynthia purred.

"Something like that," Finch replied, ignoring Cynthia's inappropriate interest.

"You military?" Dante wondered.

"Former."

"What branch?"

"Air Force."

Grady apparently couldn't help himself. "Why'd you get out? Couldn't hack it anymore?"

Before anyone could respond, a sharp gasp cut through the silence. "I knew your name sounded familiar," Cynthia cried, holding her phone. "You're that helicopter pilot who saved Marcus Rayne." She held up her phone to show an article featuring the story of when the A-list actor was injured on a hike and needed to be rescued by the Nighthawks.

"What are you talking about?" Grady grabbed her arm to move the phone into his line of sight.

"He's a Nighthawk."

"Never heard of it," mumbled Grady.

"They're heroes," Cynthia proclaimed.

"Whatever," Grady muttered, turning back to his beer.

"They help people, jackass." Their relationship was so bizarre. When they looked at each other, you could see the love there. But otherwise, they acted like bitter enemies. Strange.

"I help plenty." He gave her a look that said there was something Jolene was missing. She tried to remember what Grady did for a living but couldn't think of it.

Cynthia deflated slightly. "Oh, well, yeah. I guess you're just as good. But that's your job. The Nighthawks don't get paid."

"Then how do they pay their bills? Fuel for that fancy helicopter ain't cheap."

"Jesus, you're ignorant. They get donations."

A tingle rushed down her spine as Finch leaned in and whispered in her ear. "Do they need us for this argument?"

She snickered. "Probably not."

"Good. Let's get some food. I'm starving."

They moved to an empty spot at the bar. Dante had retreated to his position behind it before the argument had even reached its peak. Jolene grabbed two menus and handed one to Finch. She didn't know why she'd grabbed one for herself since she could recite it by heart. The menu had remained unchanged for as long as she could remember. Her father had never altered it. Predictable as always. That was Gorden Pritchett.

After placing their order, they chatted with Dante some more. The conversation eventually circled back to her father, and a familiar knot of fear formed in her gut. The doctor told her he would be fine, and logically, she understood that. But the mere thought of losing another parent brought a bit of panic. Her mom's death had been devastating. The thought of losing her dad too had become a constant source of worry for her. If he was gone, who would she share recipes with? What would happen to the pub? The house? It was hard enough knowing her mom wouldn't see her get married or have babies. It would be unbearable if her dad missed those milestones as well.

A young waitress setting their meals down in front of them distracted her from her spiraling thoughts.

Jolene's stomach growled in anticipation of her favorite toasted cheese sandwich. The cheddar that her father had shipped in from Scotland was gooey and oozing out of the sandwich, just the way she liked it. With the first bite, she was transported back to her childhood. The salty cured ham and sharp cheddar combination was just as she remembered.

A moan from Finch caught her attention, and she turned to see him happily devouring his Scotch egg. The hard-boiled egg surrounded by spicy sausage meat, then deep fried was a staple at the Dafty Neighbor. She wondered if she should think about adding it to her own menu. Maybe as an appetizer.

"You like it?" she asked.

He wiped his mouth with a napkin before answering. "It's good. But your bar will always be my favorite place."

A warm feeling spread through her body, causing her cheeks to flush as she smiled. It was a sweet thing for him to say. Despite receiving acclaim from various area publications and blogs as one of the best restaurants in Southwest Michigan, it was still validating to hear her friends say the same thing about her bar.

Her father's recipes were missed more than she had realized. Perhaps she should add a bit of her heritage to her own restaurant. She hadn't wanted to go there after the disaster that was Noitiña. That dream was crushed by Harrison, just like her trust in him. Maybe it was time to rekindle that dream and make it a reality.

She'd retained ownership of Noitiña's recipes. They were hers, after all. Her creations. It had been a smart move on her part to add that caveat into her contract with Harrison when opening Noitiña. When she'd left, she'd taken all the recipes that had made the restaurant so popular with her. She was indebted to her dad for that wise business advice.

"You been to the house yet?" Dante asked.

For a moment, she wondered why he was asking. Then she remembered what condition the house had been in the last time she'd been home. The old place had been in dire need of repair when she last saw it, and she shuddered to think of its current state. Caring for the house had been more her mother's purview. Her dad had focused on the pub and was a mess when it came to home maintenance.

"Not yet. We wanted to grab a bite before heading over there. It's gotten worse, hasn't it." It was more a statement than a question. She knew what her dad was like. She'd pushed him to hire someone to make the repairs, but like she'd said, he was a stubborn ass. Insisting he could do it himself. Only, he never made the time for it.

"He was working on the porch when the heart attack happened."

He used two fingers on each hand to indicate quotes when he said "working on."

"The railing gave way when he collapsed against it. That's how he got the broken leg."

Jolene's heart twisted at the thought of her father being hurt in such a manner. "I'll see what I can do while I'm here."

"That's not your responsibility."

"I know. But I've got some time. I can handle a few of the projects."

Dante let out a deep sigh and shook his head. "Just as stubborn as your old man."

As she ate a salty french fry, Jolene's grin took on a mischievous quality. "You know it."

"Fine. But if you need help, let me know."

Jolene was shaking her head even before he'd finished speaking. "I need you here. You know you're the only one dad trusts with the pub."

"I know, but—"

"I'll help her with the repairs," Finch interjected. Jolene shot him a look of surprise.

"But shouldn't you be getting back to Lake Haven? What about the Nighthawks?"

His gentle smile did not have the intended calming effect on her. Prolonged exposure to Finch was dangerous to her heart. She needed him to go home as soon as possible.

"I told you I wasn't going to leave you alone with this."

"I know. But what about work?"

"Graham understands. And they're covered. Now that Hollynn learned to fly the helicopter, she'll help out if needed. Besides, Natalie would kill him if he called me away from you. She didn't want you to be alone."

Dammit, Natalie. Her friends were determined to keep pushing the two of them together. She'd never explained to any of them what had happened. It really wasn't her secret to tell.

As far as she knew, Finch had never divulged the status of his marriage to any of his friends. There had never been any whispers or knowing glances exchanged between them. She had always assumed the women would make a big deal out of it if they'd known, but they never did. A sense of unease curled in her stomach as she sat there, wondering why he had chosen to keep such an important aspect of his life hidden from those closest to him. She had a nagging feeling that there was a reason for that.

"Fine," she relented. "But if you need to leave, feel free to go."

"Not gonna happen, but okay."

Chapter 8

After promising Dante they'd stop back in soon, they were back in the car, heading toward her childhood home. Trepidation pervaded her thoughts as she approached the house, wondering if Dante's description of its condition was accurate.

"If you want, I'll get a room after we get you settled in your dad's house. Just point me in the direction of a hotel."

The suggestion surprised her, as she had assumed he would be by her side at all times. Based on his repeated promises that he wouldn't leave her alone, she figured he'd stick to her like glue.

She should give him the name of any of a dozen hotels in the area, but she found herself instead saying, "That's not necessary. There's plenty of room at the house." *Shit.* Why did she say that? She wanted distance from him, not the tight quarters of cohabitating. She felt like the protagonist in one of her beloved romance novels. Only she was pretty sure there wouldn't be a happy ending for her.

Finch darted a glance at her as he drove. The sun had set, and the SUV's interior was now shrouded in darkness, except for the faint glow of the dashboard lights. Kicking herself for her suggestion, Jolene kept her eyes transfixed on the road as the headlights created a tunnel-vision effect in front.

"Are you sure?"

"Yeah. There are four spare bedrooms. Plenty of space." Keeping her true feelings to herself, she bit her lip and looked away. She could feel Finch's eyes on her as he considered her words.

Finally, he said, "Okay. If you're sure. That'd make things easier to get the work done faster."

"Right. Yeah. Okay." Internally, she groaned at her stilted words. Could she sound any more like an idiot?

"You okay?" Yup. He'd noticed her descent into stupid land.

"Sure. Fine. Just tired." More stilted words. What was wrong with her?

He was silent for a long time before he finally relented. "Okay."

Thankfully, they pulled into the driveway of the house. The sight of the overgrown lawn and peeling paint on the exterior made her uneasy. If the outside was this rundown, she couldn't imagine what the inside looked like.

As she walked toward the house, her heart beat a little faster. The creaking sound of the old wooden and warped boards as she climbed the porch steps echoed in her ears, and she could smell the musty scent of neglect that lingered in the air. Broken spindles and remnants of the railing lay in a tangled heap, surrounded by overgrown weeds in the flowerbed. The sight of the gaping hole in the porch railing where her father had fallen through made her stomach clench. She ignored it and focused on the front door.

Her hand trembled slightly as she reached out to unlock the door. She turned the knob, the metal cool against her fingertips. Pushing the door open, a cloud of dust rose up, tickling her nose and making her eyes water. As she stepped inside, the uneven floorboards creaked beneath her feet, and an uneasy feeling about what else she would find only added to her anxiety. She braced herself for the worst.

Walking farther into the house, she was overwhelmed with sadness at seeing the once bright and sunny home in its current state. The musty smell of old furniture and damp walls filled her nostrils, making her feel a little dizzy.

Memories bombarded her as she walked through the family room. This was her home. The place where she'd been a happy-go-lucky child. She could still hear her dad's booming voice echo through the house as he called to her mother in the kitchen, asking about his keys. The man couldn't keep track of a single item if his life depended on it. She had no idea how he'd managed since her mother had died.

A moonbeam and dust moats danced in the light, illuminating the corner where they put the Christmas tree every year. The dust and grime had accumulated in every nook and cranny of the house, and it desperately needed a thorough cleaning. Regular household chores were not her father's thing, and it showed.

The squalid conditions her father had been living in left her feeling heartbroken. A single lamp in the corner lit the room dimly, casting shadows on the empty food containers and clothes strewn across the floor. The threadbare couch her father often napped on was stained with God knew what, and the musty air made it hard to breathe.

She made her way through the house, her footsteps echoing on the hardwood floors. When she reached the kitchen, she flicked on the light switch and was met with the sight of overflowing garbage bins, grimy dishes piled high in the sink, and a thick layer of dust coating every surface. She wrinkled her nose at the putrid smell, which made her stomach turn. The sound of buzzing flies filled the air, and the only light came from a flickering bulb hanging precariously from the ceiling. What had happened to the pendent style light fixture that had once been her mother's pride and joy?

She recoiled in horror and let out a sound of disgust when a cockroach scurried across the filthy floor. The revolting creature made her back away, but the hard wall of muscle behind her stopped her. Startled, she realized Finch had been following her all along as his hands rested on her shoulders.

His voice was filled with concern as he asked, "Are you okay?"

The weight of what she had seen in the house was too much for her to bear, and she allowed herself a moment to rest against him. He held her loosely in a hug, with one arm wrapped over her upper chest while the sink's leaky faucet dripped steadily. His presence radiated warmth and steeliness, which seeped into her and provided a small boost of encouragement.

She sighed. "Yeah. I'm good. It's not as bad as I thought."

She felt him nod behind her. "Aside from the porch, most of this looks cosmetic. A little elbow grease and a fresh coat of paint should do it."

Jolene's skin crawled as she watched another cockroach skitter across the floor, causing her to grip Finch's arm tightly. He chuckled. "And maybe a pest exterminator."

"Most definitely," she agreed. Jolene's phone chimed. Absentmindedly, she took the device out of her pocket and glanced at the message. Every muscle in her body tightened at the threat.

YOU DESTROYED EVERYTHING. IT WILL BE EASY TO DESTROY YOU TOO.

"What's the matter? Is it the hospital?" Finch asked, picking up on her reaction.

She shoved the phone back into her pocket and forced her body to relax. "Nothing. Just a sale notification," she lied, stepping out of his embrace. She had no idea who kept texting her and tried to ignore the tremor of trepidation that hit her every time another message came through, even as she still tried to convince herself it was a wrong number.

"I'm too tired to deal with any of this tonight," she continued before he could question her further. "Let me show you to one of the spare rooms so we can go to bed." Her eyes widened at how suggestive her statement sounded, and she hastened to add, "Separately, of course."

His low chuckle rumbled through the room. "Of course."

She led him out of the kitchen and back into the family room. He grabbed their bags that she hadn't realized he'd brought inside and followed her up the stairs. She pointed out the bathroom and where he could find the towels before leading him to the room across from hers. She felt a moment of trepidation, wondering if it was too close to her own, but she told herself they were both adults. They could handle sleeping across the hall from each other. The closed doors would be enough of a deterrent . . . she hoped. And she wasn't talking about deterring him.

Taking her bag from his hand, she said, "Thanks for everything today. It meant a lot to me."

"Happy I could help." As she was preparing to say good night, he looked into her eyes and uttered, "I'd do anything for you."

In the dim hallway, his gaze locked on hers, and everything else faded away. He studied her with a spark of some unknown emotion in his eyes. His closeness made her acutely aware of the warmth emanating from his body, and her focus shifted to his lips.

He leaned in closer, and the scent of his cologne enveloped her. She held her breath, feeling her heart race, as he moved closer, and her face instinctively tilted toward his. At the last moment, his lips landed on her forehead. Even that simple touch had her knees—as well as her resolve—weakening.

His warm breath ghosted against her skin as he whispered, "Good night, Jolie," before moving back and stepping into his room, closing the door behind him.

Chapter 9

F INCH LEANED AGAINST THE kitchen counter, a mug of coffee in his hand as he stared at the empty sink. Unable to sleep, he'd gotten up and searched through the cabinets for coffee. He was going to need plenty of caffeine to combat the day ahead. After preparing and downing his first cup, he tackled the dishes moldering in the sink. The dried, caked-on food and gunk had been left to fester, emitting an unpleasant odor that made him cringe.

Now that the sink was clear—the dishwasher running quietly in the corner—and the overflowing trash had been taken to the cans outside, the smell had dissipated. The window he'd opened over the sink helped to clear the air as well.

The aroma of freshly brewed coffee wafted through the kitchen and filled his nostrils. A warm cup nestled between his palms provided a sense of comfort and relaxation. As he took a sip, the rich, bold flavor of his second cup of coffee danced on his tongue, and his mind wandered back to the night before.

He was making progress in breaking through Jolene's walls. Or maybe it was just exhaustion that had her lowering her barriers. His hope was fueled by the way she leaned against him and let him wrap his arm around her.

He couldn't forget the way she looked at him in the hall, her eyes lingering on his lips for a moment. When she tilted her face up as though anticipating his kiss, his heart had nearly pounded out of his chest. He struggled to control his desire to take what he believed she was unknowingly offering. He knew better than to take advantage of her emotional distress to win her back.

He yearned to break down the emotional barrier that had been built between them. Breaking down her walls was the only way he could see to bring them back to the way things were before. So he could have another chance to make things right. Building a future with her was his goal, but he knew they had to get through this crisis with her father first.

His phone trilled, shattering the silence and bringing him back to the present moment. He pulled his phone out and swiped to answer. "Hey, boss."

"How's Jolene's dad?" Graham asked. Graham Whitaker owned and operated Nighthawk Search and Rescue with his brother David. After spending years traveling to every natural disaster to lend his assistance, Graham had decided to bring his knowledge home, opening facilities that offered training and certifications. The job offer came just in time for Finch, who was desperate to leave Maryland and get away from Angelica. He was indebted to Graham for all that he had unknowingly done for him.

"He's in high spirits and stubborn. The heart attack was mild, but he broke his leg when he fell. He'll need rehab for it but should make a full recovery."

Graham sighed. "That's good news. How's Jolene holding up?"

"Exhausted but okay. You know how strong and tenacious she is. She's determined to take care of everything her dad needs."

Graham chuckled. "Sounds like her. Now I can tell Natalie to stop worrying."

He glanced around the mess of the house, which he knew would be overwhelming for Jolene to handle alone, causing Finch to conclude that he would need to ask for an extension on his time off.

"Listen, boss. Mr. Pritchett's house is in disarray and needs a bit of work to make it safe for him to return to. I don't want to leave Jolene alone to handle it all."

"Say no more," Graham interjected, anticipating his request. "Take all the time you need. We can handle things without you for a few weeks. Jolene is family. Take care of her."

"Thanks, and I will."

"You ever gonna tell us what happened between the two of you?" Graham asked, taking him off guard.

All his friends at one time or another had asked the same question. Embarrassed by the truth, he left his answers vague. Angelica's harsh words echoed repeatedly in his ears, leaving him feeling emasculated and demoralized. The weight of her abuse still bore down on him, suffocating him with shame and humiliation. It was an impotence that he would never forget, one that left him feeling broken and defeated. Explaining that to a group of formidable badass men was an indignity he wasn't ready to face.

"Maybe someday. I've got a few things to take care of first." Including finalizing his divorce.

"Does that include apologizing profusely for whatever it is you did to push her away and trying to win her back?"

Finch's laugh was sardonic to his own ears. "Something like that."

"Good." After a brief pause, Graham continued. "You guys need any help with the house? Brodhi is doing a training seminar down in Atlanta. I can send him your way when he's done."

He didn't know how to answer that question. Having another person around would create a buffer between Jolene and him, which she would probably welcome. But did he really want a witness to his bumbling attempts to get back into Jolene's good graces?

"Let me assess the true condition of the house over the next couple of days. I'll get back to you," he answered, hoping it was the right one.

"Sounds good. If you need anything, don't hesitate to call."

"I won't."

"Good. Take care of her."

"Always."

After hanging up with Graham, Finch drained his coffee mug, then rinsed it out and set it on the drying rack since the dishwasher was still running. He could hear Jolene moving around upstairs, so he decided to see what he could find to make for breakfast.

The contents of the fridge and pantry revealed that Gorden relied on a diet consisting of mostly canned soup and a few frozen dinners at home. The pantry was dimly lit, and the shelves were cluttered with boxes of crackers, cereal, and a line of neatly stacked cans. Picking up a can of soup, he noticed the label was faded and peeling, the expiration date unreadable. Desolation and disregard hung heavily in the air, and he couldn't help but worry about Gorden's unhealthy diet, as evidenced by the stacks of empty takeout containers scattered around the house.

Gorden would have to change his eating habits completely if he wanted to avoid another heart attack. The man's stubbornness had been apparent to Finch from the moment they met. Therefore, the chances of him altering his eating habits based on his doctor's recommendation were slim to none.

Shaking his head at the meager food supply, Finch grabbed the box of cereal, his options for breakfast limited. A quick check of the expiration date told him he was about half a year too late, but that had never stopped him before. Flipping the flaps of the box open, he silently cursed the lack of resealable cereal bags, but he unrolled the bag and grabbed a handful of cereal anyway. The little circles of oats looked innocent enough, but after popping them into his mouth, he realized looks could be deceiving. It was like trying to bite down on wood.

He rushed over to the trash can and spit out the mouthful of woodchips.

"What in the world are you doing?" Jolene asked just as he'd shoved his mouth under the faucet in the kitchen sink to wash it out.

Startled by her sudden voice, he bumped his head on the faucet and was immediately drenched. And, of course, the water went up his nose, the stinging sensation making his eyes water. He shook his head vigorously, snorting like a bull, trying to dislodge the water.

Once his head was clear of the water, both inside and out, he could hear the tinkling melody of Jolene's laughter behind him. That sound almost made his clumsy bumbling worth it.

"What the hell were you doing?" Jolene snickered, holding a dish towel out for him.

Wiping his face, he grumbled, "Trying to find breakfast."

She had a hand over her mouth as if to suppress her amusement. "Under the faucet?" She couldn't contain her laughter and threw her head back, her eyes sparkling with mirth. Her cheeks turned rosy and her eyes crinkled at the corners, making her even more beautiful.

He took her in and felt relieved to see she seemed less fatigued than yesterday. The dark jeans she wore showed off her figure while the heather-gray T-shirt emphasized her curves. Emblazoned across her chest were the bold words: *Being a chef saved me from becoming a pornstar*. The statement elicited a smirk of amusement. With her casual attire and confident demeanor, she seemed full of energy and ready to take on the day.

Her laughter was so captivating that he forgot his embarrassment about his near drowning and laughed along with her.

Once their amusement faded, he said, "There's good news and bad news." She lifted a brow, and he continued. "The good news is that if the zombie apocalypse ever comes, your father will be just fine if he hunkers down in his pantry. The bad news is that not a single can in there has a readable expiration date."

Incredulously, she stared at him with her jaw open. "What are you talking about? Wait . . . did you clean?" Her eyes darted around the kitchen, taking in the empty sink and lack of garbage.

"A little," he replied, dismissing it and quickly adding, "And judging by the number of takeout containers I had to throw away, your dad's diet sucks."

He grabbed the box of wood chips masquerading as cereal and threw it into the trash can. As she watched him, Jolene's face contorted with confusion. Then she turned and opened the door to the pantry to take a quick look. "I don't understand. Da loves to cook. He used to cook for us all the time when I was growing up. Why would he be eating nothing but canned soup?"

"Well, maybe it's just not worth it when you're cooking for one," Finch reasoned, which appeared to be the wrong thing to say as her face blanched.

"Oh my God. You're right. It's been so long since I've been able to visit. I should have been checking up on him more. I'm the worst daughter. And now he's in the hospital after suffering a heart attack. This never would have happened if I had been here to take care of him."

She was lost in guilt, pulling on a strand of hair that hung over her shoulder from her ponytail and chewing on her lip.

"Jolie," he tried to interject while wiping the last of the water from his face. He couldn't do anything about his damp shirt at this point. Stopping Jolene's spiral was more important.

"And look at this place," she continued, ignoring his interruption. "It's a mess." His eyes darted to the drops of water on the counter and floor, and tension built in his chest.

"Look at this mess," Angelica shrieked. "I swear. It's like living with Pigpen. Can you do anything right?" With a sudden movement, Angelica grabbed a dish-towel and whipped it at him. "Make yourself useful for once. Clean up those spots." Finch bit his tongue, refraining pointing out that the water spots on the coffee table came from her glass in order to avoid irritating her. That never went over well for him.

He rushed to wipe the kitchen counter and floor as he heard Angelica's voice in his head. He could feel Jolene's eyes on him but couldn't help himself. *Fuck.* Would that woman's voice ever leave his head?

After making sure the water was mopped up, he slowly rose to his feet, ignoring the questioning look from Jolene. "We'll get things sorted out for him," he said as he meticulously folded the dishtowel and set it on the counter. He adjusted it until it was perfectly aligned with the sink, and his shoulders immediately relaxed.

Once he felt like he could breathe again, he met Jolene's gaze and stifled a curse. Her eyes flicked between him and the dishtowel as she regarded him with curiosity. He prayed she would overlook what he had just done. With a miniscule movement, he shifted the dishtowel, unable to stop himself.

Jolene's lips twitched in amusement, then she shrugged. "I know we'll get it all cleaned up, but it never should have gotten like this in the first place. The least I could have done was hire a cleaning crew or something. Maybe had one of those mail order food delivery boxes sent to him."

"You could do all that moving forward," Finch suggested.

"But who am I kidding? He won't accept that type of help. He'll probably be pissed at the work I want to do here before we leave. He's such a crabbit."

Finch tilted his head, his eyebrows furrowing as he tried to comprehend the unfamiliar word. "A what?"

"Crabbit. It means a grumpy or ill-tempered person. He's a crabbit and a stubborn old goat."

"Well, it's not like he's going to undo everything we fix."

Jolene scoffed. "He might. He's that set in his ways."

Finch put his hands on her shoulders to stop her anxious pacing. "Let's not borrow trouble. We'll do the repairs and clean up to make it a safe place for your dad to come home to. Then we'll see what happens."

"Yeah, okay. You're right. It needs to be done."

"As for the rest of that little freak-out you just had—"

"I didn't have a freak-out," she insisted, cutting him off mid sentence. One of his eyebrows arched in a challenge. She huffed out a breath in annoyance. "Fine. I had a momentary lapse, but I'm fine now."

His lips twitched, betraying the smile he was trying to suppress. "As I was saying, the rest of that stuff you said will work itself out, too."

"Maybe you're right," she admitted grudgingly.

"Darn tootin'."

Another laugh burst from her. "You're a loon."

"I can accept that moniker." The overexaggerated way she rolled her eyes amused him. He'd missed this. The easy camaraderie they'd always had. Though he enjoyed the banter with his fellow Nighthawks, there was a certain spark that came with the back-and-forth between two people with a mutual attraction.

As if she'd just been doused with cold water, her expression shuttered, and she stepped out of his grasp. He attempted to hide the pain caused by her withdrawal, but it cut him deeply, nonetheless.

Moving to the coffeepot, she grabbed the mug he'd left out for her and poured herself a cup, adding a couple of spoonfuls of sugar. After taking a sip, she faced him once more, her expression devoid of emotion, as if the laughter they had just shared never happened.

"What were you saying about the food?" she asked.

"Just that if we want something for breakfast, it's probably best that we go out. Then we should probably stop at the store if we want more than soup to eat while we're here."

"Yeah, good idea. We can go to the diner, then visit dad. I need to talk to his doctor again. Then we can go to the store. We're going to need cleaning supplies, too."

"Sounds like a plan. You ready to go now?"

"Don't you want to change your shirt?"

He looked down at the wet spots on his shirt. "Oh yeah. Give me a sec." He dashed out of the kitchen and ascended the stairs two at a time, her lighthearted chuckle spurring him on.

"WHAT ARE YOU STARING at?" Jolene asked after finding Finch in the bread aisle.

"It's just not right," he muttered. Jolene had no idea what he was talking about, but he appeared troubled by whatever was bothering him. She wondered briefly if he had found out about the disturbing texts she'd been getting. Another one had come in while she was visiting her father. She ignored it until she could excuse herself to the bathroom to check it.

ARE YOU SCARED YET? YOU SHOULD BE.

The vagueness and highly disturbing nature of the threats unsettled her, especially since she didn't know who they were from. She wanted to turn her phone off and ignore them but worried she'd miss a call from the hospital. Each time one came in, she told herself she wasn't going to read it, yet she couldn't stop herself.

The messages were coming more frequently. She had no trouble ignoring the first few that had trickled in, thinking they were to a wrong number. Despite the fact that the threats may not have been directed at her, the thought of someone else being in danger weighed heavily on her mind. But what could she have done about it?

As the messages continued to pour in the last couple of days, she became increasingly convinced that she was the intended target. She should probably ask Emma to look into it. Her friend's skills with a computer were mindboggling, and yet she was reluctant to ask for help. Emma was with her fiancé on his movie release tour. Jolene hesitated to bring it up, not wanting to trouble her with what was likely trivial.

Watching Finch struggle with some inner conflict in the grocery store disturbed her. She knew if he found out about the messages, he wouldn't rest until the sender was unmasked and stopped. She didn't want to involve the other Nighthawks, but he'd do so without hesitation. Her Nighthawk friends had been through so much over the last couple of years. She didn't want to cause unnecessary worry about a few threatening anonymous texts.

"Look at it sitting there all innocent-like," Finch said to bring her attention back to the moment.

If he'd found out about the texts, she thought he would be angry and overprotective, but he didn't sound like that at all. His words were baffling.

"Innocent?" she asked.

"Yeah, look at it," he said, waving his hand toward the towering wall of bread loaves.

"Look at what?" Now she was really confused. What the hell was he talking about?

"That one. Right there in the middle." She looked where he was pointing, but the lack of any visible indication of his agitation made her doubt its severity. And his sanity, if she were being honest.

"I don't understand."

"It's unnatural," he repeated. "Look at it there in that bag. It's upside down. All its brothers and sisters are perfectly aligned in their wrapping. But not this one. The poor thing is breech."

Jolene looked closer at the row of bread he was indicating. That's when she saw that one was different from all the others. One loaf was indeed wrapped upside down in its packaging. Amid the sea of loaves, this one was the only one that looked different, almost like it was from a different batch. An oddball among the others, as if it didn't quite belong. The melody of "One of These Things Is Not Like the Others" triggered a fit of giggles that she just couldn't suppress.

She couldn't stop laughing, and it caused her to bend over, holding her stomach. Tears streamed down her face as her mirth became even more uncontrollable when Finch patted the loaf as if to comfort it.

"You are such a loon," she said between fits of laughter. The surrounding customers were edging away from them, shooting odd looks in their direction. She didn't care if she looked just as loony as he did. She had to hand it to him—the man had a knack for making her laugh, and she couldn't help but appreciate it.

Once she had herself under control, she wiped away the tears from under her eyes, hoping her mascara hadn't run. "If it bothers you that much, then pick another loaf," she suggested.

He went to do just that, then hesitated. "But what if nobody else picks him? He's the runt. The other loaves probably bully him. What if he becomes like that kid on the playground who's the last one picked for the game because nobody wants him on his team? If we don't take him home, we'll be just as bad as all the other playground bullies." He glared over his shoulder at a little old lady who chose a perfectly packaged loaf of bread.

Jolene bit her lip to suppress her laughter as he glared daggers at the old lady. In the end, he decided to take the challenged loaf home. He also grabbed the two on either side of it, claiming they were probably "friends." The man was crazy, but he'd kept her in stitches, which in turn kept her mind off all the things going wrong in her life at the moment.

Until her phone rang as she walked through the front door of her dad's house.

"Hey, Jolene. Sorry to bother you," Ox began after she answered.

"That's okay. What's up?"

"Well . . ." He hesitated, which wasn't a good sign. It had her blood pressure rising as she anticipated the bad news he had to share with her. Ox was a beast of a man. Former military, muscles for days, and a big ole teddy bear. He'd started working behind her bar years ago and had quickly made himself at home. Ever since, he'd become indispensable to her. It was a no brainer to leave him in charge while she was in Georgia. "A couple of our vendors didn't deliver today."

"What? Why not?"

"It's weird. They claim they got a call saying you were closing the doors, filing for bankruptcy, and would no longer need their services."

"*What*?" she shouted with an unnaturally high-pitched voice. Thankfully, Finch was still out at the car and couldn't hear her losing her shit.

"They refuse to deliver until they talk to you," he continued.

"Jesus Christ."

"I questioned everyone on staff, and no one knew anything about the calls. It didn't come from one of our people."

"Shit. Who would do such a thing?"

"Do you think it could have been one of your competitors in the area?"

"I can't imagine any of them doing something so underhanded. They've all been pretty friendly with me." She thought of the other restaurant owners in Lake Haven. Most were down-to-earth type people focused on making their businesses the best they could be. Some were owned by corporations but run by locals. She'd met most of them and never detected animosity from any of them.

The text messages popped into her head. It had to be related. Which meant those threats *were* directed at her. The last one asked if she was scared. Hell no, she wasn't scared. She was pissed. How dare some random no-name do this? They were not just hurting her, but her employees as well. If her business failed, everyone was out of a job. Some, like Nan Ryan, who was raising two little ones alone, needed their jobs to make ends meet.

The vendors who depended on her business to survive would also be impacted if she had to shutter her doors. Everything would domino. All because some anonymous shit decided to fuck with her.

No way. The thought of that happening was unacceptable to her. She had failed to defend her career vigorously enough the first time it was threatened. Not again. The memory of what Harrison and his wife had done to her burned in her mind, and she vowed never to let it happen again.

Ox's voice rose above the din of the bustling customers in the background to say, "I emailed you the list of vendors and phone numbers. As well as the names of those I talked to."

"Okay. Thanks Ox."

"I'm sorry I couldn't do more."

"It's not your fault."

"Let me know if I can help in any other way."

"Sure."

"Jolene . . ." He hesitated again. "Is everything all right? Are you all right?"

"I'm fine. It's gotta be a misunderstanding. I'll make some calls and get it straightened out." Though it was far from true, she tried to sound as convincing as possible, her voice unwavering.

His extended silence made her think the call had been disconnected, except the audible background chatter remained. She crossed her fingers, hoping he wouldn't question her further. "Okay. Well, if you need anything else from me, let me know."

"Will do. And thanks Ox."

"Anytime."

She hung up and immediately opened her email with a shaky hand. Four of her most reliable vendors were listed at the very top. Whoever had done this went to a hell of a lot of trouble. It wasn't like her vendors were public knowledge. So how did this person get this information? The conundrum had her stumped, but she refused to let it defeat her and was determined to solve it.

After helping Finch unload the groceries, she excused herself, claiming she had work for the bar to do. Locking herself in her dad's messy office, she felt the weight of the task ahead of her as she dialed each vendor's number. She made it clear to them that her business had not suffered any setbacks. Even offered to pay a little extra to get them to deliver as soon as possible.

By the time she was done, she was exhausted and thought nothing of checking the text message that had just come through. The device shook in her hand as she read the message, and she couldn't help but feel a sense of unease wash over her.

HOW DOES IT FEEL KNOWING YOU ARE ON THE VERGE OF LOSING EVERYTHING?

Something was going on with Jolene that had Finch worried. It went beyond the stress of her father being in the hospital. Beyond the stress of a house that was in less than stellar condition.

She'd spent hours locked away in her father's office. Occasionally, he could hear her conversation. It sounded like she was trying to clear up some kind of misunderstanding. Instinctively, he knew she wouldn't tell him if he asked what was going on. He hadn't earned that right yet. Her trust in him had been shattered since she'd learned about Angelica. And he couldn't blame her. He'd really fucked up by not telling her he was married but separated and working on a divorce.

As he wiped down the walls in the family room, his mind drifted to the morning after the truth had come out. Her anger had been palpable, and he'd felt like shit for causing her so much hurt.

Finch's list of rotten days was extensive, but that night after the awards banquet was the worst one yet. Things had been going so well. It thrilled him to have the opportunity to dance with Jolene, and he'd savored every moment. Holding her close. Feeling her body mold to his as they danced. He closed his eyes and savored the memory; it truly had been heaven. And when she'd asked him to come up to her room . . . even now, his dick twitched in response.

Angelica's appearance caused everything to fall apart. He had gone to great lengths to avoid any kind of personal interaction with her for over a year and had succeeded. Everything had gone through their lawyers. Until that night.

All the media attention surrounding the Nighthawks, including their heroic rescue of Marcus Rayne and receiving an award from the governor, had led Angelica right to him. And she'd pounced, determined to get her claws back into him. She was a miserable woman and took great pleasure in ruining any bit of happiness he could find for himself. As evidenced by her malicious attack that night.

The ding of the elevator announcing Jolene's floor was like music to his ears. He felt a knot of excitement in his stomach as he anticipated the evening ahead. Adrenaline coursed through his veins and he couldn't help but grin.

The doors slid open, and he eagerly stepped out, only to freeze on the threshold. She stood just beyond like a harbinger of doom. The scowl he'd grown to hate etched into her features. The knot of excitement twisted and morphed into something dark and sickly, threatening to burn up his esophagus. An ugly feeling of foreboding and dread took hold, and a pit in his stomach formed as a sense of impending doom washed over him.

This woman's effect on him had lasted for years, and he still hadn't shaken it. He despised himself for the way he reacted to her presence.

"Angelica," he croaked, his voice strained and raspy. He hated how his voice took on an unnatural tone whenever he was around her. It seemed to lose all its natural inflections when he had to converse with her. Taking a deep breath, he cleared his throat and tried again, this time with more conviction in his tone. "What are you doing here?"

"I came to see my husband. I've missed you." He couldn't stand the feigned affection in her voice. He had fallen for that same trick countless times before. His desperation for love had blinded him, and he'd failed to remember how quickly she could turn on him.

That's exactly how she'd groomed him. She had convinced him that he was so undeserving of love that no one else would ever offer it to him. He was unworthy and should be thankful that he had her.

Seeing the truth required time and distance. But the moment he saw her again, all those negative emotions resurfaced. He was crazy to think a woman like Jolene would want to be with him. He should walk away before *she saw him for the loser he was. He didn't want to expose his self-perceived inadequacies to her.*

No. That was Angelica in his head again. He had worth. He'd served his country with honor. He was a respected member of the Nighthawks. His mom instilled in him the importance of treating women with respect and reverence. Watching his father's devotion and commitment to his mother had taught him how to cherish and value a woman. His father had taught him the art of being a gentleman. In short . . . he was a catch.

But none of that had done him any favors in his interactions with his wife. No matter what he did, she always found fault with him, which made their relations unpleasant. Even though she hurled insults and abuse at him, he remained restrained due to his ingrained gentlemanly habits. He'd suffered through it for ten years when their dirty little secret was revealed. He left her, then delayed the divorce process, lacking the strength to face her. It had been easier just to hide away and lick his wounds in private.

But then he'd met Jolene and knew she was going to change his life. He found the fortitude to request a divorce and, as he predicted, Angelica's reaction was explosive. He was thankful for the time apart because it gave him the opportunity to reflect and grow as an individual. Even though he still struggled with hearing her voice in his head some days, therapy helped him immensely.

And because they lived in two different states after he'd taken the job with the Nighthawks, he didn't have to deal with her in person. Everything could go through their lawyers.

Then, just weeks ago, he'd learned an awful truth she'd hidden from him from the beginning. Now, everything she said to him was suspect.

"Don't give me that bullshit," he spat. "Why are you here?"

"Is it so hard to believe I wanted to see you? You're my husband."

"Not for much longer."

"You can't mean that. We were good together once."

He snorted. "If your definition of good together means constant fights, abuse, manipulation, gaslighting, and belittling, then I guess you're right."

"I can't believe that is how you saw our relationship. I loved you."

No longer vulnerable to her false words, he scoffed at her feeble attempts to manipulate him. "You loved controlling me." Her true intentions for pursuing him became clear to him at that moment. "That's why you're here, isn't it? You're unhappy because you can't control me anymore."

"I don't know what you're talking about. I wanted to discuss repairing our relationship."

"Right. After all this time, you wanted to discuss..." He broke off as a thought occurred to him. "How did you know where I was? Have you been having me followed?" Based on her past behavior, it was highly likely that she would pull a stunt like that. There had been one time before they'd started dating in high school when he'd gone out with another girl. He thought that maybe Angelica had followed them because he had spotted someone who looked like her at the same movie they had attended. But he could never be sure. When his date had come back from a trip to the bathroom, she'd appeared spooked and asked him to take her home. Despite his best efforts, he couldn't win her over for a second date. He wondered if Angelica had said something to

the girl to scare her away, even though he could never prove it.

He noticed a flash of irritation in her eyes before she concealed it. "It's no secret your little group has made the news channels since that Marcus Rayne thing," she reasoned.

He ignored the "little group" taunt. "That's true. But this awards banquet is a local thing. A Michigan thing. There's no way it would make the news in Maryland." She still lived in the house they'd owned near Joint Base Andrews where he'd been stationed. A state awards banquet wouldn't have made the news there. Not unless she'd been looking.

She shrugged. "What can I say? Guess you guys are more popular than you thought." He could see the lie clear as day. She probably had a Google alert set up for his name. Either that, or she was having him followed. Both were cringeworthy, and he'd be discussing it with his lawyer.

"Cut the crap, Angelica. I have plans, and they don't involve standing here arguing with you."

Her eyes sparked with fury. "Oh, I know what your plans are. You and that little tramp. If you think you can fool around behind my back, think again." She stepped closer, and the surrounding air seemed to vibrate with her anger. His guard was up. There was a certain volatility to her when she was like this. The closer she got, the more intense the buzz of electricity in the air became, crackling with her anger.

"What the fuck do you think you're doing?" her shrill voice hissed.

"Angelica," he said, his words measured and deliberate as he tried to choose them carefully. There was no telling what would set her off. He was in a public place. If she lost her shit, it would reflect poorly on him and the Nighthawks.

Jolene's sudden appearance in the elevator vestibule startled him, and his heart raced as he tried to compose himself. He could sense her shock as she took in the scene in front of her, her eyes widening.

Standing too close, Angelica's anger was almost suffocating, and he could feel the intensity of it in her piercing gaze. He could only imagine what they looked like to Jolene.

Then Angelica opened her mouth and made it worse. "Is this her?" she ranted. "Is this the little whore you think you can cheat on me with?"

All the color drained from Jolene's complexion. It was as if everything stopped, and all that remained was the feeling of dread. She was still in her evening gown and holding an empty ice bucket. The crinkling of the plastic lining crackled through the suddenly quiet vestibule. As the elevators' machinery clanked and whirred, Angelica's voice pierced through the noise, filling the space, making him cringe.

"How could you, Atty? How could you do this to me? And with her?"

"Angelica," Finch chastised, pissed at her feigned offense. Finch's patience was wearing thin. This was his worst nightmare. He never intended for Jolene to learn about Angelica like this. It had taken him an immense amount of effort and time to break free from her. And he was nearly there. He felt the weight of impending disaster bearing down on him. "Please keep your voice down." Angelica's lethal stare should have killed him, but he had grown immune to her wrath.

The sharp clatter of a small plastic disk crashing against the tiled floor abruptly jolted their attention back to Jolene, who stood frozen in place, gawking at them in utter shock. The acrid scent of disinfectant hung heavily in the air, mixing with the cloying aroma of Angelica's perfume. The fluorescent lights overhead buzzed loudly, casting a cold and sterile glow across the room. The temperature in the hall was noticeably cooler than the rest of the building, causing him to shiver. Yet a single bead of sweat trickled down the length of his spine, reminding him of the anxious tension that had been building. Every sense seemed heightened as he watched all his hopes for a happy future die.

He gazed at the stunning woman in the green gown and saw all that he had imagined with her crumble. Her initial shock quickly turned to a look of distrust and anger. He desperately tried to think of something to say, but his mind was completely empty. And Angelica wasn't helping the situation.

"You're nothing but a hussy, aren't you?" With a look of contempt, Angelica scanned Jolene from head to toe. With a sneer, she spat, "Slut."

Jolene set the ice bucket down on the brass table across from the elevators and turned back to face them. She gave Angelica a quick once-over of her own. "And who are you?"

"I'm his wife. That's all you need to know." Finch closed his eyes. Shit. The truth was out. It wasn't his intention for Jolene to find out this way. Shame washed over him as he thought about their plans for the evening.

Jolene stumbled over to the wall on unsteady feet. Her ragged breath resonated through the silent room.

Finch made a move to go to her but pulled up short when she raised her hand. Her eyes burned with a deep sense of betrayal that cut straight to his core.

Angelica laughed. The sound pierced through his brain, causing him to flinch. "I see he didn't tell you. Typical. He never could do anything right."

When Jolene looked at Finch, he could see a fire in her eyes that he had never witnessed before. Desperately, he gazed at her, imploring her to understand.

Despite the anger he saw in her eyes, her voice remained steady as she asked, "Is it true?"

His gaze dropped to the floor, and he felt the hot flush of shame creeping up his neck. The crushing weight of his guilt was like a vise, twisting his insides into knots. He could feel the sweat on his brow and taste the metallic tang of panic in his mouth. His heart was pounding so hard he thought it might burst out of his chest.

"Oh God," Jolene gasped, her eyes wide with horror.

"Jolie." When he whispered her nickname, she flinched hard, hitting him like a punch to the gut. "Let me explain."

He perceived a swarm of thoughts whirling through her mind. Each one hardening her expression further. When she threw her shoulders back and straightened her spine, he knew he was done.

"No. I don't want to hear it." With that, she turned around and fled. He called out to her, but his voice was lost in the sound of her footsteps.

The hall was suddenly suffocatingly hot, and the sound of his own labored breathing rasped in his ears like sandpaper. The acrid smell of sweat mingled with the floor cleaner and Angelica's overwhelming perfume made him feel sick to his stomach. His heart lay shattered at his feet, and Angelica was there to stomp the remaining pieces into dust.

As he'd stared down at his wife's smug smile, he'd decided enough was enough. He had been willing to turn a blind eye to the betrayal he had uncovered despite his lawyer's urgings, but that was no longer possible.

He leaned in to whisper in her ear. "You think you've won something, don't you? Well, I know the truth. And the truth will free me from your deceitful and malicious actions. No more mister nice Atticus." The wide-eyed look of trepidation was all he needed to know he'd hit his mark. With a half smile, he'd turned away from his past, hitting the bar on the stairwell door with more force than he'd intended. Though he was angry, his determination remained unshaken. He wouldn't stop until he turned his dream future into a reality.

Jolene still wouldn't let him explain the situation of his marriage to her. But he could sense her walls weakening. The fact that she'd laughed so heartily at his lunacy a couple of times now was a good sign.

And yet he couldn't help but feel something was wrong, aside from her anger at him. Something had her on edge. The telltale prickle on the back of his neck was a sure sign that something wasn't right. The nagging feeling wouldn't go away, and he was determined to uncover what it was.

After dinner, she'd excused herself and gone to her room, claiming she was tired. Finch tackled a few more chores, and the sound of the broom fluttered through the empty house. As he cleared cobwebs that had accumulated in corners, he felt a sense of satisfaction from making the space cleaner and taking one more task off Jolene's shoulders. He was unwavering in his resolve to alleviate her stress, even if it meant doing something seemingly insignificant.

He turned off all the lights, double-checked the locks, and sat down on the couch to answer a few texts from the women at home who were asking about Jolene. Despite everything that had happened, he reassured them she was still holding strong. He wouldn't worry their friends with his concerns. There was nothing they could do from Lake Haven. It was up to him to keep an eye on her.

Unknowingly, he had fallen asleep on the couch until racing footsteps on the stairs startled him awake. Jolene dashed to the front door, struggling in her haste to get the locks open. With a frustrated growl, she finally got the last lock released and wrenched the door open. Finch was on his feet and flying after her as she shot through the door, down the porch stairs, and around the corner of the house. He caught up to her when she'd stopped dead in her tracks, staring into the woods behind the house.

"Jolene?" He approached cautiously, not wanting to startle her.

"Did you see that?"

"See what?" he asked, peering into the darkness, trying to spot what she'd seen.

"Someone was here."

Adrenaline pumped through his veins, immediately putting him on alert. "What?"

"Someone was here. Under my window."

"Are you sure?" He hadn't heard anything moving around, and the windows in the family room where he'd been napping were directly behind them. If someone had been standing out here, surely he would have heard them.

He took a few steps closer to the house until he could see Jolene's bedroom window past the big tree in the side yard. The flower beds were a mess, with weeds and wildflowers growing everywhere, but he could see that someone had been in there recently, as there were clear depressions in the soil. There were indications of trampling on some of the plants. The grass was wet with dew, and he could clearly see the path the intruder had taken to escape into the woods.

"Stay here," he said before he followed the path. He should have known she wouldn't listen. When they reached the tree line, he heard her wince. Looking down at her feet, he swore softly. "Jolie, you're not wearing shoes. Go back to the house. I'll see if I can track their path."

He could see her gearing up to argue, but he wouldn't have it. "Please, honey. Go back inside. Lock the doors. I can't do my job if I'm worried about you getting hurt." With wide, anxious eyes, she stared at him and nervously bit her lip before nodding in agreement and quickly turning to make her way back to the house.

Turning on the flashlight app on his cell, he followed a clear path the amateur stalker had made until he reached the road. They must have hopped into a car since that's where he lost their trail.

Making his way back to the house, he was more determined than ever to get to the bottom of what was going on with Jolene. He hoped he'd made enough headway in their friendship that she'd trust him with the truth. And he prayed that her faith in him was strong enough to believe he would always protect her.

Chapter 11

JOLENE PACED THE FOYER as she waited for Finch to return. When she'd spotted the person below her window, she thought her overactive imagination had conjured them. That her worry over the threatening texts had her manifesting some nefarious being.

But the proof was plain as day in the flowerbeds. Someone had been there. Was it the same person who'd been texting her? As if she'd conjured it, another text notification dinged, startling her.

I WILL NOT STOP UNTIL I'VE DESTROYED YOU.

Her hands shook as she stared at the message. She wanted to scream. She wanted to yell at the device. Demand it tell her who was tormenting her. But, of course, it couldn't do that. Maybe it was time to get Emma involved.

"Jolene?" Finch's voice jolted her so badly the phone flew out of her hand and crashed to the floor. Her heart thumped loudly in her ears, drowning out all other sounds.

Finch bent and retrieved her phone. She stared at the thing as if worried it would bite. When she didn't make a move to take it from his hand, he placed it face up on the little table next to the front door.

"You ready to tell me what's going on?" Finch asked, making her tear her eyes away from her phone. He had a concerned look on his face, but there was also an underlying fierceness that showed he wouldn't back down until he found out the truth.

God, she wanted to trust him with this. She knew inherently he'd do everything in his power to protect her no matter what was happening between them. But did she really want to thrust him into the middle of this? The situation was so perplexing that even she couldn't fathom what was happening. How could she expect him to help?

He was already giving up so much to help her out here. He was resolute in his decision to support her, determined to be a source of comfort as she dealt with the stress and worry of her father's illness. It had gone a long way toward building a bridge between them.

She thought about the last year. He'd done every-thing she'd requested without argument. When she'd asked, he'd backed off. He'd stayed silent when she was resolute in her stubbornness. He tried to tell her about his marriage, but she shut him down before he could even begin. She'd begun to assume his marriage was a bad one, especially since she hadn't seen his wife since that night. But she never gave him the chance to set the record straight, and he'd respected her wishes.

He'd taken her aloofness, never once protesting. He'd taken her silence. She could see how her indif-ference hurt him, but he never once complaining. She'd needed the distance, and he'd given it to her. Absorbing the sting when she'd snubbed him. He'd never once been anything but patient and kind.

Now, thinking back over everything . . . God, she owed him an apology.

Maybe confessing what was going on would be another support beam in the bridge he'd been trying to build.

She was still mulling it over when her phone took the decision out of her hands. The notification tone echoed in the silence between them. The brightness of the screen lit up the dark foyer as the message preview flashed on the display.

I LOST EVERYTHING BECAUSE OF YOU. HOW MUCH DO YOU HAVE TO LOSE?

Finch grabbed the phone before she could. "What the hell?"

"It's . . ." she started, not knowing how to explain it.

"Is there more?" She could tell he knew the answer just by looking at her expression. "Unlock the phone. Let me see," he said, holding the phone out to her.

She took it and hesitated only briefly before doing as he asked. She opened the long text thread and handed it back to him, knowing she couldn't do it alone anymore. The fact that someone had been outside her window had scared her. More than the threatening messages had managed to do. She could ignore words. She couldn't ignore the tangible proof that someone had been there.

Finch's jaw tightened as he read through the messages, anger evident on his face. His eyes narrowed on the screen, looking at it as if he could reach through it and throttle the person behind the messages. She took solace in his anger, knowing that he was on her side. If the last year had taught her anything about the man before her, it was that he would never turn his anger on her. She'd given him so many reasons to do just that. He never did.

"Any idea who these are from?" he asked, thumbing through the messages again.

She scoffed. "If I knew that, wouldn't you think I'd do something to put a stop to it?" She winced, realizing her attempt to lighten the mood had instead come off as snarky.

She should have known he wouldn't take it personally. The slight upward twitch in his lips told her that. "Yeah, you would." His smile faltered as he continued to read, his expression growing more concerned. "These are escalating. Both in tone and frequency."

"I know." Even she could hear that her voice didn't sound like her. The slight wobble was a dead give-away, and Finch noticed, too. She bit her lip, trying to keep her emotions in check. She had a feeling if she let it go from between her teeth, it would tremble noticeably.

He moved closer, his steps uncertain and hesitant. She wanted to cry. She'd done that. That tentative-ness in him was her fault. All she wanted was to keep her heart from being shattered again. She had learned the hard way that vulnerability only led to heartache.

But things were different now. There was a renewed sense of connection, a rekindled friendship. If she desired, she could walk through the crumbling walls.

She closed the distance and threw herself against his chest, wrapping her arms around his waist. "I'm scared," she whispered.

He pressed his lips to the top of her head, murmur-ing her name. "Jolie." When his arms wrapped around her, the tension inside her eased. She snuggled into his embrace, letting his powerful presence envelop her.

His strength and vitality made her feel safe and protected.

"Come on," he said, loosening his hold, which had her feeling suddenly bereft. "Let's go sit and talk about this."

She nodded, and he took her hand, leading her to the couch. In her periphery, she noted he'd done some more cleaning and felt guilty for not doing her part. Just more proof that she needed to give this man a chance.

He sat and pulled her down right next to him, keeping her hand in his as if he was reluctant to let her go. "What can you tell me about what's going on?"

She drew in a deep breath, then blew it out slowly. "I don't even know what's going on," she confessed. "The texts started a few weeks ago. One every couple of days. At first, I thought they were a wrong number. I kind of still thought that until tonight."

"Okay, I can see how you'd feel that way. The increase in frequency is concerning, though." He looked down at her phone, which had gone dark in his hand. "The texts mention destroying you, which I can only imagine means physically." She could feel his hand tighten around hers as he spoke. "But they also suggest destroying everything you've built. I heard you on the phone with Ox earlier. Is everything okay at the bar?"

The idea that everything was connected had nagged at her, but she pushed it to the back of her mind. She couldn't ignore it anymore; it was all front and center now. All the things that had been happening. The messed-up orders. The incorrect invoices. The glitch with payroll. And then today with the weird calls to her vendors.

"Oh shit. You're right."

"What's going on?"

She told him everything that had been happening at the bar since that first text message had come through. Her anger grew. At herself for not seeing what was happening. And at whoever was attempting to destroy everything. It was like they knew how to hit her where it hurt the most. She'd already lost one restaurant through no fault of her own. She couldn't handle losing another.

Harrison popped into her head. Could he be behind all this? But to what end? He was the one who forced her out of Noitiña. The restaurant was his. The awards stayed with him. The notoriety as one of the best restaurants in New York City remained his.

She was the one who'd lost everything. She was the one who'd had to start over. He'd ruined her. What would be the point of doing it a second time? She hadn't seen or heard from him since the day she'd walked away with her recipes.

Was that it? Was he angry she'd maintained her ownership of the recipes?

"What was that thought you just had?" Finch asked, breaking into her thoughts.

Could she tell him about New York? Even Emma didn't know exactly what happened. She'd been too ashamed to tell anyone. Her dad only knew because he'd met Harrison a few times. She had no choice but to tell him about the disgraceful actions done to her by him and his wife. How he'd fooled her. Played her. Ruined her. Then she'd cried in her dad's comforting arms.

Maybe it was time for her to let go of the shame that had kept her silent for so long. It wasn't her shame to carry anyway. She wasn't the asshole who'd done all those things. There could be a sense of justice in disclosing the appalling deeds of Harrison Walker Winston III.

"I was thinking about my ex," she admitted, and Finch's body tensed up next to her. "While in culinary school, I met a man. He was older. Refined. Attractive. Everything a naïve, young woman would find appealing in a man. He wooed me over the next few years. And when I graduated, he offered me everything I dreamed of. We opened a restaurant in the heart of New York City together. He was the money. I was the talent. It was my kitchen. My recipes that put Noitiña on the right lists. Our notoriety was growing. The logical next step was getting married."

"What happened?" Finch asked softly, squeezing her hand.

"His wife happened."

Finch's gasp was audible, and she knew he was thinking about what had happened between them. She'd been duped. Twice. And hadn't seen it coming either time.

Finch sat stiff as a board beside her, but she ignored his anguish in order to continue her story.

"Harrison's wife was everything I wasn't. Rich. Beautiful. Refined. And a complete and utter bitch. She confronted me at the restaurant. In my kitchen, in front of all my employees. Harrison stood beside her like some sort of lapdog. There was absolutely no remorse in his expression. He'd led me on for years. Made me complicit in adultery. Then he stole everything away from me as if I'd never meant anything to him.

"He and his wife, who, as it turned out, held the purse strings, fired me that day. Forcing me out of my own restaurant. My dream. They ruined me. I ran home with my tail between my legs. If it wasn't for my dad's advice about maintaining ownership of my recipes, I would have lost everything."

"God, Jolene," he uttered, his voice full of anguish. "I'm so sorry."

Her gaze drifted down to their joined hands, taking in the smattering of freckles on the back of his and up his arm. The curse of a redhead. The faint scar on his arm caught her attention, and she couldn't help but wonder about its origin.

With a deep breath, she squeezed his hand, offering comfort while gathering courage from the connection to continue. "It took me a long time before I felt confident enough to try again. Emma and I had been close in college. She invited me to visit while she was in the Coast Guard, and I never left. The moment I drove through Lake Haven, I was drawn to its quaint charm. It reminded me so much of my hometown. I opened Jolene's bar and never looked back."

"And then you met me, and I brought it all back up for you," he said, his voice heavy with remorse. He let go of her hand and sat forward, his elbows on his knees and his head in his hands. "Fuck, Jolene. No wonder you don't want anything to do with me."

"I'm beginning to see that the two situations may be as different as night and day," she confessed.

He quickly lifted his head and turned toward her. She could see the regret and anguish that he'd caused her pain in his eyes. And that was how she knew he was nothing like Harrison. It was then that she resolved to hear him out when he was ready to discuss it once more.

"I never wanted to hurt you," he implored. "I'd been separated for years. After I met you, I filed for divorce. It's taking forever. You were a breath of fresh air. Things with her . . . my marriage . . . hadn't been good. I hadn't intended to take things so far with you. At least not until my divorce was final. I just . . . couldn't stay away." His gaze dropped from hers, and he fidgeted with his hands. "You must hate me."

"I thought I did. But lately, I've begun to see things differently. Seeing the anguish you feel at this moment, I can tell you are nothing like Harrison. I think I'm ready to hear you out."

Her phone dinged with another text, interrupting the moment. Another threat flashed on the screen.

DON'T GET COMFORTABLE. I'LL SEE TO IT YOU LOSE EVERYTHING.

"Jesus Christ. This person is relentless," Finch muttered. "We should contact Emma. See if she can work her magic to find out who's behind this."

"I thought about it, but she's on tour with Marcus. I don't want to disturb them."

"She's your best friend and cares about you. She'd want to help. In fact, I think she'd be pissed you've waited so long."

Jolene snickered to herself, knowing full well that Emma would definitely be thoroughly annoyed. "You're probably right. I'll call her in the morning."

"Do you think you can go back to sleep?" he asked, his hand slipping hesitantly over hers once again.

Could she? Now that she remembered the shadowed figure under her window, she wasn't sure. "I-I guess."

Finch reached up and cupped her cheek, the warmth from his palm giving her more comfort that she ever thought possible. She leaned into it, closing her eyes. "We're going to figure this out. I'll keep you safe. I promise."

She nodded, feeling the sudden sting of tears at the veracity in his words. She knew without a doubt that he would do everything in his power to protect her. Her faith in that truth never wavered, even when she hated him.

"Tomorrow we'll go get some cameras to set up around the house. Maybe some motion sensor lights.

Nobody will get that close again without us knowing."

"Thank you, Finch. After this past year, I never thought I'd say this, but I'm glad you're here."

The smile he gave her shot straight to her heart. It was so incredibly childlike and uncomplicated. It was the way she'd once believed Finch navigated life, what he was truly like inside. But there was more to him than met the eye. Something deep inside that he kept hidden from the world. Some inner wound that had sliced him up. And was probably still slashing through him.

"Go on up," he prompted. "I'm gonna do a perimeter check, then make sure everything is locked up tight."

"Okay." She rose to her feet, and he mirrored her action. He stood so close she could feel the heat from his body. An invisible warmth wrapped around her, and she drank in the comfort of his nearness.

She couldn't resist taking in the sight of his well-defined arms and broad shoulders. Her eyes roamed over his tempting form, taking in the way his clothes hugged his body. He really was devilishly handsome.

His sharp cheekbones cast shadows over his chiseled jawline, and his piercing hazel eyes sparkled with a mischievous glint. His tousled hair seemed to beg for a woman's touch.

She struggled to battle the intense need to be near him. It was too easy to get lost in the way he looked at her. She was so tired of fighting. Couldn't she have this one moment to lose herself, forget all her troubles, and just feel?

Yeah. She was taking it.

Fisting his T-shirt in her hand, she took a chance. She slowly rose onto the balls of her feet, the wood floor cool beneath her toes as she lifted herself onto her tiptoes. Their laborious breathing filled the air as she leaned in closer to him, her heart racing in anticipation. The outdoorsy scent of his cologne, mixed with the subtle aroma of candy, caused her senses to heighten. As she touched her lips to his, a rush of warmth spread throughout her body, making her heart skip a beat.

She played her lips across his, teasing them open. He acquiesced, and she slipped her tongue inside the warm recesses of his mouth. At the first touch, he let out a growl. His arms encircled her, one hand on her back, the other at her nape as he held her tightly to him. His embrace was entirely male, and she melted.

With his mouth moving over hers, she felt every inch of his soft lips. His kisses were slow and drugging, making her feel like she was lost in a dream. His tongue sent shivers of desire racing through her. Her eager response shocked her, but she knew it was too late to hold back now.

His lips broke from hers and traveled a fiery path along her jaw, then to her neck, and finally up to her earlobe. He whispered into her ear, sending tingles throughout her entire body. "I know what a gift you're giving me right now." The warmth of his breath and the sound of his voice sent a shiver down her spine. "I won't squander it."

He recaptured her lips with a dreamy intimacy that left her weak and confused. And so incredibly turned on. She was burning up from the inside out. But before she could truly lose herself in the power of his kiss, it was over.

His eyes were heavy-lidded and so tender it took her breath away. "Go get some sleep. We'll talk more tomorrow." He kissed the tip of her nose, making her heart flutter, before he backed away with a smile. "Good night, Jolie."

She watched him walk away, her senses reeling as if short-circuiting. With every step he took, she sensed a fierce strength coiled within him. A powerful presence that she could feel within herself.

With a last glance at her that spoke volumes, his broad shoulders disappeared around the corner to the kitchen. She realized she had been holding her breath and took a deep, satisfying lungful of air.

The man could kiss. The taste of his lips lingered in her mind, and she knew that she would have to overcome her stubbornness for more.

Chapter 12

THREE DAYS HAD PASSED in a blur of activity. The morning after Jolene had spotted someone under her window and told him about the threatening text messages, he'd gone out to see if he could discern anything about their visitor in the daylight. There wasn't much, but the impressions in the dirt were smaller than the ones his feet made and not as deep. Which made him think that maybe this was just a kid pulling a prank and not related to the texts at all. But he wasn't about to risk Jolene's safety on an unconfirmed hunch.

They'd gone to the store that day and picked up cameras and motion sensing lights. Then he'd spent the day installing them all over the house. Nobody was getting close again without them knowing about it.

After that was done, they'd spent more time getting the house cleaned up and making a list of repairs that needed to be completed. Since the porch was at the top of that list, Finch began that first. He'd spent the day before pulling up boards that couldn't be salvaged and replacing them with new.

Jolene was with her dad, moving him into a rehab center. With his broken leg, they believed it would be the best place for him to recover as he gained his strength back after the heart attack.

He couldn't stop thinking about that kiss. Like he'd told her, he knew she was giving him a gift. Her renewed trust in him was like a balm to his wounded heart. Tasting her lips again had been like rediscovering a long-forgotten memory. One that he hadn't realized how much he missed until it was unlocked. But he should have known. Just in the time they'd spent privately together before Angelica blew it all to hell, he'd known they'd be electric together. He'd never experienced anything like it before. Just one kiss from Jolene had far surpassed anything he'd ever had with Angelica. Even at his horniest teenage self, he had never felt the same level of desire as he did when Jolene kissed him.

But just like everything in his life, Angelica had to take control. She wasn't happy unless she was lording over him in some manner. Seeing him happy with another woman had sent her over the edge. But she'd made a fatal error. Angelica could mess with him all she liked. He could take it. But fucking with Jolene . . . he wouldn't stand for that. She'd made it easy for him to make the decision he'd been struggling with for their divorce.

As he affixed another post on the porch's railing, his mind wandered back to the morning after that disastrous night when he'd begged Jolene to hear him out. Even after all this time, the memory still felt like a punch to the gut.

Angelica wasn't done fucking with him. Just when he thought he was free of her, she popped up again, like a bad penny. This was the last straw. He wanted to be free of her and vowed to do everything in his power to make that happen.

In an early morning call to his lawyer, he finally gave permission to use the reprehensible information they had uncovered about her. Disgust and revulsion pervaded every time he thought about Angelica's actions and her attempts to conceal it. It sickened him that he'd been so oblivious. A deep sense of shame permeated through him as he recognized how ignorant he had been.

But no more. His eyes were wide open now. And since she was still pulling shit to ruin his life, he'd had enough. He was more than ready to fight fire with fire. She'd been fighting him over the divorce, refusing to compromise anything. He'd been willing to go the easy route and try to work with her, but no more.

Discovering the previous week what she had done early on in their marriage and how'd she'd played him for so many years combined with her little stunt last night put an end to his easy-going attitude. No more Mr. Nice Guy. She was going down, and he'd finally be free.

But first, he had to fix things with Jolene. Which was why he was standing outside her hotel room with two cups of coffee at six o'clock in the morning.

She answered the door wearing a T-shirt that matched her eyes and black leggings. His heart stopped, turned over, and started thumping hard against his chest. She looked exhausted but still so incredibly beautiful. And she had almost been his.

"What do you want, Finch?" she asked, her tone harsh and weary. Her blank expression made his gut twist with worry.

He held out one of the cups to her. With a frown, she gingerly took it from his hand, avoiding his touch as if he were contaminated. A twinge of foreboding settled in his stomach.

"I've come to offer an explanation and beg your forgiveness."

"I don't want to hear it," she sniped, then sighed. "I'm really tired and I still need to pack up to go home. Another time, maybe." She nearly closed the door in his face. He blocked it with his foot. With an irritated sigh, she moved out of the way and let him into her room. She set her coffee cup down on the dresser before crossing to where her open suitcase lay on the bed. He watched her, and regrets assailed him, weighing him down like a steel weight.

The despair in his throat made it hard to speak, but he pushed through it. He set his cup beside hers, before he shoved his hands in his pockets and hunched his shoulders. "Please. I'm sorry you found out that way. Let me explain."

"It's not necessary."

"Jolie—"

"Don't call me that," she hissed, her eyes blazing briefly before she shuttered them. It was the first sign of emotion she'd shown him since she'd opened her door.

"Sorry," he mumbled. "I won't use it again. But please, give me a chance to explain."

"I really don't need to hear it. It's probably better this way, anyway." She shook her head. "The fact of the matter is, you lied. And I can't abide liars."

"Jolene, please. You don't understand. Let me explain—"

"No," she blurted, cutting him off once more, then shrugged in mock resignation. "Maybe she did us a favor. Maybe it's better if we just remain friends. I've got my hands full with the bar. I haven't had time to even visit my dad, let alone devote time to a relationship." Her face contorted with pain as she paused and pinched

the bridge of her nose. He longed to make the hurt go away with every fiber of his being but felt helpless. Her hand fell, and with it, all emotion drained from her as she peered at him with empty, glassy eyes.

"Jolene." His plea to her was fueled by his desperation to explain.

She raised her hand, and he clamped his mouth shut. "Your silence about her makes me feel like I don't really know you, and now I'm carrying a secret that I don't want to keep."

Fuck. When put like that, it made him sound horrible. A stab of guilt struck deep in his chest. "I just need you to hear me out, and I can clear everything up."

She was shaking her head before he'd even finished speaking. "I'm tired, Finch," she uttered. "I'm tired of being hurt . . . duped. I refuse to go through that again."

His throat ached with defeat. In an attempt to conceal his emotions, he hunched his shoulders even further and stared at the ground. Overwhelmed with grief and guilt, he couldn't comprehend her words. "I'm sorry. I didn't mean——"

"I don't need excuses. Let's just forget this ever happened. It probably wouldn't have worked out between us anyway." His gaze shot up to hers, surprised that she actually believed what she said. With each passing word, the sense of loss grew stronger within him. "Then what would have happened? We have friends in common. If it didn't work, it would have created an uncomfortable situation for everyone. We're better off as friends. I need you to respect that."

He could read the desperation in her eyes, which made his spirits sink even lower. He ran an unsteady hand through his hair, accepting defeat reluctantly. His frustration was so palpable, he really wanted to tear his hair out by the roots. If he could just get her to listen, maybe he would still have a chance. But the hurt and longing that lay in her eyes gave him pause.

With a heavy heart, he decided to give her what she wanted. For now. He'd give her time. Then perhaps someday, she'd be open to listening to his story. He clung to the idea that the day would arrive sooner rather than later.

"Okay. I'll respect that."

"Good," she said, walking past him to open her hotel room door.

Picking up on the subtle cue of dismissal, he approached her by crossing the room. His fingers brushed against her skin as he cupped her cheek, unable to stop himself. His touch startled her, causing her eyes to widen as they locked onto his. "I'll always be here if you need me, Jolene. That will never change." Then he kissed her cheek and walked out the door, almost colliding with Emma.

"Ahh, the walk of shame," Emma teased. "About time the guy gets to feel what that's like." He knew he was turning bright red, and Emma confirmed it when she burst out laughing. "Oh my God. Are you blushing? Wait. Let me get a picture. I have to document this. The day Finch blushed."

She was reaching into her pocket for her phone when, with a groan, Finch blushed even deeper. He took off down the hall before she could get her picture. "Very funny," he called over his shoulder.

"But I didn't get my picture," she shouted after him. He flipped her the bird over his shoulder, and she laughed harder.

"Leave the poor man alone," Jolene admonished just before the door slammed closed. The sound was deafen-

ing, even at a distance. It reverberated through him like a physical blow to his shattered heart. It was a sharp and conclusive end to everything he had hoped for, leaving him feeling empty and alone.

He could still hear the sharp bang of the door in his mind, as if it had just happened. Could still feel the reverberations beating against his heart, slicing it with its finality.

Now that he knew about her ex, he understood how completely he'd fucked up. It was truly amazing that she was even talking to him, let alone kissing him.

Learning about what that man, Harrison—even the name was douchey—had done to her, he could feel her anguish and anger. That man and his wife had stolen away everything that was important to her. Including her trust in people. It was no wonder she hadn't wanted to hear any excuses from him. He could have talked until he was blue in the face about the truth of his marriage, but it wouldn't change the fact that she felt duped. Again.

He'd taken that knowledge like a sucker punch to the gut. By omitting the fact that he was separated from his wife while they had been getting to know each other, he'd betrayed her trust. He was no better than Harrison.

But after that kiss a few nights ago, he couldn't help but think they were on the verge of putting the past behind them. She'd said she was ready to hear him out. That the two situations—him and Harrison—were as different as night and day. He had to draw strength from that. It wouldn't be easy for him to talk about what his marriage had been like, but if he couldn't tell Jolene, a woman he'd come to care for greatly, then who could he tell? The only way for them to move forward was for the truth to come out.

The SUV pulling into the driveway caught his attention. He could see the vivacious redhead who had the capability to change his life forever in the driver's seat. She was the one who held his future, whether she realized it or not.

Chapter 13

FINCH WAS ALMOST DONE with the new porch stairs the next day, only one nail left to go, when his cellphone interrupted him. As he wiped his brow with the hem of his shirt, he fished the phone out of his pocket. His body immediately stiffened with tension upon seeing that the call was from his lawyer.

He took a deep breath, praying for good news, and swiped to answer. "Hey, Alan. I hope you have something good to tell me."

"I think you'll want to hear this. You got a minute?"

"Yeah, go ahead." Apprehension stabbed through Finch's body, feeling like a thousand needles. The weight of the call's potential impact hung heavily on him. He'd been fighting relentlessly to achieve a positive outcome, with no end in sight. This was the closest he'd ever been.

"It's done. The judge signed off on it. And all the paperwork has been filed."

Uncertain, Finch shook his head in disbelief as he listened to Alan's words. The words were muffled by the buzzing that had suddenly begun in his ears.

"I don't . . . I . . . what?" As he tried to speak, Finch's mind raced, his thoughts a jumbled mess that he couldn't make sense of.

"You're free, man."

Finch collapsed on the porch steps, his legs giving out and the phone slipping from his hand. The buzzing persisted, drowning out all other sounds. Dizziness hit him hard, making his head spin. He shook his head, and the world around him slowly came back into focus as the ringing in his ears dissipated. Distantly, he heard Alan's voice. In a stupor, he clumsily reached for his fallen phone.

"Finch? You still there?"

"I-I'm here," he sputtered. "It's done?" He still couldn't wrap his brain around the truth.

"Yeah, man. It's done. She can't come after you for anything more now. You're a free man."

Finch struggled to regain his equilibrium, hunched over with his head nearly between his knees. "Free." The word rang through his head like a bell. Could it be true? Was he finally free of her?

"The judge said it was an open and shut case. Between your witness statements and the evidence presented, it was a slam dunk. She didn't have a leg to stand on."

"Are you sure?" He needed the reassurance. He'd wanted for so many years to be free of her. It took seeing Jolene's disappointment and hurt for him to truly do what was necessary and fight back. It had taken most of the year, but if what Alan was telling him was true, it was worth it.

Alan's tone softened. The man knew exactly what this meant to Finch. He'd been by his side throughout the whole battle. Finch could never repay him for the help and support he'd shown him. "Yeah, man. Absolutely sure. She's gone from your life. Go out and celebrate. Better yet, go out and win that saucy redhead back."

Finch snorted. Winning Jolene's affection again was his greatest desire. But first, he needed to give her the whole story. He hoped she'd meant what she'd said and would be willing to listen. This time spent in Georgia with her had a positive impact on his progress. With each passing day, their friendship was becoming more solid. But he wanted more than friendship.

"I'll do my best," he promised Alan.

"That's all I need to hear. I'll email you the final documents. If you have any questions or need any-thing else, don't hesitate to call."

Finch ran a hand through his hair. "I can't thank you enough. What you've done … You've managed to do the impossible. I just … thank you." There weren't adequate words to express his gratitude.

"Just doing my job."

"Maybe. But it means everything to me."

"I know, man. Now go out and live your life."

"Yeah. Okay." Sitting in a stupor, he gazed out at the row of tulips, their petals swaying in the gentle breeze. As he replayed the news in his mind, it slowly began to sink in.

The sound of the screen door slamming startled him. Jolene stepped out onto the porch. "Oh, you finished. I was just bringing you . . ." She paused when she glanced at him. He wondered what his expression was truly conveying. Shock? Confusion? Hope? It was the last one he felt deep in his soul. He had hope now. The nightmare he'd lived with for fifteen years was finally over. "Are . . . are you okay?"

He got unsteadily to his feet and smiled. "I feel like celebrating. Let's do something fun tonight."

Jolene tipped her head, confusion marring her brow. "Like what?"

"I don't know. Any exciting things to do around here?"

"Well, the Firefly Festival is happening this week. It's usually fun. At least it was when I was little."

"Let's do it." He felt a sudden bout of nervousness that she would turn him down as he bent down to pick up his tools.

Jolene narrowed her eyes, carefully studying him. "You're acting different. Are you sure you're okay?"

He pulled his ever-present bag of gummy worms out of his pocket and offered it to Jolene, who declined before biting his own in half. "I'm great. I just got some news I've been waiting a really long time to hear. I'll tell you about it later." He grinned as he popped the other half of the snack into his mouth, savoring the sweet taste before putting the bag back into his pocket. Guiding her with a hand on her back, he held the screen door open for her and led her back inside the house. "Go get ready. I'll take a quick shower. We can leave in fifteen minutes. How does that sound?"

No matter how hard he tried, he couldn't shake the gnawing feeling of apprehension in his gut that she might reject his proposal. He wanted to do this with her. He was bursting with happiness now that he was free. Celebrating with her was the only thing he wanted to do.

Her eyes still held a hint of suspicion, but a small smile gave him hope. "Sure. Sounds good."

Her smile held him transfixed, and he couldn't look away. He longed to hold on to every smile she gave him, as they had become rare occurrences lately. He wanted to make sure to cherish every one he received.

She playfully jostled him out of his preoccupation with a little push. "Don't dawdle," she reprimanded with a grin. He saluted her with a smirk, then dashed up the stairs.

******

Something was different with Finch, and it was making her nervous. His strange energy was palpable, leaving her with a mix of curious fascination and uneasy apprehension. She was curious about the good news he had received, but he remained tight-lipped. He seemed to relish the sights, sounds, and smells of the festival without a worry in the world. It had an unsettling effect on her, for some reason.

They had arrived at the Firefly Festival a few hours ago. Sunnyvale loved to pick any random event to throw a party, and the impending appearance of the first fireflies of the year was a good enough reason.

The town went all-out. Most of the stores that lined the main drag had set up a booth to sell their wares. Food trucks formed a circle around the large open-air tent where a few dozen picnic tables were set up. The grandstand was alive with performances by bands, both local and from out of town, creating a festive atmosphere. Kids danced with abandon in the open space, while their parents looked on lovingly from the outskirts.

But the largest portion of the fairgrounds was dedicated to the rides. Everyone, from children to grandparents, found the festival rides to be the best part of the event. And that included Finch. He eagerly stood in line to buy their wristbands for the rides, his excitement ridiculously adorable.

They decided to hit the food trucks first. Finch was like a kid in a candy store as he flitted from truck to truck. Jolene laughed as he debated the merits of each item he wanted to try. He chose three distinct things and declared he would return to sample the remaining options later.

Finch suggested sharing his pork shots with Jolene, who had chosen the deep-fried PB&J sandwich, pointing out that she shouldn't limit herself to just one dish. They found an empty spot at a table with a bunch of teenagers and dug in. Jolene watched in wonder as Finch ate. The way he savored every bite made it seem like it was his first time eating from a food truck.

She shook her head as he arranged the paper baskets overflowing with food in front of him. Taking a bite of her sandwich, she moaned as the flavors erupted on her tongue.

Finch looked over at her plate, longing in his eyes. "Your reaction to that sandwich is making me wish I'd gotten one, too," he said as he peered into his chicken and macaroni waffle basket. The dish was huge, and he appeared to be at a loss as to how to begin. A large waffle sat like a boat on the bottom, topped with macaroni and cheese and a spicy fried chicken drumstick. The entire thing was coated in honey, adding sweetness to the spiciness.

"Shut up and eat your own food," Jolene teased, snatching a pork shot. The hollowed-out center of the smoked sausage wrapped in hickory smoked bacon was filled with creamy mac and cheese, complementing its savory flavor when she bit into it. "Oh my God, this is so good."

In a swift motion, Finch switched from his drumstick to a pork shot, gobbling it up in one bite. The look of pure joy on his face as he bit into the food was priceless. Sticking with the bacon theme, he next bit into his bacon-wrapped corn on the cob. Little did he know the bacon hid jalapeno peppers underneath. She couldn't hold back her laughter when his face turned red and his eyes watered as he fumbled for his water.

After downing half the bottle, he gasped, "Warn a man next time."

"Where's the fun in that?"

"I'm going back to my waffle. Seems safer."

"Aww. You afraid of a little spice?"

The way he shot her that heated look left no doubt that his interpretation of spicy was much hotter than hers. "Depends on what's being offered and by whom," he stated, digging his plastic fork into his mac and cheese waffle. Unsure of how to respond, she stayed silent and focused on finishing the last few bites of her sandwich.

"Hey, man. Where'd you get those bacon sausage things?" One of the nearby teenagers asked. Finch pointed the kid in the truck's direction and struck up a conversation with the rest of the group at their table.

He asked them about which rides they recommended, and they launched into a litany of the pros and cons of each ride. There were the classics, including the carousel and the Ferris wheel. Then there were the more daring ones like the Fireball and the Ring of Fire.

"I loved the Ring of Fire," a kid with shaggy brown hair claimed.

"Dude, I ate my fucking knees on that ride."

"Just because you can't handle some G-forces doesn't mean shit," the kid who asked about the pork shots said as he returned to his seat with a basket of them.

"Fuck off," the surly kid barked. He looked younger than the others and bore a striking resemblance to the pork shots kid. Jolene figured they must be brothers.

"You should try the Ultra Swings," stated a cute blond girl. She was so petite Jolene worried she didn't reach the height requirements for that ride. "It's so high it's kind of like being a god. You can see the whole area from up there."

"If I wanted to be like a god, I'd probably choose immortality or the power to smite rather than the ability to see a whole bunch of stuff from up high," grumbled the younger brother.

Finch burst out into laughter at the kid's reasoning.

They talked about the Scrambler, which the same kid warned one shouldn't ride if you'd eaten in the last year. When talk turned to the Inversion ride, which lifted the riders eighty feet in the air, then tossed them upside down, he complained the ride had no regard for a person's internal organs.

"Derrik, dude! What is wrong with you?" the older brother bemoaned.

Derrik angrily shoved his ball cap back on his head. "Nothin'. I just don't like the crazy rides."

"Maybe you should ride the carousel with all the other babies."

Jolene felt bad for the kid and wanted to step in to stop the teasing, but Finch beat her to it.

"I've never gone on a carousel before," he told the kids, then turned to Derrik. "Let's go together. It might be a good palate cleanser since we just ate."

Derrik's jaw dropped open in disbelief. "You've never ridden a carousel? Dude, you're like what? Fifty? How have you never been on a carousel before?"

"Dude," Finch mocked, playfully throwing the term back at the kid. "I'm only thirty-three."

"Like I said . . . old." The teasing glint in the kid's eyes made Jolene laugh.

"You have a warped sense of what old is," Finch complained.

"You're over double my age," Derrik howled. Jolene found the situation so hilarious that she couldn't stop laughing.

Finch shot her a withering glare. "You're older than me, remember?"

"Hey," the older brother said. "She's hot. I could go for a cougar. How 'bout it, darlin'?" His lecherous gaze drifted over her as he spoke.

Finch stiffened beside her. "Mark," Derrik called. "Not a good idea to be hitting on this guy's girl. He looks like he knows a dozen ways to kill you."

"Try more like a hundred," Finch mumbled.

Mark's eyes widened as the color drained from his face. "You some sort of SEAL or something?"

"I was in the Air Force."

The boys at the table burst out laughing. The one with the shaggy hair said, "Isn't the Air Force like the joke of the military?"

"Yeah. The Navy has SEALs. The Army has those Delta guys. And the Marines . . . well, they're marines. What does the Air Force have?"

"Who do you think those guys call when they need a ride?"

They laughed harder. "A glorified Uber," Mark cawed.

Finch narrowed his eyes at the group, and Jolene felt a tingle run up her spine. "Sure. You can call me an Uber if you want. But imagine you're one of those SEALs and pinned down by enemy fire. You're bleeding out from a gunshot wound. Your teammates are in worse shape than you. You only have a few dozen rounds left. And you wonder if you'll ever see your family again. The only thing going through your head is you hope your *Uber* arrives soon to save your ass."

The weight of his words hung heavy in the air as the kids sat in stunned silence. Finally, Derrik spoke. "You flew into war zones like that?"

"That and more."

"My cousin is in the Army," the petite girl shared. "He told me a story about the men who flew into enemy fire to pick them up. He said he'd never seen anything like it. They were, like, crazy skilled. Said he owed his life to those pilots."

"Are you still in the Air Force?" Derrik asked, seeming enthralled by the information.

"No."

"Why'd you get out?" Mark asked.

Finch shrugged. "It was time." She sensed there was more to it than that simple answer. They'd never gotten around to discussing his military career back when they were circling around each other. Now she wished they'd talked about it more, but seeing him shut down the kids with such a curt answer, she doubted he would have shared the story with her anyway. There was a momentary flicker of inner turmoil and anguish on his face, but it disappeared so quickly that she wondered if she had imagined it.

"Dude," shaggy-haired boy said. "What does one do after leaving a career like that?"

Jolene stepped in to answer when Finch seemed hesitant to speak. "He's now a Nighthawk."

"What's a Nighthawk?" Mark asked.

The girls at the table all gasped. "I know what that is," the petite blonde said. "They're those rescue guys who saved Marcus Rayne."

"The Titan?" Mark asked, speaking of Marcus's most famous movie role. The girls all nodded with dreamy looks on their faces.

"That's sic," Derrik stated.

"Jolene here is the best friend of Marcus's girlfriend," Finch deflected, putting the attention on her and sending the girls into fits of excitement.

"No way!"

"Oh my God!"

"So you, like, know him?"

The girls all spoke at once and continued to bombard her with questions about Marcus. The boys rolled their eyes, trying to act like they didn't care. But Jolene could see interest in the way they surreptitiously listened.

They talked with the teenagers a little longer before they ran off for the rides. Finch was nearly on their heels, his excitement uncontainable and adorable.

"Why do you act like you've never been on one of these rides before?" Jolene asked, laughing at his exuberant energy.

"Because I haven't," he stated simply. Jolene stopped abruptly and gazed at Finch's back. He realized she wasn't with him and stopped to look back at her. She stood there, mouth gaping, trying to process what he had just revealed.

He stepped back to her, his brow furrowed in confusion. "What's the matter?"

"You've never been on an amusement ride before?"

"No." There was something in his eyes he wasn't saying. But before she could decipher it, he dropped his gaze to the dusty ground.

"Why not?" It was shocking that a thrill-seeker like Finch had never done this before. His excitement about going on the rides was palpable.

He slid his hands into his pockets, refusing to meet her gaze as he muttered, "It's complicated."

"Did you never go to Six Flags or Busch Gardens when you were little? Amusement parks are everywhere. I mean, who hasn't been there at least once in their lives?"

"We didn't go on too many vacations when I was young. My parents were busy with work."

Jolene tilted her head to the side, considering the feasibility of the explanation. "Wow. Okay, then."

"Why does this surprise you so much?"

"I mean, you're you. You love a good thrill ride. Right? You flew dangerous missions. It seems like you enjoy the rush of adventure. You and your buddies never did anything like this when you were on leave or something?"

There was a hint of embarrassment in Finch's body language as his shoulders contracted. "I almost did. Once."

His tone revealed that there was a story he was hesitant to share. Or maybe he was uncomfortable. Jolene was struggling to decipher his cues. "What happened?"

Finch shrugged. "Just didn't work out."

Tilting her head, Jolene studied him intently, trying to read his thoughts. The way he shifted his weight from foot to foot and avoided eye contact indicated that there was more to it than that. She stepped closer and put a hand on his arm. "Finch?" she questioned gently. "What is it?"

He sighed. "I want to tell you everything. I promised myself I would." He stood still and ran a hand through his hair, his gaze fixed on his feet. "It's just difficult to talk about."

"I don't understand."

Someone bumped into Jolene, making her stumble into Finch. His arm wrapped around her waist, steadying her as the person mumbled an apology and passed by. Suddenly realizing they were in the middle of the thoroughfare, he steered them to the side out of the path of excited fairgoers.

"You sure you want to hear this?" he asked once they were out of the way.

"Well, now I'm worried. More than I was before."

Finch nodded, then quickly removed his arm from around her waist, as if suddenly aware of the intimacy. Abruptly dropping his chin, he took a step back, looking as if he was worried he'd crossed a line. She felt unusually bereft at the loss of contact. She took his hand and led him over to the split-rail fence that surrounded the fairgrounds. Leaning against it, she looked up at him, concerned when he still didn't look at her. She gave his hand a reassuring squeeze. "Tell me," she urged softly.

After taking a deep breath, he slumped against the fence, his shoulders sagging in defeat. "I met a girl in high school. By senior year, we were pretty hot and heavy and spent as much time together as we could. That spring, a traveling fair like this came through town. My buddies and I were planning to go. She hated these places, so I was prepared to go without her. One last hurrah with the guys before we graduated and went our separate ways."

"You never made it?" she asked when he paused. "Did something happen?" She was curious about who the girl was, but worried something had happened to her since it was obvious his plans had fallen through. She really hoped he wasn't going to tell her his high school sweetheart had died or something.

"No, nothing happened. She wouldn't let me go."

"Who? Your mom?"

He shook his head. "No. Not my mom. My girl-friend complained that since I was leaving soon for the Air Force, I should spend as much time with her as I could rather than going off and doing stupid things with my friends. She claimed it hurt that I was choosing them over her. She cried nonstop. Eventually, my friends gave up waiting for me and left. While I stayed home with her, she voiced her worries about my decision to join the military, questioning my motives. She called me selfish and accused me of not loving her like I should."

"Wow. She sounds like a piece of work. I'm sorry she did that to you. What happened to her? I hope you dumped her ass."

Finch released a snort with a burst of laughter. "Un-fortunately, no. I married her."

Chapter 14

FOR THE FIRST TIME since he'd started this conversation, Finch looked up at Jolene. If he hadn't been so worried about what he was sharing, her expression would have made him laugh. Her eyes bulged as she stared at him in disbelief.

She opened and closed her mouth several times as if she wanted to say something but couldn't find the right words. Her mouth moved soundlessly for a moment before she finally found the words to speak. "I don't . . . why . . . that woman," she finally pushed the words out, making the connection.

Yeah, she'd connected the dots. The girlfriend who'd ruined his night with his friends was the same one from that night in the hotel. His wife had a knack for ruining things he wanted. He'd never be able to erase from his mind the look of horrified betrayal on Jolene's face as Angelica had screeched at them.

"She was your high school sweetheart?"

"Yeah. We married just after graduation. Before I left for the Air Force."

"Wow. So young." She glanced around the fairgrounds, and he waited for her to gather her thoughts. He held back, knowing there was more to tell, but unsure of how she was processing the information.

"Too young," he confirmed, running his gaze over her beautiful face. The colorful lights and bustling crowds of the fair disappeared into the background as he watched her. That night, when Angelica appeared, Jolene had shut down. She'd become completely closed off and refused to listen to his explanation. Tonight, she seemed more open to hearing him out.

It had been over a year since they'd been this close, and he reveled in every moment. He couldn't help but notice she still held his hand. Her grip was firm, and he took it as a good sign. There was hope there that he couldn't suppress.

"So, that woman . . . what was her name?"

"Angelica."

"Angelica," she repeated. "She really is your wife?"

"Was," he replied, feeling elated that he could finally say that.

"What do you mean?"

"I married her when we were eighteen. We separated after ten years, one year after I left the Air Force. My divorce finally went through today."

He held his breath, waiting for her response to those words.

"Divorced?" She murmured the word back to herself, as if tasting it on her tongue to understand its meaning.

"That night was the first time I'd seen her in months. Even though we were separated and working toward a divorce, she'd show up like a bad penny every now and then." He shifted to face her. "Jolie, I'm so sorry. It was never my intention to hurt you. I just wanted . . . well, I guess it doesn't really matter what

I wanted. I hurt you and I'll never forgive myself for not telling you the truth before that night."

She bit her lip and nodded. She rapidly blinked away the moisture that swelled in her eyes. As if she'd just made a decision, she took a deep breath. "You know what? I know we have more to discuss, and I'm ready to hear it. But not now. We're here to have fun. You've never ridden rides like this, so let's get to it."

He blinked at her, stunned by her words. "Are you sure?"

She stepped away from the fence, pulling him along with her, their hands still clasped together. "What should we go on first?"

They rode as many rides as they could, and Finch enjoyed each and every one of them. But not as much as he enjoyed the company of the woman beside him. She was a breath of fresh air. Angelica had controlled him for so long that he felt invigorated to be himself around Jolene.

Angelica would have complained about every aspect of the fair. Too many people. The lines were too long. It smelled like manure. She would have hated getting dirt on her shoes. And she would have criticized him for every part of it, then blamed him for her misery.

As much as he hated to compare the two women, he couldn't help but notice the world of difference between them. Jolene didn't once complain as he dragged her around to all the rides. The lines were nothing to her as they passed the time talking to each other and to those around them. She wasn't offended by the smells, even when they visited the animals and fed the goats. Their little tongues slurping at her hands to get at the food made her laugh.

Finch watched as she effused joy. He hadn't seen her this happy in so long. It was as if she'd decided, at least for a few hours, to forget all her troubles and just have fun. He'd seen her worries stacking up over the time they'd been in Georgia. With her father's health, the state of his house, the threatening messages, and the problems at her bar, he'd noticed she had grown increasingly agitated.

He was trying to help as much as he could, hence the repairs he'd done.

He'd been enjoying himself so much he hadn't noticed the sun had set. The festive carnival-like lights lit up the area like it was day. It was as if the fair was under its own bubble. The fairgoers' enjoyment was not hindered by the darkness that enveloped them.

After a quick break for more fair food—a red velvet funnel cake for Jolene and fried pickles for him—they were now in line for the Ferris wheel.

Jolene moaned over her funnel cake. The sound shot straight to his cock. Holding a piece out for him, she said, "You've got to try this. It's so good."

As he leaned in to accept the treat, he noticed the way her breath hitched and her fingers trembled slightly. He tasted the sweet flavor of the treat on his tongue, and the sound of their breathing became the only thing he could hear. Her citrus scent, mixed with the smell of the treat, created a unique aroma. When he took her fingers into his mouth, he felt the velvety texture of her skin against his tongue. He wanted to freeze time and live in that moment forever.

Despite the flashing lights of the amusement rides and the crowds of people around them, her unblinking luminous green eyes were fixed on him. She gasped for breath as he let go of her fingers, and he enjoyed the sweet flavor of the funnel cake in his mouth. The scent of powdered sugar and fried dough mingled with the sound of her quick, shallow breaths. He savored the tasty treat, locking eyes with her, and a smile tipped the corners of his lips.

He loved the way his actions caused a hooded look of desire in her expression, but he didn't want to risk going too far too soon. They still had a lot of things to discuss. "You're right," he said after swallowing. "That was good."

"Yeah, it was," she murmured, and he sensed that she wasn't referring to the food.

Just as he was getting lost in her eyes again, a tap on the shoulder snapped him out of the trance she had him in. "It's your turn," the stranger said, gesturing toward the ride attendant.

"Oh, thanks," he uttered. With a hand on Jolene's lower back, he guided her into their pod. Once seated with the door securely closed, Finch threw his arm across the back of the seat. Jolene leaned into him, her head tilted back onto his shoulder. He could feel her body pressed against his, and his heart raced with excitement. As they sat waiting for the other pods to load, he absently twirled the silky strands of her hair around his fingers. The scent of fuel and machinery and the sound of whirring engines and clanging metal filled the space. The seats were hard and uncomfortable, but he didn't mind as long as she was beside him. The dim lighting cast a warm glow on their faces, and he couldn't help but feel a sense of excitement and anticipation about the journey ahead.

As they neared the top, Jolene's thoughts from their earlier conversation finally spilled out, breaking the silence. "Your divorce? Its final?"

"Yes."

"You said you've been separated?" He nodded. "For how long?"

"Five years."

"Why did you wait so long to get a divorce?"

"I really have no excuse."

Looking up at him, she furrowed her brow, creating deep lines on her forehead. "I don't understand."

"I was just so tired of fighting her. With the separation, I had the semblance of freedom from her. It was enough at the time. I knew that if I filed for divorce, she would have responded poorly."

"How do you mean?"

He sighed. "It's difficult to explain. In order to explain it properly, I need to give you a sense of what it was like to be in a relationship with her."

"Okay."

He remained silent for one cycle of their ride. The words were hard to find. He'd kept it private from everyone for a reason. As a man, what he'd been through with Angelica was humiliating. It was embarrassing that he didn't put a stop to it sooner. Hindsight being what it was, he knew he should have never married her in the first place.

"This is hard for me to talk about. Only two people outside of Angelica and me know the whole story."

"If it's too difficult, you don't have to—"

He cut her off with a finger to her lips. "I need to. You deserve to know. I want a future with you, Jolie. To get that, I need to tell you everything. Once you have the truth, you can decide whether you want to move forward with me."

The bright neon lights and deafening roars of the carnival rides slowly dissipated into a distant hum as he gazed into her mesmerizing jade eyes, imploring her to hear him out and understand the words that were about to escape his lips. The scent of cotton candy and fried food lingered in the warm breeze. Despite the chaos surrounding him, he remained numb to the sensory overload. It was as if he was in a bubble, detached from his surroundings.

The weight of his confession felt like a boulder resting heavily on his chest, making it difficult for him to breathe. His own heart pounded wildly in his ears, and the sound of his labored breaths filled the pod. The air in the confined space was thick with tension, and the scent of his anxiety hung in the air like a bitter perfume.

His stomach twisted with nerves as he thought about what he had to tell her. His palms were slick with sweat, and he could feel his nerves getting the best of him. There were so many unknowns. Would she look at him differently? Would she think less of him?

For years, he had carried the crushing weight of humiliation and shame like a boulder on his chest. He had tried to bury it deep inside, but it lingered like a foul odor that refused to dissipate. The memories played like a broken record in his mind, causing a dull ache in his temples. A burning flush crept up his neck as every demeaning moment played through his thoughts. He longed to shed the heavy burden, to feel light and free once again. He wondered if sharing his secret with Jolene would alleviate the heaviness he felt.

As Jolene shifted, the sound of the pod creaking filled the space. Suddenly, the scent of fresh citrus wafted toward him, calming his nerves. It was as though an orchard of orange trees surrounded him. A lighter feeling washed over him, and he took a deep breath, savoring the moment. He drew strength from her presence, gathering the courage to speak.

"One year into it, I knew I had made a mistake by marrying her. But that wasn't even my biggest mistake. The fact that I stayed with her for so long resulted in that designation.

"I was busy soaking up everything the Air Force could teach me. I was so busy that I didn't notice what was happening at home. We'd moved into base housing together after basic was over. It was nice to have someone to come home to after a long day. Though soon, I began to dread going home."

The weight of his memories caused him to grow quiet and retreat into himself. A lump of trepidation in his throat felt heavy like a rock, making it difficult for him to speak. The thumping of his heart was so loud that it felt like it was echoing in his ears, making it hard to gather his thoughts. The pod felt suffocatingly warm, and the stale smell of the space made him feel claustrophobic. Every breath he took felt like he was inhaling thick, heavy air, adding to the pressure in his chest.

Putting voice to the words that only two other people in his life knew about was overwhelming. The sheer magnitude of it all left him winded, and he struggled to keep his composure.

Jolene's soft hand squeezed his tightly, urging him to overcome his hesitancy and speak. With renewed confidence, he opened his mouth and continued sharing his story.

"It's taken me a long time to put it into words. I had to come to terms with the reality of what it was. And the shame I felt because of it. There were daily criticisms, threats, and constant demands that I should act in a way to support her, followed up with justification that the relationship was failing due to me. This slowly became my truth—I was a failure. I was responsible for her unhappiness and was not trying hard enough. I couldn't reason out the argument or provide a response. I feared expressing an opinion—any opinion about anything.

"It literally tears you apart, wrecks your psyche and makes you believe all the wrong things about yourself. Your mind becomes a battleground, and the negative thoughts it inspires can tear you apart from the inside out."

A sniffle caught him off guard, momentarily distracting him from his anxiety. When he looked down at her, tears streamed down her face. He reached up with his free hand and wiped them away.

His heart racing, he continued with newfound courage. "I never saw myself as a victim. She'd convinced me it was all my fault. I was the one with the problem. I was deployed a lot. It was damaging to our relationship. She had a knack for deflecting blame and making me feel responsible for every problem we faced. Her chronic emotional blackmail kept me under her control, exactly where she wanted me. I wanted to be the good guy. I wanted to work hard to fix things. I wanted to make her happy. It took me ten years and some harsh truth from my father to finally figure out that even as I altered every minute detail about my personality, she'd always find fault. I was complicit in her actions by staying silent, which led her to believe they were okay."

As he spoke his truth, the tension in his body began to release, but he was still uneasy and avoided looking at her. His eyes were fixed on a single rivet, just across from where they sat. As she shifted, the rustling of her clothes seemed to echo in the silence around them. The warmth of her hand on his cheek comforted him. She applied some pressure to make him look at her.

"I'm beginning to understand. If you need to stop, it's okay. It's clear that this is not easy for you, and I don't want you to struggle."

He closed his eyes, leaned into her hand, and let out a sigh of relief. It was the best reaction he could ask for. She wasn't angry. She wasn't upset. She exuded a calm and cool demeanor. She offered comfort through her understanding. Her ability to grasp the matter fully gave him a sense of calmness.

"I want to tell you more." Their pod jolted abruptly as it came to a halt, catching them off guard and sending them lurching forward. The attendant opened the pod in front of them, and people shuffled out. They'd be next. "But this probably isn't the place."

Jolene's lips tipped up in a small smile. He loved the peach perfection of her lips and longed for the right to taste them again. He shoved that desire deep down, willing his dick to do the same. "Probably not. What do you say we get some ice cream and head home where we can talk some more?"

"Sounds great."

As the pod's positioning adjusted, they readied themselves to leave. The door screeched in protest as the attendant forced it open. The bubble burst, and suddenly, he was hit with the overwhelming combination of sweet and savory smells, mixed with the sounds of carnival music and chatter.

Quietly, he trailed Jolene as they disembarked from the ride. The whirring of machinery blended with the excited screams of riders created a symphony of noise distracting him from his thoughts. The smells of fried food and sweet funnel cakes filled the bustling park, and the early spring air was refreshing on his skin.

When they arrived at the food area, Jolene made a beeline for the ice cream truck. She ordered a cone and handed him one, too. They navigated through the throngs of fair goers while savoring their ice cream cones, heading toward the SUV.

His thoughts were a cluttered, chaotic mess. The cacophony in his mind was as crowded and loud as the fair. The noise of countless thoughts and worries echoed loudly, creating a deafening roar to compete with the screams from the roller coaster. His head felt heavy and overloaded, like a messy desk that had accumulated too many papers.

The act of voicing his secret had been cathartic, but he remained on edge, the silence from Jolene making him uneasy. He was anxious to hear her thoughts. His heart raced as he imagined what she might say, his palms growing sweaty with anticipation.

He figured it could go one of two ways. Either she would be repulsed by his previous marriage and would have no desire to involve herself with a man as worthless and contemptible as him. Or she could be disgusted by his wife's treatment and motivated to restore their bond. He hoped it would be the latter, and she would give him a second chance to make things right.

Once they reached the SUV, he held the passenger door open for her, his focus on the crushed grass and dirt underneath. Before she entered, she gently touched his cheek once again. Her unexpected move caught him off guard, and he quickly shifted his gaze to her.

"Are you okay?" she asked.

"Yeah. I'm fine."

She narrowed her eyes and scrutinized him, as if she didn't believe what he was saying. "Thank you for telling me. You've been holding a lot in for so long, haven't you?" His only response was a brief, chin-dropping acknowledgment. "I want to hear more. I'm here for you, Finch. I promise."

She leaned in and brushed her soft lips on his cheek before she got into the car, making him feel a little lighter.

Chapter 15

F INCH WAS LOST IN his thoughts as he drove them home, which was the only excuse he had for not seeing the speeding truck until it was nearly too late. The blinding high beam headlights made it difficult to see as it charged at them from behind.

"Do you have your seat belt on?" he asked Jolene, afraid this nutjob would cause an accident.

"Yes. Why? What's wrong?"

"Looks like maybe a drunk driver on our tail." The bright lights made Jolene squint as she glanced over her shoulder. "I can't see the driver," she said, turning forward again.

Finch pressed down on the gas, speeding up just a bit to put some distance between them. The other driver matched his speed. Noting a long stretch of open road in front of him, he slowed and pulled slightly to the side, hoping the guy would get the hint and pass them.

He didn't. The massive truck stayed with them. While Finch contemplated whether to pull over and stop completely, the truck backed off. He drove at a regular pace, his attention divided between the road ahead and the rear-view mirror.

Just as he was about to enter a section of road that had narrow curves, the truck sped up again, this time not stopping when it reached them.

"Shit. Hold on," he yelled to Jolene, just as the truck hit their back bumper. The jolt rattled them, but he maintained control of the SUV.

Jolene grabbed the oh-shit handle and tried to peer back at the other vehicle. "What does this guy think he's doing?"

"I don't know. But I'm not sticking around to find out." He pressed down harder on the accelerator, pushing the SUV to dangerous speeds as he approached the curves. The truck stayed plastered to their back bumper. The first curve lay ahead, and he knew he'd have to reduce his speed to safely traverse it. He lifted his foot off the gas pedal just as the truck swerved and clipped them on the rear driver's side bumper.

Jolene squealed, and Finch gritted his teeth as he fought to keep them on the road. He noted the severe drop-off out of his side window. If the guy hit them at the right angle, they could veer off the road and tumble down the steep drop.

"Call the police," Finch cried when the truck hit them a third time.

Jolene scrambled for her phone, and he could hear the edge of panic in her voice as she talked to the 911 operator. They were making their way through the next curve when the truck clipped them again on the rear driver's side. It was a big enough hit that the SUV's back end slid off the road on Jolene's side. At the speed they were going, it took everything in Finch to bring them back on the road. The driver in the truck took advantage and smashed into them again, sending them across the road and perilously close to that steep ravine.

Finch overcompensated, and the SUV started to spin. With a final clip from the truck's massive front grill, they were plummeting backward over the drop-off. Finch was powerless as Jolene's screams echoed around them, unable to do anything to stop their descent.

Something stopped their freefall with a jolt. The sudden impact caused Finch's head to collide with the window, leaving him momentarily dazed and disoriented. Something warm trickled into his eye as he struggled to figure out what had just happened. In a flash, it came rushing back. Jolene.

He sat up quickly and looked over at her. "Jolie?" he asked, his voice barely audible as it shook with fear. She wasn't moving, but her eyes were open. One hand still gripped the overhead handle, the other was braced on the dashboard in front of her. He could see the rapid movement of her chest as she breathed.

With clumsy fingers, he unfastened his seat belt and turned to her. He placed a hand on her stiff arm, startling her. "Are you okay?" he asked, raking his gaze over her for any sign of injury.

It took her a moment to reply, and during that pause, she took a deep breath. With a hesitant tone and a slow blink, she responded. "I-I think so." She turned to face him and gasped. "You're bleeding." She reached over and touched his cheek near the gash on his temple. He caught her hand before she could get blood on it and kissed her palm.

"I'm okay. Hit my head when we stopped. We need to get out of the SUV." He looked up the incline, suddenly worried whoever had run them off the road may be waiting up top to finish them off another way. "On second thought, let's stay here until the police arrive."

"The police!" Jolene lunged for something between her feet. She came back up, grimacing, with her cell phone in her hand. He noticed her wince as she rubbed her chest where the seat belt had been strapped. He probably had matching bruises on his chest.

"Hello? Ma'am? Are you still there?" the 911 operator was saying.

"Yes, I'm here. We got run off the road."

"The police are nearly there. Is anyone hurt? Do you need an ambulance?"

"Yes." She answered at the same time he said, "No."

Jolene sent him a glare that told him she wasn't messing around.

The sirens grew louder until it sounded like they were right on top of them. Soon, there was a responder tapping on Jolene's window.

"Everyone all right in here?" he asked, shining a flashlight through the window at them.

"He's hurt," Jolene insisted.

"I'm fine," he mumbled in return. "Just get her out and up top, please."

They easily opened her door and helped her out. She was a little shaky as she stood next to the SUV, but that was to be expected after the adrenaline dump. Finch, however, was not getting out of the vehicle on his side. The tree that halted their progress had also smashed the door. He gritted his teeth, preparing to climb over the console. He could already feel the aches and pains from the numerous jolts they'd sustained.

The psychedelic strobe effect of lights from all the emergency vehicles up on the road was dizzying, and his head pounded as he followed Jolene up the ravine.

"Grady?" Jolene's shocked voice caught his attention. She was staring at the asshole from the bar. The one who'd been Jolene's first kiss. He hated the guy on that pretext alone. But then he'd been a dick that night in the bar. Finch was surprised to see the badge on his chest. "You're a police officer?"

"I'm afraid it's worse than that," he replied a bit sheepishly.

"How is it worse?"

"I'm the chief of police."

"Get out," Jolene hissed, her voice laced with surprise.

"Yup. So, wanna fill me in on what happened here?"

They spent the next few minutes recounting the events. Jolene insisted he be seen by the EMTs while they talked. As he suspected, it was just a small cut. It didn't require stitches. The headache was a killer, though, and he'd be happy to be away from all the flashing lights.

Grady seemed like a decent cop. He took their statements, listening attentively as they relayed the story. He sent his officers down to the wrecked SUV to take pictures and samples of the paint the truck left behind each time it hit them.

The chief even went so far as to give them a lift back to Jolene's father's place, promising them he'd keep them informed of his progress in the case.

Finch could tell Jolene was close to a crash, the exhaustion weighing on her shoulders. He sent her up to bed while he double-checked all the locks. The fact that someone had so callously run them off the road, then disappeared, worried him. He was glad he'd already gotten the security cameras and lights up the other day. Nobody was getting into this house, yet he still checked the camera feeds on his phone to make sure everything was functioning as it should. Jolene's safety was not something he was willing to compromise on.

He climbed the stairs in the dark, his hand brushing against the rough wall to guide him. His body felt as old and creaky as the wooden steps beneath his feet. When he approached Jolene's door, her light was still on and the door was slightly ajar. He rapped his knuckles lightly on the doorframe, and she looked up from her position sitting up in bed. She resembled every dream he'd ever had about her in bed. The vibrant red locks of her hair fell gently over her shoulders. Her skin was dewy and radiant after she'd scrubbed the makeup off. His heart leaped at the sight of her beauty, causing his already dizzy head to spin even more.

"You okay?" he asked.

"Not particularly."

"What can I do?"

She hesitated, playing with the edge of her blanket between her fingers. "Can you . . . I-I don't want to be alone." The raw intensity of her fearful expression tore at his heart.

"I can sleep on the floor in here with you if you want," he offered.

"No. Yes. I mean, not on the floor." She turned back the corner of her blankets and scooted over to make room.

"Are you sure?" He longed to slip into the warm embrace of the bed beside her and hold her all night long, but his doubts made him hesitate.

She patted the empty spot next to her. "Please."

His gut tightened at the vulnerability in her tone. The weariness in her voice made him ache. She was a strong, confident woman. But the last few weeks had taken their toll on her. If he could ease her mind for even one night, he'd do whatever it took.

As he stepped into Jolene's room, the warmth of the space enveloped him. The gentle light of the bedside lamp cast a soft glow on her tired features. He toed off his boots, then reached for his belt, but paused.

"Is it okay if I sleep in my boxers?" It was how he usually slept, boxers and nothing else. But if it made her uncomfortable, he'd keep his pants on.

"It's fine." She watched him strip down, as if unable to tear her gaze away. She sucked in a breath when he took his shirt off and folded it precisely. Looking down, he could see the line of bruises from the seat belt already beginning to form. "They look as bad as mine."

A knot in his stomach twisted at the idea of her being hurt. "I'm sorry." He carefully folded the rest of his discarded clothes and placed them neatly on the corner of her dresser.

"Nothing to be sorry for. We're both fine. That's all that matters. Bruises will heal."

Nodding and feeling more nervous than the situation called for, he approached the bed. She slid down and settled her head on the pillows as he climbed in beside her. Once he was situated, she reached over and turned off the light, plunging the room into darkness.

In the silence, the sound of their breaths was excessively loud. They lay next to each other, not touching. He didn't want to assume she'd want him to touch her, but the need to pull her into his arms was nearly overwhelming.

As his eyes gradually adjusted to the dimness, he discerned the subtle details of her room. The soft rustling of the curtains against the open window, the faint fragrance of lavender emanating from her bed linen, and the coolness of the air against his skin all added to the sensory experience. He noticed the dainty trinkets adorning her dresser, the photos of her friends and loved ones shoved into the corners of her mirror, and the stack of cooking books on the edge of her desk. Despite the dark, the room felt welcoming and comforting, as if it held secrets and stories of the girl who resided here years ago, just waiting to be shared.

He yearned to uncover all those secrets and stories.

With a loud sigh, she growled, "This is ridiculous." She rolled toward him, lifting his arm until she was positioned under it with her head on his chest. "Just hold me, Finch. Please."

He let his arm settle around her, his hand resting on her hip. Her hand lay on his stomach, and he covered it with his own, stroking the soft skin of her wrist with his thumb. He leaned in and pressed a soft kiss to her forehead. "You never have to beg me for anything."

He lay still, counting the seconds between each breath, until her breathing finally evened out in a steady rhythm. As she rested in his arms, he felt the weight of her body against his chest and was overwhelmed with gratitude. Her body was warm and soft against his, and a sense of contentment washed over him as he found his own sleep.

Chapter 16

A TEXT MESSAGE JOLTED Jolene awake the next morning. The night before came rushing back. The festival. The talk in the Ferris wheel. The accident. Her asking Finch to stay with her. But the space beside her was empty, the sheets cool to the touch.

With a sigh, she rolled over and picked up her phone. Another text threat, which she took a screenshot of. Then she texted Emma about it. She'd talked to her days ago, and Emma promised she'd look into it as soon as she could get to her laptop.

Climbing out of bed, she threw on some grubby clothes, ready to get to work cleaning up her father's house.

After working to the bone all day, they decided to break for dinner and got cleaned up. They picked up takeout and brought it to visit her dad, the excitement in his eyes evident as he saw the delicious food. Apparently, the food at the rehab center wasn't up to snuff.

They talked and laughed as she translated several of Gorden's more colorful phases for Finch, who was obviously lost.

"What's your whiskey?" Gorden asked Finch, and Jolene rolled her eyes. This was one of her father's favorite questions.

"Da," she warned. There was no telling how he'd react to any answer Finch gave him.

"I haven't had an opportunity to try whiskey from different regions, but I appreciated a Johnnie Walker Gold Label Reserve once."

Gorden made a disgusted sound in his throat. "That stuff's like making love in a canoe."

Finch tilted his head, obviously trying to understand Gorden's meaning. "What?"

"It's fuckin' close to water."

A moment passed before Finch erupted into laughter. The unrestrained, joyous sound resonated off the walls and filled the air. It was infectious, causing Jolene to join in, their laughter mingling together in a harmonious cacophony. As Finch laughed, his body shook with each chuckle, and his face lit up with pure delight.

Jolene savored seeing him so carefree. It had been a long time since they'd laughed together. At least like that. Sure, she'd laughed at his looniness over the past couple of days, but it wasn't like this. This was uninhibited. This was freeing. This was a release of stress and worry. Despite the weight of their looming troubles, for this one moment, they could forget it all and just laugh.

At one point during their evening, Finch stepped out to take a phone call, and the grilling from her dad began.

Gorden gave her that look. Like he could see everything she wouldn't say out loud. "He's a canny lad. Are you graftin' him?"

"Jeez, Da. I'm not in high school anymore. I can be friends with a guy without you questioning whether I like him."

"Dinnae be an eejit. It's clear you two are more than friends."

Jolene's gaze was directed downward. Her hands rested in her lap while she picked at her thumbnail. "It's complicated."

"Isne everything? That's life. Love is worth it, though."

Jolene snorted. "I don't think I'm destined for love like you and Mom had."

"Haud yer wheesht. Dinnae talk like that. You are worthy of so much love. And with the way that lad looks at you, I'd say he wants a chance to show you."

"Maybe."

"There's no mibbe about it. You can't keep letting what that dobber did to you stop you from finding something special with someone else."

"I'm not," she insisted.

"Mm-hmm."

"Seriously, I'm not. Finch lied to me about something. I'm working through it."

"Aye. That sleekit bastard left you with trust issues."

"Can we not talk about Harrison?"

"Mibbe we should talk about him. He was a right bastard. Unworthy of you. Whatever Finch lied to you about, I'm thinkin' he had a good reason. There's pain there. He's suffered. But when he looks at you, that pain lessens. He's a good man. I feel it in my bones. Give him a chance to prove it to you."

"You tryin' to marry me off?" she teased, uncomfortable with the serious turn of their conversation.

"Mibbe." She laughed at his answer. "Can't have you always comin' down here. Up in my business. I know you're messin' with things at the house. We're gonna have words about that."

"No, we're not. You need a safe place to come home to. That's all we're doing. And for Christ's sake, hire a cleaning service or something."

"Isne as bad as all that."

"It was disgusting."

"It was lived-in."

"There were cockroaches."

"That was just Charlie." She snorted. Gorden had an answer for everything.

"And the other ones?"

"Mibbe he be havin' a bevvy with his lads. A chance to get pished with the boys."

"I don't think cockroaches get drunk."

"You never seen a blootered cockroach before?"

"Jesus, Da. You'll say anything to excuse your aversion to household chores."

With a knock, Finch returned to the room. "Everything okay?" she asked him.

"Yeah. Everything's good." There was something in his expression that told her he had more to say but didn't want to say it in front of her dad. They'd decided not to tell him about the text threats or the accident the previous night. She didn't want to worry her dad unnecessarily.

"Good. Now I'm knackered. Oan yer trolley."

Finch had that look on his face again. The one that said he had no idea what Gorden just said.

"That's his more pleasant way of telling us to get out."

Finch chuckled. "Right. We'll get out of your hair."

"Get some rest, Da." She leaned over and kissed his cheek.

"See you on the morn."

Once in their replacement rental car heading back to the house, Jolene asked about the phone call Finch had taken.

"It was Grady. They found the truck abandoned in an empty lot."

"That's good, right?"

"It was stolen."

"Oh." Another dead end. She wanted this over and hoped the truck would lead to somebody. She should have known better. This waiting on pins and needles thing was for the birds. She hadn't gotten another text since the one this morning. It was only a matter of time before the next one came in.

"And there weren't any cameras in the area."

"Well, that sucks."

Finch reached across the cab and grabbed her hand. "We'll figure this out. Whoever this is will screw up eventually. In the meantime, I'll keep you safe. I promise."

She squeezed his hand tightly, feeling the rough texture of his skin against hers. She experienced a sense of safety and comfort in his touch, as if nothing could harm her while he was holding her hand.

"I'm glad you're here with me."

"Me, too." A quick glance from him was enough to communicate a thousand emotions she couldn't decipher. Then he lifted her hand to his mouth. He brushed his warm lips against the back of her hand and whispered, "Me, too."

The unfinished conversation from the festival weighed heavily on her. When they got home, it was time to finish that heart-to-heart that had been interrupted.

The silence of the house greeted them when they walked through the front door. Only the gentle creaking of the floorboards and the steady hum of the refrigerator broke the stillness. Dim moonlight filtered in through the windows, casting long shadows across the floor.

Despite its age, they'd found the house was in remarkably good condition once cleaning and repairs had begun. Thanks to the work she and Finch were completing, the house would soon be safer for her father's return home. Now that the biggest problems with the house had been managed, she could focus on the little things—like cleaning. If she managed to finish that, she might be able to squeeze in some time to paint a few rooms. The house could use a facelift, even if it was just a fresh coat of paint.

None of that mattered in the moment. Her concern was for the man who followed her as she made her way into the kitchen. She could feel the weight of his presence behind her as she moved through the house. His boots made an obnoxiously loud noise as he walked through the otherwise silent space.

Her lips twitched in amusement. No surprise, his footsteps were like thunder. The man's substantial size made him difficult to ignore . . . at least for her. It was what had first attracted her to him. Harrison had been nearly the same size as her. He couldn't stand it when she wore heels, since it made his perceived height inadequacies noticeable.

She'd loved the way Finch's height had made her feel. Loved that she had to look up to meet his eyes. And when she'd been in his arms . . . A feeling of safety and protection encompassed her. Despite never needing a man in that way, she couldn't help but relish that feeling she'd had with Finch. She was always independent and self-sufficient, yet with Finch, she'd discovered a new desire. She felt ready to take hold of what she wanted. A sense of purpose and clarity flowed through her. She knew exactly what she wanted and how to get it.

And it all started with being open to what Finch had to say. He wasn't Harrison. There wasn't a deceitful bone in Finch's body. From what she'd gathered of his story so far, he had a valid motive for the lies he had told. The shame he carried was clear as day. She knew how difficult it was to deal with feelings of shame, so she promised to do everything in her power to help him quash that mindset.

Her thoughts were on her own battle with shame as she stepped into the kitchen. With the dim light from the stove hood as her guide, she made her way to the refrigerator. She opened the door and grabbed two beer bottles by the neck. The cold glass sent a shiver down her spine as she remembered how she'd drowned her sorrows after Harrison's betrayal.

It took her a long time to come to grips with her shame. Eventually, she realized that the shame she was carrying wasn't hers to bear. It was Harrison's. He was the one who'd lied. He was the one who'd led her on for years. He was the one who'd cheated on his wife. She bore no responsibility for his misdeeds.

She and Finch were similar in that way. Neither one was at fault for what had happened to them. The shame they carried was not their own, but something that had been placed upon them.

"Let's take these out to the deck and talk," she suggested. She headed for the back sliding door with a detour to the family room to grab a blanket. With effort, she slid it open, adding *WD-40 the door* to her mental to-do list.

They settled on the loveseat. Finch took the bottles from her so that she could spread the blanket out over their laps. As the nighttime temperatures began to drop, the air felt damp against her skin, the humidity level reminding her that storms were forecasted.

Finch twisted the cap off the bottle. The snick of the pressure escaping filled the air, and he handed it to her. She took a deep sip from hers, pausing to savor the rich, bold flavor before glancing over to see him do the same.

The crinkling of plastic caught her ear. Finch pulled a bag of gummy worms from his pocket and held it out to her. Laughing, she took a worm and bit it in half.

Settling back into the love seat with his own gummy worm, he flung his arm across the back and exhaled deeply. "This is a nice spot."

Jolene leaned against him, and she could feel his warmth seeping into her skin, just like it had on the Ferris wheel. Just like it had in bed the previous night. After absorbing the feel of him against her, she glanced out over the land behind her house. The flat area of the backyard gave way to foothills. The picturesque town of Summervale was nestled in the lush Chattahoochee National Forest. The view from their spot was breathtaking; the dense canopy of trees seemed to go on forever, and the Blue Ridge Mountains provided a stunning backdrop. Taking a deep breath, she filled her lungs with the invigorating air scented with pine needles.

She'd always loved sitting here. After the debacle with Harrison, she'd come here with her tail between her legs. She'd spent long hours breathing in the crisp, rejuvenating north Georgian air.

Lake Haven had a similar effect on her. The breeze coming off Lake Michigan was always refreshing, and she loved that she could enjoy it any time from her bar.

But there would always be something special about home. "This was always my favorite spot," she told him.

"I can see why."

He gazed at her, transfixed, as if he could see their entire future together in that moment.

She'd decided she wanted to know everything with no expectations. No promises would be made. No vows or declarations. Just the unvarnished truth. "Will you tell me more?"

Chapter 17

"LOVE, LAUGHTER, AND RESPECT." Finch paused to think. "These are the pillars of my parents' relationship. I soaked up every aspect of it during my childhood. They were high school sweethearts, just like Angelica and me. I think that when you are raised in that type of atmosphere, you assume you'll have the same type of relationship with a significant other. How could you not? You've seen what true love looks like."

He lifted his beer to his lips and took a much-needed sip, letting the cool liquid soothe his parched throat. Dread filled him, making his body rigid and his breath shallow. He was terrified that Jolene would be unable to accept his truth and would turn away from him.

"When things start to go wrong, you live in denial at first. You make excuses. *She's just having a bad day.* Or *she's high strung and passionate.* Then comes the guilt. *Maybe it was my fault. Maybe if I had done* xyz *she wouldn't have gotten mad.* There is a loneliness that comes with thoughts like that. You can't talk to anybody about it because you start to believe the bullshit she tells you. After all, she loves you and only has your best interest at heart, right? So she lets you know of all the ways you've failed her under the guise of 'talking things out' and helping you 'see the errors of your ways.' She tells you that if you hadn't left the light on, she wouldn't have gotten so angry. Anything that sets her off is something you will always be at fault for, even if it's something as natural as turning over in your sleep.

"As a man, you're raised knowing it's wrong to hit a woman. There is no way to fight back when the violence starts. So when she's punching you, kicking you, biting or cutting you, you can't retaliate. You tell yourself *you're a man. You can take it.* You are much bigger than her, so if you fight back, she could get hurt.

"Then there's the worry about her accusing you," he continued, picking at the edge of the label on the bottle. "She kicks you or threatens you with a knife and you grip her wrist to keep the knife from cutting you. She'll cry abuse. And you know who they're going to believe. No one will ever believe a woman half your size is the instigator."

He stopped and looked down at their clasped hands. The scar on his wrist caught his attention. A memento from a particularly nasty attack. Angelica was accusing him of some made-up bullshit about a woman he worked with. She was convinced he was having an affair. She came at him with a knife. As an airman, he had the military training to disarm her easily, but he feared he'd hurt her in the process. So he'd tried to dodge her attacks as best he could while attempting to calm her down. A few swipes with the knife made contact, the pain overshadowed by the shock of the attack. The worst of his wounds were on his wrist. Once she had exhausted herself, he'd left and stayed in a hotel room for the night with a detour to the pharmacy for supplies. Alone, in his room, he'd stitched up the wound on his own. He'd been too embarrassed to go to the hospital, afraid he'd hear the same derision as before. "What kind of man lets his wife hit him?"

The realization struck him hard that things were awry in his relationship, and he had no idea how to set them right. Accepting the harsh reality that he'd let his marriage deteriorate to physical abuse, he'd felt lost and helpless, with nowhere to turn.

"You live with the shame every day. *You* let your marriage fail. *You* did something to upset her. *You* are at fault for all of it."

"None of it was your fault," she said softly. "You know that, right?"

His desire to agree was overshadowed by years of conditioning that caused him to constantly second-guess himself. Theoretically, he knew it to be true. Angelica was unstable. He often questioned if she had an untreated mental illness and had once begged her to seek professional help. That had backfired in a big way. In her warped mind, she was never the one with the problem. It was always his fault she had lashed out at him. The inconsistency of it all was frustrating and hard to predict. A maddening way to live. She'd once stabbed him in the hand with a fork for making a noise as he ate.

And still, he'd hoped she'd get help. She'd finally see what she was doing to their marriage. That her moments of rage and violence were not normal. He couldn't help but think that if she'd gotten help, maybe it would have saved them. Saved *him* from years of suffering and shame.

A furrow appeared on Jolene's forehead as she tipped her chin up to look at him. Her expectant expression made him realize he had been silent for too long, leaving her question unanswered. The weight of it hung in the air, leaving him vulnerable and exposed.

Her expression changed, becoming full of strength, shining with a steadfast assuredness. "You are *not* at fault," she insisted with unwavering eye contact. "I will keep telling you that until you believe it. You. Are. Not. At. Fault." Speaking with a quiet, desperate firmness, she punctuated each word with absolute certainty. A smile played at the corners of his lips in response to her vehement tone.

Shifting his hand from the back of the couch to her shoulder, he gently stroked her skin, feeling the goose bumps rise as he drew her closer. He closed his eyes and savored the sensation of her body pressed against his. She adjusted the position of their clasped hands until their fingers intertwined. Palm against palm. As he gazed down at their hands, he suddenly became aware of the stark disproportion in their sizes. Her fingers were delicate and slender. In contrast, his own seemed rough and calloused, the skin weathered from years of hard work. He couldn't explain why, but seeing their mismatched hands together made him feel an overwhelming desire to shield her from harm. It was a strange moment, and one that he couldn't quite shake. The fear of something happening to her was like a living beast inside his chest, constantly clawing at him.

He leaned in and kissed her temple, breathing in the refreshing scent of citrus that surrounded her. "Thank you." Her head rested on his shoulder as she settled into the crook of his arm. He couldn't believe that she had chosen to be here with him in this moment. He was touched by the fact that she had put aside her hurt and anger and was focusing completely on him. The fact that she was fighting his internal demons with such fervor filled him with wonder and gratitude.

As they sat there, surrounded by the beauty of nature, she idly twirled his fingers between her own. The gentle rustling of leaves in the breeze and the soft chirping of crickets provided a soothing soundtrack to the moment. He took a deep breath and smelled the sweet fragrance of budding spring flowers and the fresh scent of cut grass from his morning work on the lawn. Yet the air held the pungent tinge of ozone that preceded a storm. Despite being lost in thought, they were both fully present, soaking in every sensation that the natural world had to offer.

"What made you finally decide to leave?" Jolene asked.

He took a deep breath before responding, the answer heavy on his tongue. "My dad." The memory of the humiliating experience lingered in his mind long after it was over. The fact that his dad—his role model—had witnessed his shame still tied his gut up in knots, even to this day. "My parents came for a visit and arrived earlier than expected. They'd gone to the guest room to rest before dinner. Angelica arrived home and didn't know they were there yet. She laid into me immediately because I'd left a spoon in the sink. It escalated quickly. Before I knew it, she was punching and kicking me. Her favorite target was my balls, and she got in a good kick that sent me to my knees."

"Oh God," she gasped, as if she could feel his pain.

"That's when she noticed my father standing at the end of the hall. He had his phone out. I thought he was calling the police, but no. He was recording the whole ugly scene. It was like someone had flipped a switch on her. She reverted into the sweet, affectionate woman my parents knew and loved.

"By that time, my dad had seen enough. He threatened to call the police if she didn't get out. She laughed and told him nobody would believe him. When he showed her the video he'd taken, she slammed out of the house."

He couldn't believe she had backed down when she'd stormed out. She'd never once backed down when he threatened to report her. Even with the proof of his injuries, she always maintained that no one would take him seriously. It was as if a huge weight had been lifted from his shoulders and he could finally breathe again. His parents had helped him pack up and leave that night. His mom had been confused at first, but after his dad had talked to her, she was all-in. To this day, Finch still didn't know what his dad had told her, but he was sure he'd never shared the video with her.

They took him to their home in western Maryland and hooked him up with a lawyer. It had been a humiliating experience telling Alan everything that had happened in his marriage. He'd been documenting things for years. All the injuries. The weapons she'd used on him, whether it was a dish being thrown at his head, boiling water poured on his arm, or a knife. He had pictures of everything. Not to mention his dad's video. He'd filed for divorce that very day, but it still took five long years before he was finally done. Five years of always looking over his shoulder, wondering if she'd come at him. She would occasionally pop up out of nowhere like she had at the gala, but thankfully, she'd never been violent at those times. Just verbally berated him. He tried to tune it out, but her words always found their way through the cracks.

Those times had been hard enough after experiencing freedom away from her. But what really killed him the most was knowing that his dad had seen it. In those weeks after he'd left, he'd grown increasingly despondent, and his dad had noticed.

Finch sat at his parents' breakfast table one morning after his mom had left for one of her club meetings. He had a bowl of cereal in front of him but couldn't bring himself to eat. His dad had come in and sat down across from him. They sat in silence for a while. Duncan Mobey had never been a big talker. But then his dad's mouth opened, and a torrent of words spilled forth. Words that settled deep in his tattered soul.

"I'm proud of you, kid." Finch's jaw dropped as his gaze shot up to his dad. In his mind, there was nothing that could make his dad feel a sense of pride in him. "I see you now, Atty. I see the type of man you've become despite what you'd been through. And I couldn't be more proud."

The sting of unshed tears tingled at the back of his nose. Regardless of the abuse, his marriage had failed, and he had not yet allowed himself to grieve and was on the brink of a breakdown. His dad's words just might send him over the edge.

"I was already proud of you. You've served this country with honor. You've grown into a man I can respect. But now, I see you in a different light. You have exceeded my expectations and have proven to be an exceptional man."

Finch scoffed. He wasn't so sure about that, but before he could counter Duncan's words, he continued. "Ten years you've been married to her, and I'm betting that wasn't the first time she attacked you." Duncan's eyes dropped to the scar on Finch's wrist. Finch pulled his hand back and put it in his lap under the table, out of view. "She was brutal. Vicious. And you didn't raise a hand against her to stop her. That shows an incredible strength. You knew that you were bigger and stronger than her and could have very easily restrained her. But you didn't."

"I didn't want to hurt her," he admitted.

"I know. Despite everything, you still loved her."

"I hated her, too."

"I know. But you didn't let that hate control you. You kept the love first and foremost in your heart. And someday, you'll find the right woman to shower that love on. But right now, it's time to let go. It's time to heal."

He still hated that his dad had seen firsthand what he'd been through, but he'd tried to hold on to his words. "My dad said he was proud of me," he told Jolene. "He'd seen my shame, and he still told me he was proud of me. I'm still not sure I deserve those words."

Chapter 18

WITH TEARS IN HER eyes, Jolene shifted until she was straddling his lap. She wanted to be absolutely sure he heard what she had to say. "I am such an idiot." She spoke with conviction, determined to get her point across. He opened his mouth to argue, but she put a finger over his lips. "I'm an idiot because I knew the type of man you were and I allowed my past experiences to cloud that truth."

She framed his face between her hands and stared deeply into his eyes. The wind picked up and blew her hair into her face, but she ignored it. She spoke slowly and clearly, wanting to make sure her message was received. "You are a man of honor. Of integrity.

You pour your heart and soul into your work, tirelessly giving to others. You have every reason to let hate and anger eat away at you, but you don't let it. You genuinely care for people. Doesn't matter if they're stranger or friend. You have the biggest heart of anyone I've ever met. The fact that you do it with all that weighing on your shoulders is truly remarkable and proves my point.

"But I can see it still causes you pain. Listen carefully. It's crucial that you understand what I'm about to say." She paused, studying his eyes carefully, noting the tiny variations in shade and color that made them so unique. "The shame you feel is not yours to bear."

"Jolie," he muttered, and she could tell he was about to contradict her.

"The shame is not yours to bear." She repeated herself, wanting to make absolutely certain he understood. "After Harrison's betrayal, it took me a long time to understand that myself. What he did was shameful. I had to learn that his actions did not reflect poorly on me. I was not responsible for his actions. It was hard, but I had to learn to disconnect his misdeeds from my own emotions. What he did was not a reflection of my character, and I had to remind myself of that constantly. It was his shame to carry, not mine."

Finch clasped one of her hands and placed a kiss on her palm. "I'm sorry he did that to you. I wish I could hunt him down and—"

She stopped him with a kiss, pouring everything she was feeling for him in that moment. When she broke the kiss, she was breathing heavily, but she had more to say. "I see you now. I see when you struggle. I see when you try to push it down and put on a brave face. I see the way you use humor to cover the pain you feel. I'm sorry I closed my eyes to it for so long, but now they are open. And I promise to keep them that way. The shame isn't something you have to bear alone, and I will help you come to terms with that. I promise."

His expression softened as he stared at her. "I do not deserve you," he whispered.

With a shout of "Bullshit!" she caught him off guard, and his eyes widened in shock. "I call bull- shit," she said, her voice quieter this time.

"Jolie—"

"Nope. Not gonna hear it. I will not let you demean yourself anymore. You are the best man I know, and we deserve each other. Now shut up and kiss me."

The smile he beamed at her made her heart take flight. Despite the heaviness of the conversation, his smile was a marvelous thing, a ray of light in the darkness. And she loved the fact that she had made it happen. But all those thoughts flew out of her head when he took her mouth in a searing kiss.

Electricity charged the air, and she had a feeling that was more due to them and their passion than the incoming storm. She wrapped her arms around his neck while his went around to her back. His hands locked against her spine, holding her tight to the hard planes of his chest. She felt the strength of his hold, as if he was afraid she'd slip away.

His erection pressed against her, and as he deepened the kiss, she shamelessly ground herself against him. Her pussy was weeping for him, and she didn't want to wait any longer.

A loud clap of thunder jolted them apart. She couldn't tell if it was the charged atmosphere or the kiss that had just rocked her world that made the fine hairs on her arms stand at attention. She glanced over her shoulder at the ominous clouds closing in on them. Relentless bursts of lightning painted the pitch-black sky with a bright white light, exposing the otherwise invisible details of the surrounding landscape. Rumbles of deafening thunder echoed through the atmosphere, filling the air with a sense of foreboding. A pungent odor of ozone and rain hung in the air. The anticipation of the impending storm was almost tangible, creating an atmosphere of both excitement and apprehension.

All that disappeared when she turned back to Finch. The fiery intensity of his gaze was palpable, as if it could sear through flesh. His stare ignited the air around them, sending shivers down her spine. It was so intense it felt like a physical touch. His rapid breathing was loud in her ears, as if he had just come up for air after being submerged. His fingers flexed on her hips as if he was trying to convey his desire without words. The atmosphere wasn't the only thing that was charged with an electric tension. She felt like a single touch from him could ignite a fire.

Oh, boy howdy, she was itching to light a match and watch the flames dance. She wanted to burn so badly she could feel the heat rising in her chest.

The first fat drops of rain did nothing to cool her overheated skin. He pulled her in closer as if he could shield her from the rain, like some sort of human umbrella. It made her laugh. "We can go inside, you know."

She felt his smile against her hairline. "I know. I just don't want to pop the bubble."

She knew exactly what he meant. "We can create another one inside."

"Yeah?" he asked, as if he was unsure whether she was telling him the truth.

"Yeah." Before she could climb off his lap, he stood with her in his arms. She wrapped her legs around his waist and her arms around his neck, clinging like a monkey. God, she loved his strength.

He moved toward the sliding glass door. "Wait," she called. "The blanket." He stopped and held her as she bent over and grabbed it. He took the advantage and kissed her extended throat, tracing the exposed contours with his tongue. The sensation of fiery shivers ran through her.

Then he was moving again. The blanket trailed behind them, snagging on the rough surface of the door-frame as they strained to push it closed. It seemed Finch didn't want to put her down to deal with it, and she didn't mind one bit. With a yank, she freed the blanket. The fabric tore with a loud ripping sound that echoed through the room. "Oops."

"I'll buy your dad a new one." Finch's grumbled promise made her laugh. As soon as the door was shut, she let go of the blanket, and he moved swiftly through the darkened rooms. The continuous strobe light effect of lightning illuminated the way. Feeling frisky, she started nibbling on his neck as he climbed the stairs.

Only once did he fumble, possibly due to a sensitive spot that she hit. "Fuck," he hissed. His curse was a sharp exhale against her cheek, and she couldn't help but smile.

"You okay?" she teased.

He huffed out a breath. "You're dangerous."

"Sorry."

"No, you're not." He was right about that. She liked the effect she was having on him. She liked that he took the remaining stairs two at a time. It was hot as hell. Here was a man who couldn't wait to be with her. And yet, if she told him to slow down or stop, she knew he would. But there was no way in hell she'd say stop. This had been a long time coming. Over a year late. She'd been such a fool. She sighed. It made her suddenly sad for all the time they'd missed.

He'd reached her room and let her feet hit the ground in front of him. He gripped her hips, his gaze studying her. Was her remorse evident in her expression?

"Jolie, we can stop—"

Could the weight of her regret be felt through the heaviness of her sighs, seen through the furrow of her brow, and heard through the quiver in her voice? "Don't you dare." She was determined not to waste another moment on regret. It was time to move forward. Her longing for him to understand was so intense that she was willing to utilize every available approach to accomplish it. In every gesture, every glance, she sought to convey her feelings to him.

Meeting his gaze, she erased any trace of remorse from her expression, replacing it instead with a sense of desire and confidence. The unspoken love she could see in his eyes gave her the power to let go of everything and just focus on the here and now. On them.

She reached up and wiped away the raindrops from his hair, feeling the dampness on her own skin. He grabbed her wrist, and she could feel his warm breath on her skin as he brought her wet finger to his lips, sucking it into his mouth. "Are you sure?" he asked around her finger. She wanted to giggle at the muffled sound of his voice. Only Finch could make her laugh at a time like this.

"I want you. I want this. I want us. Don't stop."

"So, what you're saying is . . ." he murmured after taking her finger out of his mouth and kissing a knuckle. Jolene could hear the teasing quality in his voice.

"Omigod, Finch. If you don't strip me naked right this minute . . ."

He leaned in, savoring the moment, taking in the sweet aroma of her perfume and the softness of her skin. As he tilted his head to kiss her extended throat, he could feel the heat radiating from her body. The sight of her elegant neck and the way it curved gracefully stirred something deep within him.

Pressing his lips against the nape of her neck, he cherished everything about her. The gentle rustling of her hair filled his ears as he traced the contours of her throat with his tongue, feeling her shiver in his arms. The taste of her skin was sweet and salty, delicious like the sour gummy candy he so liked to snack on. He held her close, feeling the rapid beat of her heart against his chest as they melted into each other's embrace.

The flames of desire flickered in his eyes like a wildfire in the dead of night, consuming everything in its path. His breaths came in short, irregular bursts, making it sound like he was struggling to fill his lungs with air. Her gaze was so intense that it felt like a physical touch, sending all the blood in his body down to his cock, which throbbed with anticipation painfully in its denim confinement.

An intense, animalistic craving seemed to consume his entire being. His breaths turned ragged as he fixated on his target. His fingers flexed and twitched with anticipation, yearning to touch and possess what lay before him.

He could tell she was just as hungry as him. She pushed her hands under his shirt, tracing the ridges of his muscles with her fingers. Reaching behind his neck, he pulled the shirt off and let it drop to the floor and fought the need to fold it neatly. There was no Angelica to criticize him for the mess.

Being nearly a foot shorter than his six-foot two frame, Jolene's lips were at the perfect height to tease his nipples. He sucked in a gasp at the sensation of her tongue swirling around it. He was going to need her to stop that soon before he blew in his pants.

Reaching for the hem of her shirt, he whipped it up and off, distracting her from what she'd been doing to him. He made quick work of her lacy bra and bent to return the favor on her own nipple. He rolled her stiff bud with his tongue, savoring the sounds she made in response. She gripped his head, holding him to her as if afraid he'd stop. That was not going to happen. Not unless she wanted him to. And he hoped she'd never want him to stop.

While feasting on her other nipple, he reached between them to unfasten her pants. They slid down her legs to pool at her feet with only the slightest push from him. He stood back and raked his gaze over her body. She stood as bold as could be in front of him, unashamed of her body. Her pale skin shone like a pearl in the dim light. The freckles that dotted her shoulders mesmerized him, and he longed to explore them with his tongue. Her breasts were just enough for a handful, the rosy nipples standing prominent and begging for his touch.

Reaching up, he took hold of her ponytail and with a gentle tug, he freed her hair from the elastic tie. Finally . . . *finally* . . . he combed through the soft waves with his fingers. The silky strands slipped easily through his fingers, like water through a sieve. The sensation of her hair was so captivating that he could spend hours just running his fingers through it. But he had other plans.

With a raised eyebrow, he offered her a sly grin as their eyes locked. Then he gave her a gentle shove, and she fell back onto the bed. He crawled over her body without any hesitation, his movements deliberate as he shifted her to the center of the bed.

He worked his way down her body, using his lips to explore every dip and valley. Tasting, teasing, until he reached the barrier of her panties. He could smell her arousal, an intoxicating scent that made his mouth water. He was starving for her. Had been starving for her for over a year. Ever since their night at the gala had been interrupted. His stomach had been tied in knots since then. Hunger pangs he couldn't ease. Couldn't quench. Until now.

"I have needed this," he said, his warm breath gusting over her. "For so long. Starving for you, Jolie," he breathed, feeling desperate for her.

"Finch," she whispered. Their eyes locked, and he saw the same hunger burning in her that he felt within himself.

He quickly removed the lace blocking him from his feast and dove in. She arched against his mouth as he licked her slit, the taste of her on his tongue. Her movements turned wild when he swirled his tongue around her clit, then sucked the little bundle of nerves into his mouth. He memorized every moan, every twitch, every quivering muscle, every convulsion that conveyed to him the spots that gave her the most pleasure. He aimed to please.

And pleasure her, he did, as the room filled with the sound of her moans and the sweet scent of her arousal. The softness of her skin under his touch was like silk, and he could feel the heat emanating from her body as he continued to satisfy her.

His senses seemed heightened. He could hear the wind outside whipping through the trees. The steady barrage of raindrops drumming on the roof. His heartbeat was amplified, and he swore he could hear hers as well.

Her taste. The feel of her soft skin under his hands. The scent of her arousal. The sight of her writhing beneath him, her eyes closed in ecstasy, was an image he would never forget. Every heightened sense fueled his desire as he continued to tease and please her.

He sent her flying with skilled fingers and a deft touch. Her moans grew louder and louder as he traced circles on her sensitive clit with his tongue. He continued until she was left breathless and completely satisfied.

He lifted his head and rose over her. Her cheeks were flushed. Her fiery hair was splayed out across the pillows. Her chest rose and fell with her heavy breaths. She took his breath away.

Finally, her eyes blinked open, and he lost himself in the jade-hued treasures of her eyes. As she stared back at him with dilated pupils filled with yearning, his heart swelled. He could see it in their bottomless depths. She needed him. He thought he could live off that feeling forever.

Chapter 19

FINCH HELD HER CLOSE, whispering sweet nothings in her ear as he gently ran his fingers through her hair. Her breasts brushed against his hard pecs, setting her nerve endings on fire. A hot streak of yearning renewed, bolting to the juncture between her thighs. God, she wanted more. And she wanted it now.

Working her fingers between their bodies, she reached for his belt. He raised his hips, giving her room. She worked the belt open, too impatient to remove the thing all together from the loops. Making quick work of the button and zipper of his jeans, she pushed the material down over his hips.

He rolled off her and shucked the rest of his clothes until he was as blessedly naked as her. Then he was hovering over her. She opened her legs, allowing him to settle between them. His cock teasing her entrance.

"Shit. Condom," he muttered and went to move off her.

She stopped him, and his eyes widened in surprise. "I'm protected. And I haven't been with anybody in a really long time."

He kissed her nose. "I haven't been with anyone since my separation."

What he had just admitted left her wide-eyed in shock. She opened her mouth to say something, then closed it. She had no idea what to say to that.

Finch shrugged. "What can I say? I took my marriage vows seriously. When I met you, I knew you were going to challenge all my preconceived notions about my situation. That night, before Angelica swept in, I intended to break those vows. My marriage had been over for years. I shouldn't have felt even the slightest guilt. But it was there, nonetheless. Inexplicitly. It was baffling. After everything she'd put me through, why should I feel guilty about taking something for myself?"

"Because you're a good man. She didn't deserve you."

He scoffed. "I'm not so sure about that. I was willing to keep lying," he admitted to her, "just to be with you."

"You had your reasons. And I understand them now."

"In a way, I'm glad we got interrupted. It may have taken longer than I expected, but I'm free now. I can come to you with a clear conscience. I didn't realize how important that was to me until now."

"Then what are you waiting for?" she asked, thrusting her hips against him. His eyes widened briefly before they became hooded with desire.

With a wild thrust of his hips, he entered her. Her legs tightened around him as he pumped into her. She could feel every heavy, solid inch of him. Huge, long, and thick.

His hands roamed her body, tweaking her nipples, teasing her senses. She felt a powerful orgasm building as he plunged into her. Fast, deep, and strong.

With a commanding thrust, he lifted her, causing her to arch her back and throw her head back in pleasure. Her skin was on fire as waves of ecstasy washed over her, leaving her breathless and floating on a cloud of pleasure.

He kissed her through her climax, his tongue matching his punishing pace. His hips ground against hers. Each driving, impaling thrust going deeper, shattering her until she felt him go rigid. He shouted her name, and his body surged against hers, pushing her high and hard over another crest with a rush. Or maybe it was the same long, continuous summit. She had no idea. All she knew was that she was lost in sensation and she never wanted it to end.

They lay there for an indeterminable amount of time. His face was buried in her neck, which he showered with kisses as they floated back to earth.

"I don't want to move," he murmured. His warm breath against the sensitive skin behind her ear sent tingles down her body.

"Then don't."

"I'm probably crushing you."

"Don't care. It'll be a hell of a way to go."

He chuckled, which caused him to slip from her body. They both groaned in disappointment. He rolled beside her and pulled her into his arms. They lay there, listening to the relentless rain and wind battering the world outside.

She wanted to ask him more questions about his past but didn't know how to begin. She admired him for what he'd confessed earlier about the guilt he felt for wanting to be with her while he was still married. She was awed by the immense courage he must have had to break away from her.

It astounded her that he'd stayed with her for so long. Why would a man like him stay with a woman like that? What drove him to stay? Could he have loved her that much?

She was lost in thought when he spoke up, saying, "I can practically hear the wheels turning in your brain. Ask what you want to know. I'm an open book to you now."

She bit her lip before finally going for it. "Why did you stay?"

Lying with her head on his shoulder, her arm was splayed across his stomach. He had an arm wrapped around her shoulders, his hand resting on her hip. When she asked her question, she could feel his fingers tighten on her skin before he relaxed them.

"I ask myself that question all the time. There are only two reasons I can think of. I thought I loved her. And I believed in the vows I'd taken. Those were important enough to me to stay. Until they weren't. By the time I'd left, I was just so weary of it all. When my dad saw her rampage, it became clear to me in that instant that this wasn't love. It wasn't supposed to hurt. It wasn't supposed to be one-sided. It wasn't supposed to be full of fear."

"She twisted your love. Used it against you."

"Yes. Exactly."

She moved her hand, running her fingers through the line of hair from his stomach to his chest. "Why did you never tell anybody?"

He sighed. "There's that age-old stigma that men can't be abused by women. It's too ridiculous for some people to even fathom. She'd laugh when I'd threaten to report her. She always maintained that no one would take me seriously. Nobody'd believe me. She used the fact that I was in the military against me.

I had training. I was stronger than her. She'd tell me that everybody would believe I had started it for those reasons alone."

"That's bullshit."

"People often won't believe that men can be victims of domestic abuse. It becomes a joke. They'd laugh and say things like, 'Can't handle the little lady?' Or my favorite, 'Grow a set of balls.' It's easier to keep quiet instead of facing the ridicule."

"Jesus. I never thought about it like that before."

"Men have to be seen as passive. My military career took me out of that category. We also have to be victims with clear injuries, whereas a lot of times a woman can just make a verbal accusation and are believed much more easily."

"That's such bullshit."

"That may be, but society perpetuates it."

"How so?"

"You ever seen the animated version of *Beauty and the Beast*?"

"One of my favorites."

"There's a brief part in the marketplace scene at the beginning. Belle is walking through the town, singing.

In the background, a woman knocks a guy over the head with a rolling pin because she thinks he's paying too much attention to Belle."

"Hmm."

"They remade the movie into a live action film. Do you think they took that scene out? No, they changed the weapon. She uses a frying pan instead."

"Shit. I never noticed that before."

"Most people don't. A hit to the head like that could be deadly in real life, but in those movies, it's seen as funny. Would a man hitting a woman with a frying pan be considered just as funny?"

"No," she gasped. It was all so wrong. Things needed to change. Society needed to do better.

"Twenty-six years separate the two movies, and violence against men is still considered amusing."

"Shit. That's so wrong. I never realized. I guess I'm complacent in perpetuating society's warped perceptions." She suddenly felt a different type of shame. She'd probably laughed at scenes like he'd described before. And now that he'd opened her eyes, she could see how wrong it was.

"It took me years of therapy to understand it. Still doesn't make it right, but at least I can get past most of the anger."

"Only most of it?" Her teasing tone quickly disappeared when she saw the rage in his eyes. "What? What is that look for?"

"There's more I haven't told you."

She inhaled sharply, apprehensive that his words could damage their connection.

This was the part that never failed to kill him. The level of betrayal he'd felt was just as fresh as the day he'd first learned about it. If his lawyer hadn't uncovered the medical records, he still wouldn't have known. Ten years he'd lived with her and her lie and never knew. It was an incredibly cruel lie, too. One he never imagined she'd be capable of perpetuating.

"I always wanted a family," he started. Jolene propped her chin on her fist, which was on his chest. He avoided her gaze, but he could feel her anxious eyes on him. "After a few years of marriage, we decided to start trying. I was excited at the prospect of having children. She was, too, or so I thought. Years passed, and nothing happened. She blamed me, of course. Yet she refused to seek out fertility treatments. Anytime I'd bring it up, she'd scream and yell. She'd say if I was more of a man, she'd be pregnant by now. It was humiliating and frustrating."

"I'm so sorry."

"It wasn't until just before the gala that I found out the truth. My lawyer took it upon himself to hire a private investigator. Little did I know how deep her cruelty really went."

"What did she do?"

"After that first discussion about starting a family when I was deployed again, she went to a doctor and had her tubes tied."

Jolene sat bolt upright so fast it stunned him. "The fuck you say?"

He pulled himself up, feeling the weight of the world on his shoulders, and rested his back against the solid headboard. "During all those years of 'trying,' she made me believe it was my fault. Finding out what she'd done . . . God, Jolie. It had been devastating. There are no words to describe what I felt. The rage. The embarrassment for how badly she'd fooled me. The weird sense of relief that it wasn't my fault and that maybe kids would still be in my future. My therapist helped me work through a lot of it, but the rage still burns like embers inside."

"I can imagine." Her eyes dropped to where her hand lay on his arm and nibbled on her lip. "How did none of us know you were going through that? You found out about this recently, right?"

"Just over a year ago. After the stunt she pulled at the gala, I was done. I was ready to do whatever it took to get free of her."

She abused that lip some more, and he wanted to pull it free of the mistreatment. He let it go, understanding that she needed to do it while processing her thoughts.

"How?" she whispered, her eyes filling with tears. His gut twisted. The pain he'd felt wasn't hers, but here she was, becoming emotional about the shit he'd gone through. At that moment, he knew he loved her. It was so different from how he'd felt about Angelica. Light-years different. This was what real love was. The type of love his parents had. He'd do whatever it took to protect that love.

"How what?" he asked once he could speak past the lump that had formed in his throat.

"None of us knew. None of us noticed. How is that possible?"

He took her hand and threaded his fingers through hers. He brought it to his lips, kissing it before answering her question. "After almost fifteen years, I became an expert at hiding things. I'm the class clown, remember? It was how I learned to cope. How I learned to hide. With humor. Nobody looked too deeply at the class clown."

"God. That's so sad," she said as a tear slid down her cheek. He reached up and swiped it away.

"Maybe. But it was my defense mechanism. I couldn't stand the thought of anybody discovering the truth. I couldn't bear the shame. It was a bitter pill to swallow, especially after finding out how badly she'd played me. It was easier to hide."

"Now I want to go back and pay closer attention."

"I wouldn't have let you see anything."

She ripped her hand from his and bracketed his face. Her jade eyes narrowed, focusing on him intently as she studied him. "Promise me you won't hide from me anymore."

"Jolie—"

She jiggled his head as her focus on him intensified. He would have found it amusing if he didn't know that laughing at this moment would make her mad.

"Promise me."

She was so serious, her voice trembling with those two words. It sobered him immediately. He laid his hands over hers and looked deeply into her eyes. "I promise." And he meant it. There were no more se-crets between them now. It was a promise that would be a breeze to keep.

"Good," she declared. "Now kiss me."

"With pleasure."

Chapter 20

THE ROOM WAS STILL dark due to the storm that raged outside when Finch slipped out of bed early. The pile of discarded clothes on the floor taunted him. An irritating voice in his mind that sounded suspiciously like his ex-wife called him out for the mess. He bent and picked up the clothes, folding each item and placing them in neat piles on the corner of Jolene's dresser. He shook his head at himself as he straightened one pile until it was aligned perfectly with the edge of the dresser. He really needed to find a way to exorcise that voice. There were long stretches of time when he was with Jolene that the voice was non-existent. He hoped to have more moments like that.

Walking away from his need to tidy the room, he decided he wanted to do something special for Jolene. She'd listened to everything he'd confessed last night, and there hadn't been an ounce of judgment. Her questions were driven by her desire to understand. To truly know him. To know what he'd gone through.

It had humbled him when she'd taken on his pain as her own. The memory of it was vivid in his mind. He could still see her face, the way her eyes had softened as she took his hand. He could hear the gentle cadence of her voice as she spoke. The weight of his pain lifting as she drew it from him was a physical sensation of release and relief. It was an overwhelming moment, one that he would never forget.

The rain continued to pour, drenching the world in a monotonous gray. He glanced out the window in the kitchen as he made breakfast. The relentless rain made the outside world look bleak. But inside, he felt anything but bleak. For the first time in fifteen years, he felt . . . good. The future looked bright, and it was all because of the woman he'd left curled up in bed.

He was anxious for the toast to pop so he could go back to her.

Once everything was done, he put it all on a tray he'd unearthed from deep in a cabinet and carried it up the stairs. The door creaked as he pushed it open, and Jolene stirred. She blinked at him, pushing her hair out of her face. God, she was adorable.

As she sat up, her features remained inscrutable. "You made me breakfast in bed?" she asked.

He wasn't sure how to interpret her expression and suddenly grew nervous that he'd done something wrong. "Yeah," he replied, not knowing what else to say. He'd found with Angelica, it was best not to say anything at all.

He placed the tray down on the bed.

"You made me breakfast in bed," she repeated, this time as a statement.

"Is that . . . is it okay?"

Jolene got to her knees on the bed in front of him, causing everything on the tray to teeter dangerously. With a gentle grip on his face, she pulled his attention away from the tray and toward her. "You made me breakfast in bed. Nobody has ever done anything like that for me before. Know this, Finch. I will never complain about you wanting to do something special for me."

As her words settled, a smile broke through the uncertainty. Something inside him eased, as if the knot that had been constricting his organs suddenly loosened. He could breathe easier, and his heart felt lighter.

"You better watch out, woman. You just gave me carte blanche to spoil you rotten."

"A little indulgence never hurt anyone," she answered, using his own words from their doomed helicopter ride. Then she snatched a gummy worm from the bag he'd added to the breakfast tray and bit it in half. Swiftly, he bent down and seized the other half from her grasp with his teeth. It was hard not to laugh when her eyes widened so comically in shock.

She pounced and wrestled him to the bed. He didn't put up much of a fight. Flat on his back on the bed, she straddled his hips and pinned his hands down beside his head.

"That was mine," she complained.

"Yup," he answered, popping the P.

"What happened to spoiling me?"

"I'll start tomorrow."

Her grin took on a mischievous quality as she peered down at him, and he knew her head was going someplace dirty.

She let go of one hand to grab another gummy worm. This time, she stuck one half in her mouth while leaving the other half hanging out. As she leaned over him, her naked breasts brushed against his chest. He wanted to crush her to him and run his hands all over her silky-smooth skin, but she still had his hands pinned.

She teased his lips with the gummy worm. When he tried to snap at it with his teeth, she withdrew. His dick was so hard it could hammer nails. His missed attempts only fueled his desire. Each time she laughed, his erection twitched with anticipation. Seeking what it craved most, like he sought that gummy worm.

Finally, he caught the candy with his teeth. Or she capitulated and let him catch it. Either way, he wasn't complaining. Especially when their tongues were dueling it out with each other after they'd each swallowed their half.

She let go of his hands, and he tunneled his fingers through her hair, holding it away from her face. Her hair was so thick and silky that he found himself lost in the sensation of it wrapped around his fingers.

Lost in her kiss and the feel of her hair, he hadn't noticed where her hand had gone. He gasped into her mouth when she wrapped her hand around his cock. She had managed to push his sweatpants down just far enough to release him. How she pulled that off without him noticing would forever remain a mystery.

"Want you. Can't wait," she panted.

"Fuck," he hissed. She rose up on her knees and positioned him under her before sinking slowly down on his erection. They both groaned as he filled her.

She sat up, and he sank in even deeper. A perfect fit, like she was tailor-made for him. He never wanted to be removed from her. He could happily stay in this position for the rest of his life. She was everywhere. A sensory feast. Her scent, that tart citrusy flavor, would always spark his cravings now that he'd gotten a taste.

She began to explore, moving her hips, seeking out what gave her the most pleasure. He let go of her hair and moved his hands to her breasts, unable to resist as they bobbed in front of him with every move she made. He rolled her nipples, loving the sharp cry that burst from her lips.

The way it felt to touch her was nearly overwhelming. The feel of her tight channel surrounding him. The way she gasped his name. He gritted his teeth, determined to hold back.

"Need you to come, Jolie," he rasped, moving one hand down her body. Finding that nerve bundle that drove her wild, he pressed it with his thumb at the same time he pinched her nipple. Her legs tightened against his hips as she cried out. Her movements grew harder, more focused on reaching that ultimate high.

He moved his gaze up her body and lost his breath. Her head was thrown back, and the long curtain of her hair hung down her back. It made him think of the waterfalls that, when the light hit them just right, looked like fire. Fire falls.

The woman was fire. The moment she caught, her blaze scorched.

She came in a glorious eruption that left him breathless and unable to look away.

"Fuck, you're beautiful," he hissed. Still lost in the throes of her climax, she didn't respond, but he felt her pulse around his dick, as if her pussy heard him and appreciated the words.

He sensed her tiring, so he reluctantly removed his hands from her tit and clit to grip her hips. He held her in place as he took over, thrusting up into her. She opened her eyes and gazed down at him. He could read so much in that simple look, but it would take him a while to categorize it all. For now, he embraced the emotion that he read as love.

That emotion spurred him on. As did the sensuous smile that played on her lips. He thrust harder, deeper, but lost his rhythm when she reached up and plucked her nipple with one hand while the other moved lower to manipulate her clit.

"Jesus H. Christ, Jolie. Warn a guy. Fuck, that's hot." He wondered how his mouth could still form words, since the rest of him was lost in the sexy display writhing on top of him.

"Fuck me, Finch," she cried.

He bucked his hips hard, and she gasped. "Yes, ma'am." For once, he didn't mind being bossed around. Especially when they both gained so much pleasure from it.

"Fuck. Fuck. Oh. I'm . . . shit. Right there." Her words spilled rapid fire as she burst once more. She came with one long moan.

He couldn't hold out any longer as her body milked his. His balls twitched, and he erupted, pouring sheer fire inside her.

Breakfast did not survive their morning romp. Not that she cared. He'd made her soar not once, but twice. She'd never had a partner like him. He was fun and sexy in one hot, muscular package. He turned her on in ways she'd never imagined.

For example, during breakfast take two, they were down in the kitchen together putting the meal together. Her body was still sizzling from their earlier exploits. Therefore, every time he touched her, she felt the heat. And it built, mercilessly.

Finch, the stinker, could tell the effect he was having on her and took full advantage. The second breakfast was ruined—at least the food was—when he was unable to hold out any longer. He lifted her onto the counter, pulled her shorts off, and feasted on her. She should have been embarrassed at the display she'd made. But she wasn't. The sensations were too overwhelming for her to care that she had her legs spread as wide as they could go on her dad's kitchen counter.

But the man's tongue did things to her, and she blocked out everything else except the things he was doing to her. She came all over his face. In fact, she'd never come so hard in her life.

The next thing she knew, she was flat on her back on the couch and Finch was buried deep inside her. She was all for it. Couldn't get enough. Couldn't even stop long enough to eat, apparently. They'd have to, eventually. They'd need the fuel at the rate they were going. And the gummy worms wouldn't cut it.

But, *oh God*, when he moved inside her like that, who needed food? She could live off orgasms, right?

Apparently not, since as soon as they'd come down from another fiery eruption and gotten cleaned up, they were putting together breakfast take three, laughing over the fact that they'd have to increase their food budget at the rate they were going.

Since the rain was still coming down in buckets, they sat at the kitchen table to eat. The world was dark and gloomy outside, but inside felt all bright and shiny.

As they ate, Finch received a phone call from Matt Blankenship at the airfield where they'd landed, if one could call it that. She shuddered at the memory of the near disaster. Finch took her hand and twined his fingers with hers as if he sensed where her thoughts had gone and wanted to offer comfort.

She loved that he could sense those types of things in her and hoped she did the same for him. When his hand tightened around hers, she was definitely sensing his mood. He wasn't happy about whatever Matt was telling him.

"Are you sure?" Finch said into the phone. "Yeah, okay. Do what you can. Send the sample off. But I doubt knowing the cause will get us anywhere."

Jolene listened to his side of the conversation, trying to discern what they were talking about. It appeared something had been tampered with on the helicopter, and both men were pissed.

"How long till the part comes in? Okay. Yeah. Thanks, man." He hung up and set his phone down on the table. He took a deep breath before looking up at her.

"What is it?" she asked.

"Matt found what went wrong with the tail rotor."

"I'm guessing it's not good."

He shook his head. His expression appeared almost as if he was shell-shocked. Hoping to convey strength, she squeezed his hand.

"There was some sort of substance that had eaten away at the flight control cable."

"And that cable was important to the mechanics of the helicopter?" she asked, wishing she knew more about aircraft functions.

"Yeah. It's a steel coil device that connects the cockpit controls to other control surfaces."

"Like the tail rotor? That's what you lost control of, right?"

"Yes. The tail rotor."

"Does Matt know what the substance was?"

"No. He's never seen anything like it before. He took some samples and sent it to someone he knows that works in a lab. Hopefully, they'll be able to figure it out."

"How did something like that get on the cable?"

"That's the question, isn't it? Matt said it wasn't natural wear and tear. He said it looked like something had chewed away at the cable." He glanced down at his phone as if it held the answers for him. She empathized with the type of man he was. He was meticulous about the condition of his aircraft. The fact that he'd missed seeing this issue was probably killing him. Clearly, it wasn't his fault. But she knew it would be almost impossible to tell him that.

She thought about what could eat away at steel like that. No way it was an animal. That meant something had dripped onto the cable. Or was poured. She gasped at that thought.

"Oh my God, Finch. Do you think someone did this? Did someone—"

"Sabotage my helicopter?" he interrupted. "Yeah, I do."

"Who?"

He shrugged, but she could tell he had a name in mind. He just wasn't ready to voice it out loud. His ex-wife came to mind. From what he'd told her about the woman, she was unhinged. But would she go to these lengths? And for what purpose?

She'd been impressed with the skill with which Finch had handled the crisis. If it had been anyone else, she wasn't so sure the outcome would have been so positive. She wondered what he'd been like on missions in the Air Force. Something Matt said came to mind just then.

"Can I ask you a question?"

He looked up at her with curiosity. "Sure."

"Matt mentioned you served together," she started.

"We did."

"He also hinted that you were kind of legendary. That you used to take the risky missions without hesitation."

He dropped his gaze. "Yeah."

This was the part she was going to hate learning the truth about. His home life had been miserable. Would he have done anything to escape it? "Why? Was it because of her?"

Finch ran his finger over a line in the wood grain of the table, seeming to think over his answer. He remained quiet for so long she wasn't sure he was going to answer.

Then he drew in a deep breath. "I would fool myself into thinking it wasn't. That I volunteered for those missions because I was the best person for the job. And don't get me wrong, I was the best," he stated with a cocky grin that didn't quite reach his eyes and quickly dropped away. "But I was lying to myself. There were days when I would have done anything to escape my life with her."

Jolene felt the sting of tears. Since the moment they'd met, Finch had seemed larger than life. A big personality full of piss and vinegar. He was kind, giving, and oh, so funny. It made her a little sad now to realize some of that had been a coping mechanism. A way to hide the pain he was feeling.

She rapidly blinked back the threat of tears. Standing up from her chair, she walked toward him, the scent of fried bacon mixed with the faint aroma of coffee. She lowered herself onto his lap, feeling the warmth of his body and the softness of his shirt against her skin. His steady heartbeat as she leaned in to kiss him comforted her. They sat in silence for a moment, lost in each other's embrace.

"These last few days have been the best of my life. That's because of you. From the moment I met you, I knew you were going to change my life. I'm just so sorry it took me so long to pull my head out of my ass."

His palm was warm as he cradled her cheek, and she leaned into him, savoring the sensation. "You've changed my life, too. I will be forever thankful for you," he said just before taking her lips in a soul-consuming kiss.

A kiss that soon turned explosive. He reached for the hem of her shirt, and she was up for it. From the feel of it, he was "up" for it as well. She smiled against his lips.

"What's so funny?" he asked.

"Is it possible to have too much sex?"

"Like you said, a little indulgence never hurt any-body."

She threw her head back and laughed, which quick-ly turned to a gasp when he stood with her in his arms. He took the stairs two at a time and sent her soaring.

Chapter 21

IT HAD BEEN RAINING for three days straight, with no signs of stopping. The town of Sunnyvale was in trouble. Rivers were threatening to swamp their banks. The land was already saturated, and there was nowhere for the water to go. People's basements were flooding. A great many houses along the riverbank were vulnerable.

Finch and Jolene were doing all they could to help. Jolene was volunteering at the high school. Safely situated on higher ground, it had been turned into a temporary shelter. She was working with other area chefs to keep the displaced residents fed.

Meanwhile, Finch was doing more grunt work. With the looming threat of a flood, he and others worked tirelessly to fill as many sandbags as possible. The rhythmic shoveling of sand and the thud as each bag was filled resounded around him. Sweat and rainwater dripped down his face as he heaved each heavy bag onto the truck, his muscles straining.

Removing the work gloves he'd borrowed from Dante, he took a breather, wiping his face off and downing a bottle of water. He looked down at his calloused hands. The roughness was a testament to the hours he had spent scooping up heavy, wet sand with a shovel. Looking around at the others working as tirelessly to save their town, he felt a sense of exhaustion. The rushing sound of the nearby river was a constant reminder of the impending danger, and there was no guarantee their efforts would make a difference.

The hard work was a preemptive strike against the force of the water that threatened to destroy everything in its path. The possibility of mudslides was now a major concern as well. Finch had called Graham, hoping the Nighthawks could come down to help evacuate people if needed, but they had been deployed to Kansas after a devastating rash of tornadoes decimated a community there. After participating in a training seminar in Atlanta, Brodhi was en route to Sunnyvale to lend a hand.

In the late afternoon, Finch got a ride to the high school to meet up with Brodhi. And he was anxious to see Jolene as well.

The cafeteria was abuzz with activity as people chatted in groups and children played around them. He leaped over a remote-control car that was headed on a collision course. A parent shouted at a kid to be more careful. Finch smiled at the sheepish boy and waved away his apology.

As he entered the kitchen, the scent of onions greeted him first. He spotted Jolene immediately, and something inside him eased. At least until he saw her face. There were tears streaming down her face as she stood at the counter, knife in hand, expertly cutting vegetables. Filled with concern, he rushed to her side.

With his hands on her shoulders, he turned her to face him. "Jolie? What is it? What's the matter?"

She laughed, and he blinked at her in surprise. She grabbed a hand towel off the counter and wiped her tears away. "Nothing's wrong. I was just chopping onions. My eyes always water when I cut onions."

Her explanation caused the vise on his throat to spin open, and he breathed a sigh of relief. "I've heard it helps if you put a piece of bread in your mouth."

Her face scrunched up in disgust, and he couldn't help but laugh. "Soggy bread." She shivered dramatically, making it clear she didn't like that idea.

"You don't like soggy bread?"

"Hell no."

"But aren't you the one who brings the stuffing for our Thanksgiving feasts? And what about the tiramisu on your dessert menu?"

"Yeah, I can make the stuff, just not eat it."

"A chef who doesn't like her own creations," he teased.

She pushed his shoulder with a huff. "Oh, shut up."

He kissed her and felt the weight of the world lift off his shoulders, buoyed by their lighthearted connection. His dick went from zero to sixty with that simple kiss. "Can you take a break? I need to talk to you in private."

Her brow furrowed in concern. "Sure. Give me a minute." She got one of the other helpers to finish chopping the onions, then took his hand and led him out of the kitchen.

He found himself in a darkened hallway lined with lockers. The typical high school flyers covered the walls. It must have been close to election time, since there were numerous student council campaign signs plastered everywhere. He wondered if the kids would get the opportunity to vote after all this.

Jolene led him to a classroom door at the end of the hall. It surprised him it wasn't locked when she easily opened it. But his concern for the security of the school flew out of his mind as soon as the door closed behind them and they were alone.

He cupped her face and drew her mouth to his, thrusting his tongue past the barrier of her lips. He needed this. Needed her. Now that he'd had her, he couldn't get enough.

Backing her up against the wall, he plastered his body to hers, losing himself in the feel of her softness against his hard. Her moan of pleasure had his cock throbbing with the need for relief.

Her hands worked their way under his shirt, splaying across his back. She undulated against him, drawing her own pleasure from their embrace. He felt her heat as she rocked against him, his cock nestled snugly in the V of her legs.

Conveniently, she was wearing a button-down shirt. He released a few buttons until her lace-covered breasts were free. Then he yanked the cups of her bra down and kissed his way to her breast. He took the rose-tipped nipple into his mouth, lashing the hard point with his tongue. She grasped his head, holding her to him as he suckled. With a near painful grip on his hair, she arched against his mouth. He greedily took what she was offering, moving to the other one to give it equal attention.

While he feasted on her breasts, he slid his hand under the waistband of her pants, delving deep until he felt her warm, wet heat on his fingers. Sliding between her folds, he pushed a digit inside her. She gasped against his ear and widened her stance.

Fuck, he needed her.

Being around her was like being wrapped in a warm blanket of scents, sounds, and textures. The orange aroma that was as familiar to him now as his own but at the moment had underlying tones of onion. The way it felt to touch her, to feel her arch against him, to hear her wanton gasps in his ear—it was everything.

"Finch," she cried when he clasped her nipple between his teeth and bit down, then soothed the pinch by rolling it with his tongue. He kindled her passion until his own surged, her sounds of capitulation sending him over the edge of control.

He finished unbuttoning her shirt and pushed it off. It fluttered to the floor at their feet. Then he worked her pants open and shoved them and her panties down to her knees. Spinning her around, he thrust his hips against her, trapping her between him and the wall. She cried out and braced her hands against the wall. Her back arched beautifully as she pushed back against him. He ran a hand down her spine, reveling in the feel of her smooth skin.

Freeing himself from the confinement of his cargo shorts, he grasped her hips, adjusted her angle, then plunged inside in one agonizingly deep thrust. The pleasure was absolute and explosive. They both cried out, the sound echoing through the empty room. He clamped his hand over her mouth and bit into her shoulder to muffle any sounds that might attract unwanted attention.

He pounded into her with powerful thrusts. His hips moved with a fierce intensity, driving him deeper with a firm, unyielding force. Each surge was harder than the last, driving her wild with pleasure. He pushed deeper and harder. A raw act of possession.

Her eager response matched his. She arched her back and took his reckless fury. Her wet heat stirring him to go harder, faster. He grasped her breast with his free hand, rolling her nipple between his thumb and forefinger. He felt her suck in a breath against the hand covering her mouth.

He was close and needed her there before he lost himself. As he explored her body, his hand slid down to cup her mound, his fingers brushing against his own arousal. When he flicked at her clit, she went wild. She shattered into a million pieces in his embrace, her body pulsing with pleasure as she brought him to the brink of ecstasy with her.

He sucked on the delicate skin of her neck, marking her as he emptied himself inside her. With a final pulse, he let go of her mouth and slammed his hand against the wall, his body shaking with pleasure. With one hand still pressed against the wall, he slowly withdrew from her, his breathing as ragged as hers.

"Wow," she murmured.

His head dropped to her shoulder as he tried to catch his breath. His hand was still cupping her mound, and he could feel his come dripping from her core. It was erotic as fuck. "Yeah. Wow," he breathed into her neck.

"What was that about?" she asked as they came back down to earth. With her hands in tight fists against the wall, she leaned into him, tilting her head back on his shoulder. His hand left the cold wall and found hers, linking their fingers together when, without hesitation, she let go of the tight fist she had been holding and clasped his hand. She held on as though she never wanted to release him.

He removed his hand from between her legs and wrapped it around her waist, pulling her closer while he kissed the side of her head. "I missed you."

"It's only been like six hours since you last saw me."

"That's five hours and fifty-nine minutes too long."

"You're crazy," she said, but there was a hint of laughter in her voice. She liked that he'd missed her.

"Crazy for you," he whispered in her ear. He could tell she liked that, too, even if it was a cheesy line.

With a sigh, she straightened away from him and pulled her pants back into place. "I should get back to the kitchen," she bemoaned as she situated her bra back into place. After he tucked himself back into his pants, he bent over and grabbed her shirt. He held it out for her to slip her arms into, then pushed her hands away to do the buttons up himself. He noticed the redness on her neck and smiled. A reminder of the passion they had just shared. He felt a perverse sense of joy at seeing his mark on her skin.

He was captivated as he watched her redo her ponytail, marveling at the many facets of colors in her hair. He couldn't resist the temptation and ran his hand down the tail, feeling the soft and silky texture.

She grinned up at him. "You like my hair, don't you?"

"Yeah," he answered simply.

She flicked at an errant curl on his forehead. "I like yours, too. Especially when I can pull at it when you go down on me."

He flared his nostrils. "Fuck, Jolie. You can't put that image in my head. Now I want to drop to my knees in front of you and eat you out until you scream. But I have to meet Brodhi. We gotta get the helicopter ready in case evacuations are needed."

She gave him an impish grin and a shrug. "Sorry." He saw right through the fake apology. But he didn't care. He loved that they were back to where they were before. They were now better than ever, having overcome so much together and grown even closer. The gap between them had been bridged, and their relationship had deepened. He loved her more than he ever thought possible but couldn't tell her yet. It felt too soon, even though he'd loved her from afar for a long time. For her, they were new. He could wait. Nothing would change how he felt about her.

Hand in hand, they walked back to the cafeteria. Brodhi was there talking with Grady. Brodhi's search and rescue K9, Sorcha, was quick to welcome them with her tail wagging. Jolene dropped to her knees, laughing at Sorcha's enthusiastic greeting. Finch shook Brodhi's hand and thanked him for coming.

"Chief Smith was just telling me about a mudslide on a mountain road."

"Oh no," Jolene cried, coming to her feet.

Grady stepped closer. "Yeah, we just got word. Several families have been cut off and are asking for rescue."

"We're at your disposal," Finch offered. Thankfully, Matt had completed the repairs the day before. "We'll get the helicopter ready and be in the air in no time."

Grady looked at him skeptically. "You can fly in this weather?"

Both Finch and Brodhi laughed. "I've flown in worse," Finch said. "Although my bird isn't that big. If we're talking families, I won't have enough room for all of them."

"Take the police chopper. If you're familiar with a Bell Huey. Our usual pilot is unfortunately away for a family emergency."

"That would be a more sturdy aircraft for the conditions. I could do it with mine, but I'd much prefer the powerhouse of the Bell."

In no time, he was saying goodbye to Jolene and promising her he'd be careful. He and Brodhi followed Grady to the hangar where they kept the Bell. Despite his familiarity with the model, Finch carefully reviewed the safety checks of the helo he was unacquainted with while it was being fueled.

He, Brodhi, and Sorcha set off to rescue the stranded residents, the rain showing no signs of letting up.

Chapter 22

Two days later, exhaustion was setting in for everybody. Jolene worked on feeding the displaced families three healthy meals a day, with supplies donated by area businesses. It was amazing to see the community come together to help one another.

Ever since their first trip out after the mudslide, Finch and Brodhi had been working relentlessly. Jolene had barely seen him over the last two days. He'd breeze in for a kiss and food, then head right back out. She couldn't help but admire his dedication in saving the people of her hometown.

She missed him, but she knew there would be plenty of time for them when the crisis was over.

She'd kept in touch with her father, reassuring him that she was safe. The threatening texts were still coming but less frequently. She was grateful that the number of messages she received had dwindled down to just one or two per day. The decrease was a welcome relief, and she finally felt like she had some breathing room.

Brodhi came into the kitchen with Sorcha on his heel as she was pulling a pan of lasagna out of the oven. It was lunchtime, and the cafeteria would soon be full of families.

"Hey, you here for lunch?" she asked Brodhi, glancing over his shoulder for Finch.

"Yeah. And some rest." She could see the weariness etched into his face, his eyes heavy with fatigue. At forty-four years old, Brodhi was one of the oldest Nighthawks, but his fitness level was on par with the rest of them. His well-defined muscles, including his broad shoulders, wide chest, and bulging biceps, were proof of that.

His grizzled appearance hinted at his age, even though he was able to out-compete men who were much younger. The wrinkles on his face and his salt and pepper hair betrayed his years. He was a handsome silver fox, yet a bit of a loner. He kept his distance from everyone except Sorcha, who seemed to have a special connection with him.

"Where's Finch?" she asked, hoping her voice didn't reveal the longing she felt to see him.

"He stayed to make sure the helo got fueled up again."

Trying to mask her disappointment, she simply said, "Oh."

Brodhi's sly smile made it clear that she hadn't done a very good job. "Don't worry. He said he was right behind me."

"Okay." That pepped her up a little. The rain had slowed, and the rescue workers took advantage of the lull to regroup and assess the situation. There had been more mudslides, which were hampering ground rescues. Hence why Brodhi and Finch had been working nonstop. "Can I get you anything?"

He eyed the pan of the bubbling lasagna. "I wouldn't mind a hunk of that."

"Sit down," she said, pointing to a stool at the counter. She sliced up a large portion of the lasagna and set it down in front of him with a bottle of water and a couple of slices of garlic bread. Then she got a bowl and filled it with water before setting it on the floor for Sorcha.

Brodhi pulled out a packet of food from one of the many pockets in his vest. "Can I get another bowl for Sorcha's lunch?"

"Sure thing." She handed him a second bowl, then bent over the counter, resting on her elbows, as she kept him company. The room filled with the sounds of Sorcha chomping down on her food. "Is Sorcha the first K9 you've worked with?"

His expression turned hard, which made Jolene almost regret her question. "No. I've had others."

"That's nice. Did they retire? You were a K9 handler in the military, right? I can imagine that's a hard job for a dog to do long term."

"Unfortunately, no. They died."

"Oh, I'm so sorry. Lost in action?"

"No. There was a fire at the kennel where the dogs were housed." Jolene's jaw dropped as she looked at Brodhi in disbelief. A shadow seemed to pass over his eyes, lending them a dark and foreboding look.

It was clear that the loss had left a lasting impact on him. And who wouldn't be affected? She could only imagine how devastating something like that would be for the handlers who worked so closely with the dogs. She could see the strong relationship between Sorcha and Brodhi. It was probably even more intense when you were in a war zone and could have to risk your life for the other.

As if sensing her handler's dark mood, Sorcha ambled over and sat beside him. She leaned against his leg and looked up at him as if he hung the moon. As Brodhi scratched her behind the ears, the dog's tongue lolled out in a relaxed grin.

"I'm sorry to hear that," she said, the words feeling inadequate.

Brodhi shrugged. "It was a long time ago." Jolene had the sense there was more to the story, but she didn't want to push. Frankly, she was surprised he'd disclosed that part of his past with her. Brodhi was a private person who didn't share much with others, and she respected that. At least for now.

Her phone rang, and she looked at the screen, delighted to see it was Finch calling. "Hey," she said after swiping to answer.

"Jolie," he answered, sounding breathless.

"Is everything okay?"

"Yeah. We just got a call for another rescue. I just wanted to let you know so you wouldn't worry. I'm hoping to be done by dinner. Save me a seat."

"Sure. Brodhi's here. Do you want me to send him back to you?" Brodhi sat straighter in his seat, Sorcha almost matching his stiff posture.

"No. I can handle this one on my own. I'm just getting one person from a cabin on River View Drive. Should be a piece of cake."

"All right. Be careful."

"Always. I . . ." He trailed off, hesitating as if he had more to say but stopped. "I'll see you soon."

"Yeah, see you soon," she replied before clicking off, feeling inexplicitly disappointed. It was then she realized she'd been waiting to hear three little words. Was she ready for them?

Her gut said yes. Her head cautioned it was too soon. But was it? Too soon? She felt like she'd always loved him in some way. Even when she was so incredibly mad at him. She had been developing a strong like for him before the bombshell that had been dropped on her. A like that felt as if it had the potential to grow into more. Perhaps she'd been kidding herself and the like was already more. And that was why his perceived betrayal had cut so deeply.

The sudden influx of people reminded her that she needed to get back to work, leaving her with no time to ponder further.

Finch landed the helicopter in a clearing near the cabin he'd been called out to. After shutting things down, he climbed out and shlepped through the mud to the door. Thankfully, the rain had slowed to a drizzle. They were calling for it to end sometime overnight. Tomorrow was supposed to be full of sunshine.

He smiled at that thought. He didn't care how much it rained. Jolene made him feel as if he was basking in sunshine every day. The mere sight of her brought a burst of colors into his life, like a rainbow after the rain. The sound of her laughter was like a sweet melody, filling his ears with pure bliss. Her smile felt like a burst of sunshine, illuminating his world with joy and warmth. The refreshing aroma of her perfume sent him into an orange grove. When she touched him, the affection in her fingers was like a gentle breeze brushing against his skin, soothing his soul with its tenderness.

After the hell he'd been through with Angelica, Jolene's presence in his life was a reminder of the beauty that existed in the world, a beacon of hope and happiness. He had finally escaped from the woman who had made his life unbearable. He eagerly awaited the end of the rescue mission so he could hold his beloved tightly in his arms once more. The thought of being with Jolene again was the only thing that kept him going through the unending days of long rescue missions. With the crisis nearly over, the town would recover. They'd finish up the work on Gorden's house. Then he and Jolene would head back to Lake Haven. Their relationship forever changed.

The euphoria he felt was tinged with apprehension when he thought about explaining what had happened between them. Having to share the intimate, hellish details of his marriage to Angelica filled him with dread. He needed to keep Jolene's words in his heart. The shame wasn't his to bear. Somehow, he knew his friends would understand that.

After nearly slipping on the mud, he pulled his thoughts back to his present mission. It was strange that the person he'd been sent to rescue hadn't been standing outside waiting for him. Or at least standing on the porch out of the rain. Most of the people they'd been sent for had been so anxious to leave their situation they waited eagerly for him. Some had even met the helicopter at the landing site and he'd had to hover till they moved out of the way so he could land. But this person was going to make him work for it.

He knocked on the door, his fist pushing it open as if it hadn't been latched completely. "Hello?" he called out, sticking his head through the gap to peer into the gloomy interior of the cabin. He didn't see anybody waiting directly inside, so he nudged the door open farther and stepped over the threshold.

The pain was instantaneous. He stumbled but managed to shake off the wooziness. Another shocking blow sent him to his knees, then down to the floor. A kick to his ribs had him crumpling into the fetal position to protect the area from more pain. Which left the rest of him open to attack. The sudden impact of the boot against his chin caused his head to snap back violently, leaving him dazed and disoriented. The force of the kick was so strong that he felt his teeth rattle and his body go limp, leaving him momentarily incapacitated. With one last kick to the back of his head, he felt agony explode in every nerve. The impact sent shockwaves through his body, causing his vision to blur. Then there was nothing but blackness.

Chapter 23

IT WAS GETTING LATE. The dinner crowd had come and gone, and Jolene was getting worried. Finch hadn't shown and wasn't answering his phone. Jolene chewed on her thumbnail as she paced the high school cafeteria.

Brodhi had been nice enough to wait with her, even though he was exhausted. He gave her words of reassurance, but she could see the worry in his eyes as well.

"We should see if there's a way up to that cabin," she said for what seemed like the thousandth time.

"The mudslides have made that area nearly impassable," Brodhi explained, also for the thousandth time.

"God. I know. But there's got to be something we can do. I can't just sit here."

"Unfortunately, sometimes all we can do is sit and wait."

She growled out her feelings about that statement.

When her phone rang, she nearly dropped it in her haste to answer it. She swiped to answer without looking at the caller id. "Finch?"

"No, it's Emma."

Jolene visibly deflated. "Oh. Hi, Emma."

"Is everything okay?"

"Finch went up into the mountains to rescue someone and hasn't come back yet."

"I'm sure he's fine. Sometimes these things take longer than expected."

"Then why isn't he answering his phone?"

"You said he's in the mountains? Maybe there's no signal."

Her thumb was back in her mouth as she mulled over Emma's words. "Yeah, maybe."

"Anyway, can I tell you what I found, or is this a bad time?"

"No. Tell me. I need the distraction."

There was silence on the other end for a moment, then Emma laughed. "You fixed things with Finch, didn't you." It was said as a statement, as if Emma knew it was an inevitability that she and Finch would end up together.

She bit down on her thumbnail. "Maybe," she mumbled around the digit.

"Oh, Jo Jo. That's wonderful. No wonder you're so worried."

"Yeah, well. Hurry up and distract me with what you know."

"Okay, first, the phone calls are from a burner phone out of New York City. That's about all I can get with that."

"Hmm. New York," Jolene murmured.

"Think it's someone you knew while you lived there?"

She thought of Harrison and his wife. Would they really do something so incredibly juvenile all these years later? She didn't think so, but who knew what drove people to do stupid things?

"Maybe. But I don't know. It seems kind of far-fetched."

"Well, maybe this will help," Emma went on. "I found an image of your truck driver."

That surprised her. "What? How?"

"I retraced your route from the fair to your dad's house. I looked for CCTVs along that route, then 'borrowed' the footage to see if I could spot the truck following you." By "borrowed," Jolene knew she meant she'd hacked into the cameras to obtain the footage.

"And you found it?"

"Yeah. I did. And I got an image of the woman driving it."

"A woman?" Harrison's wife, Paris, popped into her head, but she couldn't imagine a woman who liked the finer things in life stooping so low as to drive a beat-up truck. Let alone know how to hit another vehicle to send it off the road. She could have hired someone to do her dirty work, though. That was always a possibility.

"Yup," Emma replied, popping the P. "I just texted the image to you."

"Hold on," she said, lowering her phone to open the text message. Seeing the familiar face on her screen, she gasped. It was a face that she'd hoped to never see again. And suddenly, her worry over Finch grew exponentially. "Oh, fuck."

"What? Do you know her?"

"That's Angelica Mobey. Finch's wife."

The silence on the other end was telling. "Finch is married?" Emma gasped.

"Was married. His divorce was final the same day we were run off the road."

"Oh shit. Why would this woman want to hurt her ex-husband?"

"Because she's batshit crazy. You have no idea the hell she's put Finch through. It's not my story to tell, but needless to say, it's a miracle he's finally free of her."

"Well, I look forward to grilling Finch on that story when you guys come home."

"Take it easy on him. It hasn't been a walk in the park for him."

"Okay. I hear what you're saying. Just let him know we're all here for him if he ever does want to talk about it."

"I'm sure he already knows that."

"Anyway." Jolene could hear typing on Emma's end, then a chuckle. "Well, this bitch didn't do a very good job of hiding her tracks. Searching her name, I found a VRBO rental agreement for a cabin in your neck of the woods. On River View Drive."

Jolene sucked in a breath, her worry now ramped up to eleven. "Fuck. Brodhi," she called out to the man who sat right by her elbow listening to everything.

Even though she could tell he was shocked over the *Finch was married* bomb she'd just dropped, he took out his phone and said, "I'm on it."

"What is it?" The sound of Emma's panicked voice echoed through the phone. "What's the matter?"

"That's the address Finch was sent to. She must have done something to him. Oh God! She killed him. Oh, shit!" Her worry had morphed into panic. Not Finch. She wanted to cry out. Not after she'd just found something incredible with him.

"Jo Jo!" Emma called, pulling her back from her spiral. "Calm your shit. You can't think like that. You know he'd do everything possible to get back to you. That man has loved you for years. And he never gave up. Don't you give up on him now."

Jolene sucked in a deep breath, trying to calm her racing heart. "Yeah. Okay. You're right. But if that woman has so much as harmed a hair on his head, I'm going to fuck her up so hard."

Emma chuckled, but her laugh was devoid of any real mirth. "There's my girl."

"Grady's on his way," Brodhi told her. "He has some ideas about how to get up there."

"You hear that?" Emma said, having obviously heard what Brodhi said. "Brodhi's on the case. You know you can count on him and Sorcha."

"Yeah, I know. And I'm going with them."

"Jo Jo," Emma admonished.

"Shut it, Em. You didn't sit back and let those guys hurt Marcus. You can't expect me to."

"I know. But I had training," Emma said softly, and Jolene knew she was only telling her the truth. But at this point, nothing would keep her from getting to Finch. She didn't care about her lack of training. Emma had been teaching her a few self-defense moves, and her dad had taught her how to shoot a gun years ago. If the need came, she could handle it. Even if the idea of pulling the trigger made her palms slick with sweat.

"I'm going," she said firmly.

Emma sighed, knowing there was no talking her out of it. "Please be careful, Jo Jo. I don't want to lose you, too."

She knew Emma was thinking about the night her best friend and partner died. It was part of the reason why she'd left the Coast Guard. "I know. I promise I'll be careful."

"Can you promise you'll stand back and let Brodhi and Sorcha handle the bitch when you get there?"

"Um." She hesitated. She wanted to promise that but couldn't. There was no telling how she'd react to seeing Angelica. Especially if she'd hurt Finch.

"Never mind. Don't answer that."

"I love you, Em. We'll meet up when I get home. We have a lot to talk about, and I want to hear all about the movie release tour."

"You got it. And you better not leave anything out. I want to hear all about how you and Finch got together again."

"I'll call when this is over."

"Please do. I won't be able to sleep until I know you're both safe and sound."

"Thanks for your help."

"Anytime." They said their goodbyes as Grady came into the cafeteria looking just as exhausted as Brodhi. Their little town had been put through the wringer, and Grady had done an amazing job at the helm. He'd shed the asshole persona from the other night and stepped up for his town. And now he was willing to help save a stranger.

He led them outside, where a pair of ATVs on a flatbed truck waited for them. The rain had, thankfully, finally stopped. She glanced up at the sky. Dark clouds scuttled across the expanse while the moon fought for supremacy. She was rooting for the moon.

They drove out to a trailhead, and Jolene waited as Grady and Brodhi unloaded the ATVs. She shivered involuntarily, unsure if it was from the cold breeze or the fear of what they were about to do.

Grady tried to talk her out of her decision to ride along one more time, but she was determined. Nothing would keep her away from the man she loved. Nothing.

Chapter 24

FINCH WOKE WITH A start, a pounding head, a nauseous stomach, and pain everywhere. He groaned and rolled to his side, trying to remember what had happened.

"It's about time you woke up, Atty." The harsh voice from his past blasted through his skull, and it all came rushing back. The trip to the cabin. The thoughts about his future with Jolene. The attack when he'd entered the cabin.

Angelica. She'd been behind the whole thing. She'd orchestrated the rescue mission, then attacked him. He'd been hit by her plenty in the past, but nothing as brutal as what had just happened. He was sure a few ribs were cracked, if not broken. His mouth had a metallic taste, and he felt around his teeth with his tongue, surprised they were all still there after that kick to his chin.

"You're completely out of your mind," he said, his voice shaking with anger. He moved his hands to push himself up into a sitting position, only to find them bound in front of him. With zip ties.

He shook his head at her stupidity. Didn't she know how easy it would be for him to break the plastic?

Still, he'd wait until an opportune time to break free. Until then, he'd play along. Especially after seeing the large knife in her hand. If he needed to, he could easily wrest it from her, and this time he wouldn't hesitate. He'd never fought back in the past, afraid of hurting her and having her turn him into a bad guy in front of the authorities. This time, he'd do whatever it took to disarm her. He was done being pushed around by her.

Despite the dizziness, he sat up. He braced himself against the wall, gritting his teeth as the pain continued to pulsate through his body. The night she'd cut him with the knife and he'd had to stitch himself up hadn't been nearly as painful as this.

"What do you want, Angelica?" he asked, infusing as much calm into his voice as he could, given the circumstances. It was a lesson he'd learned after years of trying to talk her crazy down.

"What do you mean?" she asked. "We're married. I just wanted to spend some time in an intimate cabin with my husband. You didn't come home after the helicopter crashed. Why didn't you come home?"

Finch narrowed his eyes at her. "What do you know about my helicopter?"

"Nothing. Nothing. You know I don't know about things like that."

"Angelica. Did you do something to my helo?"

She looked at him, aghast, but he'd seen that expression before. It was completely fake. And a precursor to her turning things around until he was to blame for everything. "How could I have done something? I don't know anything about helicopters. You're the expert. You probably didn't take care of it the way you should, as usual. You really should be more careful, Atty. You could get someone killed."

And there it was. The manipulative bitch was out in full force. She'd twist anything and everything to put the blame squarely on his shoulders. It wasn't going to work this time.

"What did you do to my helicopter?" he hissed through gritted teeth.

"Atty. I just wanted you home. If you'd gotten hurt, I would have taken care of you."

"What did you do to my helicopter?"

Her pacing quickened as her agitation grew. She began to mutter to herself. "He said it would work. He said it would work to bring you home."

Finch tried one more time. "What did you do to my helicopter?"

"He told me the gallium would work to bring you home."

Gallium? He'd never heard of it. "What's gallium, Angelica?"

"It's just a harmless acid. He said something about metal embrittlement when it interacts with steel."

Jesus Christ. She'd sabotaged his helicopter. He could have been killed. Jolene could have been killed. If he was any less of a pilot, they very well might have been. *Fuck*. He'd known she was dangerous, but he just didn't understand how far she was willing to go. He'd find a way to make her pay. And the man who helped her.

Rage flared through him. Rage unlike any he'd experienced before. He didn't care what she did to him. He could take whatever she dished out. Had taken it for years. But screwing with his helicopter? Endangering other people's lives? Endangering Jolene? No way.

"Why? Why would you do this?"

"We're married. We belong together. I just wanted to bring you home."

"We're not married anymore. I'm not your husband. I'm finally free of you."

"Shut up," she shouted, slapping the blade of the knife against her thigh.

"You need to accept that," he reasoned.

She turned her back on him, her hands going up to cover her ears, the knife still gripped tightly in one, sticking up like some macabre antenna. The blade caught the light, reflecting a deadly shimmer. His spine tingled with a sense of foreboding that he couldn't shake. The feeling grew worse as he observed his ex-wife's insanity.

"No!" she shouted. "Lalalala. I'm not listening. You are my husband. I'm your wife. There is no changing that."

"Angelica . . ."

Her singsongy voice was like nails on a chalkboard as she continued to sing "Lalala." Jesus Christ, she was bat shit crazy. How had he never seen it when they were younger? He thought of himself as a pretty observant guy. He had to be with his job. First with the Air Force, then with the Nighthawks. Flying required him to be constantly vigilant and aware of his surroundings to ensure safety. To avoid danger, he had to remain acutely aware of everything and everyone around him.

But he'd missed his wife's true personality. Had he been so blinded by love in those early years that he hadn't seen the clues? Thinking back now, they were so obvious. He'd been such a fool. And look where that had gotten him. Trapped in a cabin with an insane person.

"You have to face reality. Our divorce was final."

She spun so fast he didn't have time to react. She slapped him across the face so hard his head bounced off the wall behind him. He groaned as dizziness swamped him. He bit back the bile that burned in his throat, refusing to show that bit of weakness to her.

Breathing heavily through the worst of it, he racked his brain for something to say to defuse the situation. There would be no reasoning with her. He realized that now. She was too far gone. Maybe a little reverse psychology?

"What's the plan, Angelica?"

"What?"

"What's your plan here? You know people will miss me eventually. I have a job I need to go back to. If I don't show up, they'll report me as missing. Then the police will get involved. They knew where I was going. They know about this cabin. I was sent specifically to this cabin to rescue someone who was stranded up here. They'll find the helicopter. Then the cabin. So what's the plan?"

"I . . ."

"This wasn't very smart. You've led the authorities right to you. When they discover what you've done, you'll be arrested. Making a false police report is a crime. You lured me here under false pretenses. You used law enforcement resources fraudulently. You held someone against their will. Assaulted them. All crimes."

"No. No. That's not what happened. They'll never believe that story. You attacked me. You kept me prisoner."

"I'm the one with the bruises," he reasoned.

"I had to defend myself. You were such a brute. I didn't have a choice but to defend myself. That's why I grabbed the knife. There's no way they won't believe me. The man is always the guilty one."

"Not this time. There's too much evidence of the things you've done in our divorce proceedings. Remember my dad's video?"

"No!" The sound of the knife slapping against her thigh echoed through the quiet room. The sharp tip caught on her pants and tore a small hole. She didn't react. He didn't think she even noticed.

"Yes, Angelica. It's over. Walk away while you can."

"No!" The force of her scream was so powerful that it caused the glass in the windows to vibrate. "No. It's your fault. You came after me. They'll believe me. I'm a woman. They'll believe me. I had to defend myself."

She suddenly went still, and Finch felt a chill race down his spine. She looked down at the knife, then over at him. Whatever she was thinking couldn't be good.

"I had to defend myself." She took a step toward him. He worked his way to his feet, agony shooting through every nerve ending. He ignored it, needing to be ready for whatever she was planning. "I had to defend myself. It was the only way."

She lifted the knife, and the glint of the blade caught his eye, causing his heart to race. She advanced fast with the knife aimed at his stomach. Despite catching her wrist, the tip still managed to nick him. It was a sharp stab of pain that he brushed away. She tried to push forward with the blade, but he held her back, his grip strong and unyielding. His muscles strained. Jolene's face flashed through his mind. There was no way he was leaving her. Not like this.

The sound of an engine in the distance made them both freeze. He smiled. He should have expected Jolene to send help when he didn't show up for dinner like he'd promised. And from the darkness outside, it appeared he was extremely late for dinner.

The noise grew louder. He tilted his head to listen. Were there two vehicles? He guessed they were probably ATVs, since that was the most logical vehicle to use in this terrain in the aftermath of the mudslides.

"It's over, Angelica."

"No," she hissed.

The engine noises were directly outside now. They shut down. Then there were boots clomping across the porch. The door opened and Grady, Brodhi, and Sorcha entered. They took in the scene, and Sorcha growled. Angelica took one look at the three of them and backed away from him.

"I had to defend myself," she muttered.

"Then why is he in zip ties?" Grady stated the obvious.

"I had to defend myself," she repeated.

"Yeah, yeah, lady. Tell it to the judge."

Grady took out his handcuffs and made a move toward Angelica.

But then Jolene stepped in behind them.

She must have seen the agony on his face, since she didn't hesitate to rush to him. "Omigod, Finch!" she cried.

Angelica lost her shit at seeing Jolene. Finch could only watch in horror as his ex-wife lunged forward, her eyes on Jolene. With a scream that would live in his nightmares, Angelica's grip tightened around the knife, the sharp blade glinting in the dim light of the room. The woman he loved was caught in the crosshairs of a crazy woman's desperate attempt for control. And he was powerless to stop it.

Chapter 25

JOLENE DISREGARDED GRADY'S ORDER to wait and rushed into the cabin. Her heart lodged in her throat as she took in the sight that greeted her. The bitch was in front of an obviously bruised and battered Finch. A knife was gripped in her hand. Finch had a hold of her wrist with his zip-tied hands, but she was still putting all her weight into thrusting the blade into Finch's stomach.

Her heart pounded as she watched Angelica back off, muttering about needing to defend herself. Grady was about to put her in cuffs, but Jolene couldn't hold herself back anymore.

"Omigod, Finch!" she cried and rushed toward him. That was a mistake. Angelica spotted her, and instantly, all that rage and craziness was turned on her. The knife gripped in her hand was the only thing Jolene could see as it came at her. She sucked in a panicked breath and spun away at the last minute. The knife caught in the sleeve of her coat, ripping through the layers but not hitting skin. Unfortunately, she didn't escape far. Angelica caught a chunk of her hair and pulled. Jolene stumbled and somehow ended up with Angelica behind her, the knife at her throat.

She could hear the men yelling all around her. Sorcha growled. Jolene was only conscious of the blade's tip pressing lightly on her throat. Everything else faded into background noise.

Grady said something. Then Finch. Whatever Finch said angered Angelica. Jolene sucked in a breath through her nose as the knife dug deeper, piercing her skin. A warm, wet trickle of blood slid down into her collar, and the room rushed back into focus.

"Okay, Angelica. You win," Finch was saying. "Put the knife down, and I'll leave with you. We'll start over. Okay, baby? It'll be just you and me. Just like always."

Tears sprang to her eyes. She was in danger, and Finch was ready to make the ultimate sacrifice to save her. She couldn't let that happen. There was no way she was going to let this bitch get her claws back into Finch. Not happening. Not on her watch.

The blade started to slip away from her throat as Finch pleaded with his ex-wife. "Please. Just back away from the woman and we'll leave. What do you say? We can get remarried. It'll be just like before."

Angelica's grip on Jolene loosened further. She held her breath as she realized the blade was no longer piercing her skin. Now was her chance. Moving without hesitation, she grabbed the hand holding the knife and twisted out from under her. Angelica cried out as she wrenched her wrist at an unnatural angle. With a clatter, the knife fell to the ground, and the woman collapsed to her knees. Jolene held on tight, standing in front of her as Angelica screamed bloody murder. She still held her hand tightly in her grip as Grady rushed forward and slapped a cuff on her.

"You can let go now," he ordered, but she found herself unable to obey. It wasn't until she felt Finch's body heat behind her and his hand gently prying hers off Angelica that she was able to release it. Grady immediately had her face down on the ground and both hands cuffed behind her.

Jolene slumped against the hard chest behind her and closed her eyes as his arms wrapped around her. "Fuck, Jolene," he breathed in her ear.

She spun in his embrace, flung her arms around him, and buried her face in his neck, breathing in his scent. The outdoors and candy.

They held each other close as Angelica screeched and cursed them out from the floor. Grady's voice was dull and unemotional as he read her the Miranda rights, but she was in her own batshit crazy world, and it was evident that nothing else mattered.

Jolene tuned it all out and pulled back to rake her gaze over Finch's battered face. Her stomach twisted uncomfortably at the sight of the darkening bruises. She cupped his cheeks gently, turning his head left and right to take them all in.

"It's not as bad as it looks," he assured, and she knew he was full of shit.

"Looks pretty bad to me." Her voice broke, revealing the vulnerability she was trying to hide with bravado.

He laid his hands over hers. "I'm okay." His gaze fell to her neck, and a shadow passed over his face. "You're still bleeding."

"I'm okay." She repeated his words back to him. The fact was, she didn't even feel the cut. She was more concerned about him. It hadn't gone unnoticed to her how carefully he was moving. She'd seen the lines of pain in his face as he tried to stop Angelica. Her answer elicited a narrowed gaze from him, but she met his stare with a defiant glare of her own. Neither of them would show the other the true extent of their pain, and so they remained at a standstill. It would be funny if she wasn't so worried about him.

Brodhi approached Finch and handed him a soft gauze pad, which he gingerly used to clean her cut. She watched him apply the bandage and sensed his frustration with the limited supplies.

"That was a pretty badass move," Brodhi said to her while packing away the small first-aid kit in yet another pocket in his vest.

"Where did you learn to do that?" Finch asked.

"Emma's been teaching me some things."

Surprise flickered across Finch's face. "Remind me to thank her."

"She's the one who led us to you."

Finch tilted his head in confusion. "What do you mean?"

"She got an image of the driver who ran us off the road. It was her," Jolene said, with a tip of her head in Angelica's direction. She filled Finch in on everything Emma had managed to find. Including the fact that the text messages had come from New York City.

"I don't know where Angelica's been for the last year. She could have been living in the city. I just don't know. My lawyer might have information about her location since I last saw her. I'll call him tomorrow."

Grady hauled Angelica to her feet. "Don't worry. I'll question her thoroughly. I'll see what I can get out of her." Jolene and Brodhi had filled Grady in on the text threats as they drove out to the trailhead. She made a mental note to send him the screenshots of the messages promptly, knowing he'd need them while questioning Angelica. After she'd seen to Finch's injuries. She was worried about how gingerly he was holding himself.

"You good to fly back?" Brodhi asked.

"Yeah. I'm good. Thanks for your help."

"No thanks necessary. You know that." The wooden floor echoed with the thump of Sorcha's tail as Brodhi scratched her behind the ears. "I'll help Grady get the trash down off the mountain."

Finch nodded, and with an arm across her shoulders, he led Jolene out of the cabin behind the others. Finch stopped once outside and tilted his head back. Jolene followed his gaze and, for the first time in days, saw a sky filled with stars. She inhaled deeply, letting the damp earth and pine scents fill her.

"Let's get you down off this mountain and to a doctor," she told Finch.

He winced. "I don't need a doctor."

"Bullshit."

He smiled down at her, obviously loving her vehemence. "I'm okay, Jolie. I promise. I've had worse. I'll heal. And with some tender loving care, I'll heal even faster."

Brodhi chuckled as he made his way to the ATVs. Jolene swatted Finch's arm, her cheeks burning with embarrassment. Finch laughed at her but winced and held his side in pain. Jolene's stern expression should have been a clear indication of her belief that he should seek medical assistance, but it just made him laugh harder. Then he kissed the expression right off her face. In that moment, nothing else mattered as he kissed her, his love for her evident in every brush of his lips. The world faded away, leaving only the sensation of his touch and the overwhelming love she felt for him.

Chapter 26

JOLENE TURNED OFF THE music and began counting the cash in the register as part of her closing routine. She made sure all the bottles were properly stored and the taps were shut off. Then with a sigh, Jolene wiped down the bar and stacked chairs, signaling the end of another night. She had sent her staff home early in appreciation of the hard work they'd done for the month she'd been away.

It had taken another two weeks after the incident with Angelica for her and Finch to finish her dad's house. He was still in the rehab center, and she'd promised she'd come back when he was ready to move home. Knowing he would only fuss about it, she decided not to mention all the things they'd done in his house. The transformation would be a surprise for him. A surprise she hoped he appreciated. Her goal had been to make the place safe for him, and she was happy with the results.

Making their rekindled relationship public was met with overwhelming excitement from their friends. Needless to say, they had been shocked by the revelation about his marriage. But the support they showed him had brought her to tears. She knew how anxious he'd been about telling them the truth. Especially the guys. But the worry was unnecessary. The guys had a unique dynamic that allowed them to be themselves without fear of judgment. Finch had failed to remember that.

She took one last look around to make sure everything was secure before heading to her office for the work she wanted to take home with her. Finch had left earlier to take Brodhi home but was coming back for her, and she wanted to be ready to go when he arrived. She grabbed a canvas bag and shoved the spreadsheets she'd printed out earlier inside next to her laptop. She wanted to make sure she had successfully reestablished her relationships with the vendors after the disruption caused by the sabotage.

A sound from the front caught her attention. She stopped what she was doing and cocked her head, listening intently, but only the sound of the ice maker filled the quiet bar. Double-checking to make sure she had everything, she slung the bag over her shoulder, grabbed her keys, and locked up her office after stepping out into the hall.

Another strange noise had her walking down the hall toward the main bar area. A faint flickering light casting dancing shadows on the walls caught her eye. Stepping out from the hall, she froze in shock. The bar was on fire.

Shit. Her restaurant was on fire!

Dropping her bag, she ran behind the bar and grabbed the fire extinguisher. A line of flames went from one corner of the bar to the front door. It was strangely mesmerizing, the way the fire danced across the floor as if following a set path.

She readied the extinguisher and started spraying. The acrid smell of smoke filled the room, and she began coughing uncontrollably. It stung her eyes, and she blinked rapidly to try to clear her vision. The extinguisher was barely making a dent. Her heart raced as fear coursed through her veins, making it even harder to catch her breath.

Time to go, she thought as another hacking cough racked her body. Flames blocked the front door. She wasn't getting out that way. As she dropped the extinguisher, the sound of it hitting the floor was drowned out by the deafening roar of the fire. She ran down the hall to the back door. She didn't hesitate, running at the door and hitting the bar with full force, expecting it to yield.

It didn't.

Something was preventing the door from opening. She glanced over her shoulder. The flames had not reached the hall yet but were closing in fast. She pushed against the door with all her might, but it didn't budge.

The thought crossed her mind that this might have been done deliberately. She felt a cold sweat break out on her forehead as fear took hold of her. The smoke was so thick as it billowed down the hall toward her she had to squint to see through it, and her eyes watered as a result.

Giving up on the exit door, she hurried to her office, knowing she could use the window in there to escape if need be. Forgetting she had locked it, she searched her pockets for her keys and panicked when she didn't find them. That was when she remembered she'd dropped them with her bag. She could just make out the lump on the floor that was her bag. The thick smoke made it hard to breathe, so she got down on her hands and knees to crawl toward it.

The heat was so intense as she approached the main room it felt like her skin was on fire. Her coughing became more intense, causing her to pause and gasp for breath. Finally reaching her bag, she swept her hands along the floor, looking for the keys through the thick, black smoke. The tips of her fingers brushed against metal, and she nearly wept with relief.

She grabbed the keys amand crawled away from the heat and flames. Too bad she couldn't escape the smoke as easily. As the smoke grew thicker in the hall, she crawled toward her office, feeling her way along the ground.

She fumbled with the keys, her heart pounding in her chest, until she finally unlocked the door and fell into the room, slamming it closed behind her.

Suddenly, she remembered her phone. Grabbing it from her pocket, she pushed the button to wake it up. Nothing happened. Shit. She'd forgotten her battery was dead. Why hadn't she plugged it in while she closed up the bar? Too late now. The landline on her desk was within arm's reach, and she quickly grabbed it. After pressing the power button, she held the cool plastic to her ear and waited. The absence of the dial tone was odd. She'd used it several times today, and it had worked just fine. Now nothing.

She clutched the edge of her desk as a coughing fit racked her body. Her eyes darted around the little room, seeking a way out.

Her office had one window and it was time to use it. On unsteady legs, she moved quickly toward her salvation. It was a small window, but as she eyed it, she was confident she could squeeze through. Twisting the lock open, she pulled at the sash. Nothing happened.

A sob slipped past her lips. She yanked at the window again, her frustration building with every failed attempt, until she felt her nail snap from the strain. Putting her hands flat on the glass, she tried to push it open that way, to no avail. That was when she noticed the haphazard nails that had been hammered into the frame. She stared in disbelief, trying to get her brain to understand what her eyes were telling her. Someone had nailed the window shut.

There was no doubt in her mind now that this was deliberate.

Wispy smoke was seeping into the room from under the door. As she coughed again, her body convulsed, and she doubled over, trying to catch her breath. Her stinging eyes darted around the room, searching for something to push into the gap under the door. She had to slow the buildup of smoke in the room. She spotted her sweatshirt and snatched it up off the back of her desk chair. Falling to her knees next to the door, she shoved the material in the crack, but it wasn't long enough. She whipped her shirt off and filled the remaining space with it. It was a good thing she'd gone with her sports bra instead of one of her lacy numbers.

She gasped for breath between coughs, struggling to rise from the floor. Crawling back to the window, she scanned the room, hoping to find something to break the glass. Her body was working against her now, her energy waning.

She had to pause for several seconds between coughing fits. She tried to take a deep breath, but the burning in her chest made it impossible. Her stomach muscles hurt from all the coughing. Her parched throat begged for a sip of water. She wanted to lie down and go to sleep.

No! She fought against that suggestion. Finch was coming. She just had to hang on a little longer. Find something to break the glass. She pulled herself up on her knees and ran her hands over the surface of her desk. Her fingers bumped into her stapler. It was an old industrial type of stapler. The thing had some heft to it. Maybe that could work.

With the stapler gripped in her hand, she tried to move closer to the window, but was hampered by another coughing fit that made her lightheaded. Once the worst of it passed, she crawled to the window and smacked the stapler against the glass.

That wouldn't do. Her strength was dwindling. Her efforts hadn't even left a smudge on the window. She tried again. Coughed. Hit. Cough. The hacking turned so violent that it left her weak and unable to lift the stapler.

The stapler slipped from her grip and clattered to the floor. Her eyes were burning so badly she could barely see a foot in front of her. She slipped to the floor, trying in vain to find her stapler. She told herself to keep moving. Screamed at her body to get up. But it wasn't listening.

She was so tired. Maybe if she took a little break, she would then have more energy to try again. She lay on the floor, her cheek against the cool wooden boards. It felt wonderful after the heat building in the room.

Just a short break. Her eyes slipped shut. Finch would be there soon. She'd take a little break, then she would go back to work.

Her final thought before blacking out was about how pissed Finch would be knowing his favorite bar was now a memory.

Chapter 27

As Finch drove back to Jolene's, a strange glow on the horizon caught his attention. The closer he got to the bar, the more his gut tightened until his worst nightmare raged in front of him. Without bothering to park in the lot, he hastily pulled his truck to the side of the road, making sure it was out of the way of the firetrucks, and ran to the bar.

The front door of Jolene's bar was fully engulfed. Fingers of flames flickered while billows of black smoke rose into the sky.

"Jolene," he shouted, praying she'd gotten out and was standing nearby. No response. The flames crackled loudly, drowning out any other sounds.

The front half of the bar was a fiery inferno, with flames shooting up toward the ceiling. The burning building radiated so much heat that he could feel it from several feet away, causing him to sweat heavily. He raced around the side, where more flames licked up the walls. It was both terrifying and mesmerizing as they danced and leaped through the front half of the bar. The acrid smell of smoke wafted through the air as the fire consumed everything in its path.

He continued to call out her name as he ran. The sight of the big dumpster pushed up against the back door caused him to swear uncontrollably. There was no way Jolene would have been able to get out this way. She couldn't have moved it, even if she had used all her strength to push on the door. The massive hunk of metal was locked in place with blocks of wood shoved under the wheels.

Icy fear raced down his spine. This was deliberate. Grady had never been able to prove that Angelica had been behind the threats to Jolene. Finch kicked himself. He should have been more vigilant. He should have realized the threat wasn't over.

"Jolene!" he hollered, banging on the part of the door he could reach.

"Finch!" Hearing his name, he spun around to find Ox and Evan running toward him.

"Is Jolene still in there?" Jolene's burly bartender asked.

"I think so. Help me get this thing out of the way."

"Fire trucks are on their way," Finch's teammate Evan said, bending down to yank a chock block out of the way. Once the wheels were free, the three of them pushed the noxious dumpster out of the way.

Finch tried the door, but, of course, it was locked.

"Here." Finch assumed that Ox had been visiting his girlfriend, who lived in the same building as Evan. He was thankful the man was there as he deftly inserted his key into the lock and gave it a quick turn. He yanked the door open, and billows of smoke rushed past them. Shit. It was so thick he couldn't see anything beyond the threshold.

"Jolene," he called, while getting to his hands and knees. He felt the guys doing the same behind him, and he glanced over his shoulder at them in appreciation.

"We're with you," Evan said. If anybody could understand what he was feeling at this moment, it would be Evan. It wasn't too long ago that they'd had to rescue his girlfriend from her deranged ex. Finch had been with him through that crisis. Now Evan had his back.

The smell of smoke and burning wood filled the small space of the hallway. The roar of the flames just beyond was deafening, but he kept calling out to Jolene as he crawled.

"I'll check the kitchen," Ox said, peeling off in that direction.

"I got the break room," Evan announced.

Finch kept moving forward, his instinct screaming at him that she wouldn't be in either of those places. He felt along the walls until his fingers encountered the molding around her office door. It was cool to the touch compared to the intense heat that was being funneled down the hall from the main room.

He called out to her again. Not waiting for an answer, he turned the knob and pushed, meeting some resistance. He strained to push the door open, but the hunks of material wedged underneath made it difficult. He pushed harder until it was open wide enough for him to crawl through.

The sight of her red hair on the floor by the desk made his heart skip a beat. "Jolie," he bellowed once more. She didn't stir.

He crawled to her with his heart in his throat. Clad only in a sports bra, she appeared almost ghostly, her skin paler than usual. The smoke from the fire had left dark smudges on her face. He could see the tracks of her tears through it. She lay prone under the window. A large metal stapler sat just out of reach next to her. As he crawled to her, he strained his burning eyes to see if she was breathing. He willed her chest to move but couldn't see anything.

Approaching her side, he reached out a trembling hand to feel for a pulse. A rush of air escaped his lungs in relief as he felt it, faint but there. He started coughing as he reached for her. There was no time to waste. He had to get her out of there . . . now.

He couldn't crawl and carry her at the same time, so he gathered her in his arms and stood. Crouching as low as he could to avoid the worst of the smoke, he ran out of the room, calling for the other guys. The flames were licking away at the end of the hall. If he had been any later, it would have been too late to reach her. A painful tightening in his gut accompanied the unwelcome thought.

Ox and Evan crawled out of the other rooms and waited for him to run past. He burst out the door, coughing and gasping for breath in the refreshingly clean air. The fire engines were roaring to a stop as he kept running through the lot, getting Jolene as far away from the smoke and fire as he could. Spotting an ambulance just arriving, he made a beeline for it, calling out for help.

Firefighters scrambled out of the trucks, and chaos erupted around him, but he only had eyes for the precious bundle in his arms. An EMT noticed him and pulled a gurney out of the back, then indicated for Finch to lay her down on it. There was a flurry of activity around her, and he was forcefully but gently shoved out of the way.

He watched them work on her with his heart in his throat. She had to be okay. He had come too far and endured too much. He couldn't bear the thought of losing her now.

Another EMT was trying to put an oxygen mask on him, but he shooed them away. "Focus on her."

A large hand clamped his shoulder. "Let them help you, too. You won't be any good to her," Ox said in his gravelly voice, "if you can't breathe."

As if to indicate his point, Finch was racked with a coughing fit. "Fine," he admitted reluctantly, allowing the EMT to place the mask.

Coughing from the gurney caught his attention. He tore the oxygen mask off and rushed to Jolene's side, barely hearing the sigh of exasperation from the EMT behind him.

The guys working on her must have realized there was no way they were keeping him away from her any longer, since they made room for him at her side. He clasped her hand in his, careful not to dislodge the IV in the back of her hand.

"Jolie." He breathed her name. Her eyes popped open and fixed on him. The jade green swimming in tears was the most beautiful sight he'd ever seen. He leaned over her and cupped her cheek, careful not to dislodge her oxygen mask.

Her hand trembled as she reached out to him. Her fingers brushed something away from his cheek and that's when he realized he was crying.

"I'm okay," she rasped, then coughed uncontrollably.

He grabbed her hand and held it to his lips. "Don't try to talk. Just rest."

A tear of her own slipped out, and he caught it before it could steal into her hairline while she lay on the gurney. As he kissed her fingers, he looked deeply into her eyes, silently promising that everything would be all right. More tears slipped out, but this time, he let them fall. He'd keep holding her however he could—even if it was just her hand—while she let her emotions out. He'd hold her forever if need be.

A scream rent the air, startling all of them. A sudden rustling from the crowd that had gathered to watch drew his attention to the other side of the street. A woman was pushing her way through the people, screaming obscenities.

"No! She has to die! Why? Why can't she die?" She broke free of the crowd, her focus on Jolene. There was a crazed and intense hatred in her expression as she tried to make a beeline for them. Finch quickly moved to the other side of the gurney, determined to protect Jolene from the woman who, by this time, had whipped out a gun. She let off a few shots, and everybody scurried to safety, but Finch held his ground. She'd have to go through him to get to her.

Suddenly, the woman tripped over something and fell flat on her face. The gun skittered from her hand and across the pavement. Police officers came out of nowhere and converged on the woman who lay sobbing on the ground.

"Whoops. My bad," Sophie said with a shrug.

Evan chuckled and threw his arm over his girl-friend's shoulder. "You tripped her?"

She turned not so innocent eyes on him. "Would you believe me if I told you it was an accident?"

Evan's smile grew as he shook his head. "Not a chance."

Jolene's laugh quickly turned into a hacking cough. After the cough passed, Jolene slumped back on the gurney, exhausted. Finch moved back to where he'd been before the attack and took her hand back in his.

The police had cuffed the woman and hauled her to her feet. Jolene gasped, but this time it wasn't from smoke inhalation.

"Omigod!" she rasped and moved the oxygen mask aside. "That's Harrison's wife. That's Paris Winston."

"What? Are you sure?" Finch asked.

Jolene squinted as she looked the woman up and down. "She looks a little different. Last time I saw her, she was this refined snob in designer everything. She looks a little worse for wear, but that's her."

Deputy Ian McClintock approached them. "You know her?"

"Yeah, she's my ex's wife."

"Seems like she doesn't like you."

Jolene snorted. "Understatement."

They watched as she was placed into the back of a sheriff's vehicle. As she taunted Jolene, her voice grew louder and more piercing. "At least I destroyed what you most love. You destroyed our lives. Consider it justice," she spat as she was shoved into the car.

"Ex's wife? Does that mean . . ." Ian trailed off, unsure how to word his question.

"That's exactly what it means. The bastard was cheating on her with me. I didn't know he was married," she was quick to add, and Finch squeezed her hand to remind her of their mantra. The shame was not hers to bear. "Weird. I have no idea what she's ranting about. As far as I knew, they were happy as pie when I left New York City. My ex had everything, including my restaurant. He'd left me with nothing."

"Asshole," Ian muttered in disgust. "I'll come visit tomorrow to get your report about all of this."

"Thanks, Ian," Finch said, holding out his hand for Ian to shake.

After Ian left to handle the law enforcement side of things, Jolene squeezed his hand, drawing his attention back to her. He helped her reposition the oxygen mask while stroking her hair away from her face. Though she was exhausted and covered in soot, she remained the most beautiful woman in the world.

"Finch?"

"I'm here, Jolie."

"I'm sorry."

"Nothing to be sorry for."

"But you're gonna have to find a new favorite place."

"No, I won't," he stated firmly. "Because my favorite place is wherever you are."

"I love you."

"I love you right back." He kissed her forehead, then allowed the EMTs to load her into the back of the ambulance. They took one look at him and realized there was no way they could stop him from riding with her.

Chapter 28

TWO WEEKS LATER, AND Jolene felt like her lungs were nearly back to normal. It had been an eye-opening couple of weeks. Full of resilience, friendship, and love. And she had to admit she had felt a tiny sense of justice as motives became clear.

Paris Winston acted like a spoiled child who didn't get her way. Turned out, since Jolene had retained ownership of her recipes, the new chef at Noitiña couldn't replicate the level of cuisine their customers had been accustomed to. It went out of business not long after she'd opened the doors to her bar.

Despite his best efforts, Harrison had been unable to replicate the success of Noitiña with any of his new restaurant ventures. He'd driven them to near bankruptcy, spending most of his wife's money in his follies. Until one day, a few months ago, he gave up and took the easy way out. His wife had found him in his home office. According to the reports, he had shot himself in the head. He'd left a note, which the police think was what set Paris on the path of revenge. Ian had managed to get a copy of the note from the NYC detectives and showed it to her. Just three lines. No signature. *It began and ended with* Noitiña. *We never should have pushed her out. I'm sorry.*

And laying nearby was an article from the *Southwest Michigan Dine Out* magazine touting Jolene's Bar and Grill as one of the best locally owned restaurants in the area.

It was strange to think that Harrison's last thoughts were about her. She could take those words as an admission of regret for what he'd done to her. An apology, of sorts. But she wasn't deluding herself. Harrison was the type of man who never held on to regrets. And she wouldn't fool herself into thinking the *I'm sorry* was for her.

Frankly, she didn't give a shit. She'd found a new life in Lake Haven. A better life. She had friends who gave up their free time to help her rummage through the ruins of her bar for anything salvageable. Those same friends were planning fundraisers to help her rebuild, hoping to supplement what insurance didn't cover.

Then there were Emma and Marcus. They'd surprised her one day with a brand-new food truck with her logo painted on the side. They figured she could use it while she rebuilt. She could still keep her customers happy with a few of the favorite menu items. And furthermore, she could participate in the upcoming county fair.

Some of her employees understandably took new jobs but hoped to come back when she reopened. But her most dependable ones, like Ox, Nan, and Sophie, stayed and sweated it out with her in the back of the food truck. That was loyalty. Something she'd never had among her employees at Noitiña.

Finch had been by her side through it all. They had both learned a great deal about themselves over the weeks since her father's heart attack. Neither one of them had noticed how much their shame was eating away at their soul. It was an emotion that had kept them trapped at the moment the shame was born. The feeling never faded with time, and at any moment, it could drown them again. Shame had a way of lingering, waiting to pull you back and force you to relive the experience as if it was happening for the first time.

But by sharing their shame with each other, it began to wither. Shame's power lies in its unspeakable nature. The creature thrives in silence, and it preys on those who keep to themselves, feeding off their timidity, introversion, and distance from others. Secrecy is its lifeblood.

But it crumbles when exposed through conversation. Which was exactly what happened when they sat down with their Nighthawk family. Jolene knew Finch was nervous to confess to the guys about his past. They talked for hours among the two of them about their struggles with the shame parasite. Hearing Finch's whole story had been a privilege. And she knew their friends would feel the same. By virtue of who they were, they had earned the right to hear their stories. She and Finch were incredibly lucky to have found a group of friends—nay, family—who embraced their imperfections and vulnerabilities.

After the boost their friends had given their self-esteems, they couldn't keep their hands off each other. They'd barely made it through Finch's front door before clothes were flying.

Now, Jolene lay in his arms, content to be still for the first time in a long time. Even with everything that needed to be done with the bar, she was enjoying her down time. Probably far too much. Spending time with Finch, getting to know him on a deeper level, was a revelation, and she felt like she was seeing him in a whole new light. And she fell deeper every day.

She trailed her fingers through the springy hair on his chest. "I spoke to my dad today."

"Yeah? How is he?" Gorden and Finch had taken to each other, and Finch was slowly learning the Scottish vernacular her father often slipped into using.

"He's still his same old crabbity self."

Finch snorted. "No surprise there."

"Dante is keeping an eye on him. He won't let him overdo it."

"Good."

"He's selling the house."

"No shit? I thought he never wanted to sell."

"I guess our work on the house inspired him. He's decided now's the time to get out. He's realized he doesn't have the time or energy to take care of it anymore. He wants to move to a condo where everything is taken care of for him. And he's going to hire a cleaning crew. No more dusting. No more cleaning bathrooms. And he's most excited about not having to mow."

"Good for him. I guess he *can* see reason."

Jolene laughed. Her father was a stubborn mule. That was for sure. She was just glad he was making some changes. "Too bad it took a heart attack to make him see reason."

"Going through a scare like that can change a person's perspective."

She could tell he was thinking about what they'd been through. She wasn't sure if it changed her perspective or made her appreciate what she had more. "Did it change yours?"

She waited patiently as he took a moment to ponder her question. "There's no doubt that what happened was eye opening. I knew Angelica was capable of violence. I just never imagined she'd go as far as she did. And it kills me that I didn't see it sooner."

"You can't think that way."

"I know. I just wish I could have spared you all that hurt."

"Me? She hurt you more than me."

His fingers trailed up her back, sending tingles down her spine. She loved feeling his hands on her. She hoped it gave him as much comfort as it gave her.

"I've taken a lot of abuse from her over the years. I could handle most everything she's ever thrown at me. But seeing you with her knife at your throat..." Jolene lifted her head to see his face when his words dropped off. His features were pinched, his eyes squeezed shut as if he was reliving it. "And then the fire. Finding you lying there . . . Fuck, Jolie. I just . . ." His face contorted in agony, his eyebrows furrowed, and his teeth clenched together. His eyes were scrunched shut so hard that his lashes quivered. The room was filled with a heavy silence, only broken by his labored breathing. He seemed to be struggling against an invisible force, his muscles tense and his body shaking. His fist was clenched so tightly that his knuckles turned white. It was as though he was fighting a battle with the memory, and it was consuming him.

She could empathize with how he was feeling. She often woke up in a cold sweat after dreaming that they'd been too late to save him. The dream was always the same. She'd rush through that cabin door just as Angelica sank her blade into his gut. Then she'd hold him in her arms as his lifeblood drained away.

Every time she'd had the dream, she'd wake to find him right beside her. She took solace in his presence. Even in his sleep, he always seemed to sense that she needed him and pulled her closer. She'd snuggle in, breathing in his familiar scent, and feel the gentle rise and fall of his chest, and a sense of security would wash over her, lulling her back to sleep.

She rose up until she was hovering over him, her long hair sweeping down around her face. In an instant, his eyes sprang open, and she could see the pain and agony flicker across his face, causing her heart to clench. The torment in his eyes was palpable, almost as if she could reach out and touch it.

There was only one thing she could think of to say. She bracketed his face between her hands and stared into his eyes. "I love you. I'm right here. I'm safe. And I love you."

The tension in his muscles melted away almost immediately. His facial features softened as he met her gaze. The green in his eyes was so intense that it almost appeared to overpower the blue. She loved that she could tell his mood through his eyes. This was her favorite. It conveyed his feelings for her without words.

He raked his fingers through her hair, drawing it away from her face. "Jolene," he whispered. "My Jolie. I love you so much. My perception *has* changed. I see you. I see us. I see a wonderful future together. My happiness is immeasurable whenever you're near. And I can't wait to see what tomorrow brings us."

His fingers worked through her tangled hair, smoothing out the knots.

"Thank you for giving me a second chance. He leaned in close, his eyes locking on hers as he made a promise. "I won't let you down."

"I know," she replied, the sound of her voice barely audible above the soft hum of the ceiling fan. As she reached up to run her fingers through his hair, the sound of their breathing became more pronounced. She moved closer to him, feeling the warmth of his body, and she kissed him, savoring the roughness of his stubble against her lips. With each kiss, the intensity grew, a fiery passion that conveyed all their promises. The feel of his strong arms wrapping around her sent shivers down her spine, and she knew in that moment that nothing could ever tear them apart again.

Epilogue

Brodhi

“**C**AN I PET YOUR dog, mister?” The little voice came from a tiny slip of a girl with dark brown braids hanging over both shoulders. With her rosy cheeks and wide eyes, she peered up at him, looking incredibly cherubic. As he glanced down at her, he couldn’t help but feel a sense of warmth and tenderness in his heart.

He’d once dreamed of something exactly like this. A little girl at his side, staring up at him adoringly. But that was before. Before bitterness, grief, and rage shut him off from the world.

Sorcha sat at his heel, waiting for the order that would give her permission to greet someone new. Brodhi could practically feel the dog trembling with excitement. She had done well today and deserved a break from her duties.

"Sure," he answered the girl, wincing when his tone sounded more gruff than he intended. He gave a soft order to Sorcha, who sniffed the girl's proffered hand, then stood patiently as she rubbed her little hands over her coat. Sorcha wore a working vest that didn't quite cover all of her fur, leaving some exposed for petting. The girl rubbed Sorcha's ears and giggled when her tail began thumping against the ground. She'd found Sorcha's favorite spot.

The girl's infectious giggle and the vibrant scene of girl and dog in front of him made Brodhi's heart ache with bittersweet longing. He tore his gaze from the pair and looked around at the crowd of people all enjoying the county fair. Happy families. Gaggles of teenagers. Loving couples. People from all walks of life were enjoying the things the fair had to offer.

The Nighthawks had come out in full force to support one of their own. Since the fire at Jolene's, they'd rallied to help her begin the rebuilding process. She'd obtained a food truck, which had been doing a steady business throughout the week-long fair. Her employees had stuck by her side in the heat and humidity, making and serving Jolene's most popular offerings in the back of the sweltering truck. That was true dedication.

The significant others of Nighthawks team members had come out for Jolene as well. Natalie, Brodhi's boss's fiancée, had set up a booth to sell her paintings, while Sutton, who was Tin Man's girl, was selling her photographs nearby. The profits generated from the sales were dedicated to supporting Jolene's rebuilding fund.

Helicopter rides were being offered at the fair, with Finch and Hollynn taking turns as pilots. The profits were once again slated for Jolene's.

Even Brodhi himself was doing his part. He'd set up a course to showcase Sorcha's search and rescue skills. She'd been a big hit with the kids. During one part of their "show," he'd ask for audience participation, usually from a kid. He'd get Sorcha to get the kid's scent, then cover Sorcha's eyes and have the kid hide. She'd never failed to find them, much to their delight. The jar he'd set up for donations, which he'd pledged to Jolene's rebuilding fund, had overflowed each day.

"What's his name?" the little girl asked, bringing his attention back to the pair. Sorcha was now in full dog ecstasy, lying on her back as she got her belly rubbed, her tongue lolling out of her mouth.

"*Her* name is Sorcha," Brodhi answered.

When Sorcha licked her cheek in greeting, she giggled and said, "Hi, Sorcha."

"She likes you."

"Of course she does. All animals like me," she replied with the confidence only a young person had.

"All animals?"

"Yup. I help my mom with the animals all the time. They love me."

Brodhi looked around for the girl's parents. Not seeing any adult hovering nearby, he asked, "Is your mom here somewhere?"

"She's back at our tent."

"What tent?"

"The sanctuary tent."

He had no idea what she meant by "the sanctuary tent," and he didn't like the idea of leaving the girl out here by herself. It seemed irresponsible to let someone so young wander around the fair by herself. The girl couldn't be any older than ten, and this world had far too many predators to take the risk.

"Can you show me?"

The girl popped to her feet, and he struggled with a moment of envy. Oh, to have knees that moved so easily again. "Sure. Follow me."

Brodhi ordered Sorcha to heel, and they walked with the girl to a large tent on the outskirts of the fair. As they approached, he could both hear and smell the animals. The unique aroma of a shabby petting zoo. Sorcha's ears twitched as she took in the sounds of numerous animals.

The girl bounced into the tent, full of energy, greeting the animals as she passed as if they were old friends.

"Shiloh!" a woman shouted from the back. "Where have you been? You know you're not allowed to wander around the fair by yourself."

The woman dropped to her knees in front of her daughter and grabbed her in a hug. The mom's back was to Brodhi, but the resemblance between the two was clear. They had the same dark brown hair plaited into the same type of braids. He was surprised they weren't dressed alike. But the woman was in a pair of jeans that hugged her ass just right as she crouched in front of her daughter. Brodhi quickly pulled his gaze away from that sight and noticed the heavy combat-type boots on her feet. A strange choice in footwear for a woman. "I'm sorry, Mommy. I forgot."

She then held her daughter at arm's length, her hands gripping the girl's upper arms. She raked her gaze over Shiloh as if to assure herself her daughter was in one piece.

"You forgot," she admonished. "How could you forget something like that? It's the same rule we talk about every day. I swear, you'll be the death of me." The exasperation was clear in the woman's voice. As if they'd had this discussion numerous times.

"You know you're grounded, right?"

Shiloh dropped her gaze to her feet. "Yes, Mommy. I know."

"Okay, then. You can start cleaning out the bunny cages."

Brodhi cleared his throat, and the woman startled and looked over her shoulder at him. A stunning pair of blue eyes met his. A familiar set of blue eyes.

Marnee Monroe.

Rage consumed him like a wildfire. His fists clenched, and he gritted his teeth as he stared at the woman he'd hoped to never cross paths with again. She had played a significant role in his anger, and it was something he'd never been able to shake off. He still felt her betrayal as if it was yesterday.

"Brodhi," she gasped, rising quickly to her feet. The disbelief and apprehension in her voice was clear.

"Look, Mommy. This is Sorcha. Isn't she pretty?" Shiloh beamed, coming to pet Sorcha again.

Without taking her gaze away from him, she answered her daughter, "Very pretty dog. It's time to say goodbye to Sorcha and begin your chores. The bunnies are waiting for you."

"Okay." The disappointment couldn't be missed in the girl's expression. She gave Sorcha a hug, saying, "Bye, pretty girl. I hope I'll see you again." Then she turned those brilliant blue eyes on him. The same hue as her mother's. Eyes that lived in his dreams. And his nightmares. "Bye, mister."

He gave her a soft look and waved goodbye as she raced away toward where he could only assume the bunny cages were.

Turning his attention back to Shiloh's mother, the softness he'd felt for the daughter evaporated into something hard. "She was wandering around the fairgrounds by herself. What kind of mother lets their kid do something like that?" He knew his words were harsh, but he couldn't hold them back. The anger he felt because of everything he'd lost—everything this woman had a hand in destroying—was all consuming.

Her body tensed up, and she visibly bristled, throwing her shoulders back. "Not this mother," she stated through gritted teeth. "She slipped away without my knowledge when I was working with the animals."

"They let you work with animals again?" He could see the barb hit where it hurt.

If it was even possible, her spine stiffened further. She yanked on the bottom of her long-sleeved T-shirt in agitation. Jesus, it was in the mid-eighties. He was sweating just standing in the shade of the tent. What kind of person wore long sleeves in this heat?

"I have every right to work with animals," she argued.

"Not in my book."

"I had nothing to do with what happened."

"Tell it to someone who cares," he threw at her, then turned and walked out of the tent, Sorcha following dutifully beside him. He looked down at his best friend, feeling her confusion. Sorcha was very intuitive and could pick up on how he was feeling. Brodhi was sure he was sending out all sorts of mixed signals for the dog to sense.

Marnee Monroe had lived in his head for far too long. It was time for her to be ousted just like she deserved.

Finch

Finch retrieved a bag of gummy worms from his pocket, the sweet smell of sugar and artificial flavors wafting up to him. He took out a red and yellow one, the same colors that he'd shared with Jolene on their flight down to Georgia, and popped it into his mouth. The memory made him smile. Communication may have been strained, but they still had that common ground. He knew at that moment he had a chance to win her heart again.

As he chewed, he finished shutting everything down after the last helicopter ride of the day. He was ready to see his girl. In order to experience the fair themselves, they both decided to take the evening off from their responsibilities. He couldn't wait to spend the evening partaking in all the goodies and rides with Jolene. The fair they'd attended in Georgia had been a lot of fun and had brought them closer than ever. He was eager to recreate the experience, but they would avoid the heavy talk about his ex this time.

They were going to leave all the heavy stuff behind and just enjoy their time together. After crazy kidnapping exes, scorned women turned arsonists, fires, and floods, they were more than ready to have a fun evening. But since that thought popped into his head, he couldn't help but remember the days that had followed the fire.

Angelica was awaiting trial for kidnapping, attempted murder and a host of other charges. He wasn't looking forward to the day when he'd have to testify to what he'd been through with his ex-wife. Thankfully, he'd have the support of his Nighthawk friends.

Previously, the thought of having to explain anything to the group of intimidating men was too much to bear. The thought alone had made him feel small and insignificant, like a mouse in the presence of lions. It felt like an indignity he wasn't prepared to face. He'd braced himself for the weight of their judgment, but it never came. It was something he should have realized from the very beginning of his employment with the Nighthawks.

They were a stand-up group of men. They listened. They supported. They put his mind at ease, telling him he had nothing to be ashamed of. Then they moved on.

Jolene had been right. The shame was not his to bear.

Paris Winston was still being evaluated to see if she was competent to stand trial. He had his doubts that she was mentally insane. She seemed like the manipulative type. He should know. He'd lived with one for ten years. As far as he was concerned, the woman was guilty as hell and should spend the rest of her days locked up. He didn't care whether it was in a mental facility or a jail cell.

He'd never forgive her for nearly killing Jolene. The memory of Angelica's cruelty toward Jolene lingered in his heart, and he knew he could never forgive her either.

He strongly believed that Jolene deserved justice for all the wrongs that had been inflicted upon her. Especially at the hands of the Winston family. It was too bad Harrison had offed himself and robbed Jolene of that justice.

As he finished up his final checks on his helicopter, he heard his name being called. He turned just in time to catch Jolene as she threw herself into his arms. Her lips were on his before he could say hello, and she wrapped her legs around his waist, clinging to him. And he was completely okay with that. His response to her kiss was filled with fervent desire. He'd missed her today.

When she broke the kiss, he grinned. "Now that's a greeting I could get used to."

She laughed heartily, throwing her head back. The sunlight played with the gold highlights in her red hair, making them glimmer. She had a way of making his heart swell with love every time he saw her. *I'm a lucky guy.*

"Darn tootin'." He laughed at her reply, having not realized he'd spoken out loud. "And I'm the luckiest girl."

"Darn tootin'." He kissed her again, and she enthusiastically returned it. He was seriously debating skipping the fair and taking Jolene home. To bed.

"Not happening, Romeo," she said, as if she'd read his mind. "I want fair food."

"But I'm hungry for something else," he complained, nuzzling her neck, momentarily transported to an orchard of orange trees. He hoped she never changed whatever product she used to give her that scent.

"That can wait," she said playfully as he continued to kiss her neck.

He pressed his hardness against her center, perfectly aligned with her legs around his waist. He palmed her ass, feeling the heat of her body through the linen shorts. A smile played across his lips as she moaned. "Are you sure about that?"

Her sunny yellow tank top dipped low in front, revealing a generous view of her ample breasts. He wanted to bury his face in them. Pulling his head from her neck, he glanced around. They were alone out here on the far edge of the fairgrounds. What would be the harm in a little taste?

He turned them and pushed her back up against the side of his helicopter and buried his face in her neck once more. But he didn't stop there. Trailing his lips across her throat, he moved downward over the swell of her breast.

"Finch," she moaned. He couldn't tell whether she was scolding him to stop or begging him to continue. He went with the latter. With her propped up against the helicopter, he could have a free hand to explore. He pulled the strap of her tank top aside and halfway down her arm, exposing her silk-covered breast. The material did nothing to mask her arousal as he could see the prominent peak of her nipple, which he promptly took into his mouth. He sucked and played with the bud until she was squirming against him.

He cleared his throat before speaking, his voice husky and raw. "You ever make love in a helicopter?"

Her shudder betrayed her, revealing that the idea had sparked something inside her. Guess she'd forgotten all about getting fair food to eat.

Not bothering to wait for an answer, he pulled the rear door open. Flashing an alluring smile, she dropped her feet to the ground and climbed into the back seat, ready for the ride ahead. And what a ride it was going to be.

As he followed, he slammed the door shut, creating a bubble of privacy around them. With the door closed, the noise from the fair was muffled. The faint laughter of children and the occasional roar of a ride were now subdued, as if heard from a far-off land. Finch's heart raced with excitement and anticipation, but it wasn't because of the thrilling fair rides.

It was all for the vivacious redhead beside him. His dick throbbed, unhappy with its confinement behind his cargo shorts. He tried to send it a message to cool its jets, but then Jolene whipped her shirt off over her head. The bra was next. Then she wiggled on her seat, and her shorts and panties ended up on the floor next to the other discarded items.

His mouth went dry, taking in every inch of her gorgeousness. There was no containing his dick now. It knew what was coming next. With a growl, he pulled her onto his lap, her legs straddling him.

"Why do you still have clothes on?" she asked, working her hands under his T-shirt. He raised his arms over his head, allowing her to pull it off. Setting his hands on her hips, he pulled her tight against him and bent to take a nipple in his mouth again, this time without the barrier of her bra.

As he teased her breasts, first one, then the other, he felt her fingers at his stomach as she struggled to undo his belt. He helped her, moving his lips to capture hers. He loved the whimper that fell from her lips when she struggled with the button on his pants. Taking pity on her, he assisted her with the fastening, then the zipper. She reached inside his boxers and pulled his cock out. He moaned and thrust into her hand, which she'd wrapped around him. He nearly lost it when she used her thumb to spread the bit of pre-come that leaked from the tip around the shaft.

Unable to wait a moment longer to bury himself deep inside her, he lifted her by her hips. She held his cock firmly as she lowered herself onto him, taking her time to savor every inch. Slowly and deliberately, she took him in, and he reveled in the sensation of being completely surrounded by her. Once firmly seated, her eyes shuttered.

She began a slow rhythm, her head thrown back while she worked herself on him. He watched her take her pleasure, unable to take his eyes off the sight before him. With the rosy flush on her chest and cheeks and her red hair hanging in a curtain down her back, she was pure fire. And he wanted to experience the burn.

Losing her bar the way she did hadn't dowsed her inner flame. It burned brighter and hotter. The determination he saw in her to persevere and rebuild was intoxicating. It was her own personal brand of justice. Her unwavering resolve and confidence sent a clear message to those who tried to mess with her—she wouldn't be defeated.

He found it sexy as hell.

She picked up her pace, and he could tell she was nearly there, so he had to amend his thoughts about what he found sexy. Jolene, shattering into a million pieces around him, topped the list. Before she'd even started the descent, he took over, holding her hips in place while he thrust up into her. Her tits bounced in his face, and he couldn't resist taking a hard bud into his mouth and sucking hard. The noises she made spurred him on, taking her up and over with him. Her second ride to the peak of the day.

He found himself on the edge too quickly, his breaths coming in short gasps as he emptied himself inside her with a low grunt.

As she collapsed against his chest, he wrapped his arms around her, holding her close. She leaned heavily against him, her breaths shaky and uneven. She pressed her lips against his throat, and he felt the corners of her mouth turn upward.

"Best ride at the fair," she teased.

"Darn tootin'."

They stayed together, enjoying the quiet, until Finch remembered the gift he had for her. "Hey, I've got something for you."

"Hmm? What?"

Without dislodging the naked woman on his lap, he dug in his pants pocket for her gift. She laughed the moment she saw the colorful snack bag.

"You got me gummy bears."

"I still don't think they're as good as worms."

She tore open the bag and popped a red one into her mouth. "You are so wrong. Bears are far superior."

"Worms last longer. And they're ribbed for your pleasure."

Her laughter echoed through the helicopter as she threw her head back with abandon. Her carefree spirit was infectious, and he felt his heart swell with love for her as he watched her laugh. Witnessing her like this was nothing short of a miracle after a year of her shutting him out. He hoped there would always be laughter and joy.

Unable to resist, he kissed her. She tasted sweet, like the gummy bear, and he wanted to feast on her.

"Mmm. So good," she murmured against his lips. "More, please."

He chuckled and replied, "A little indulgence never hurt anybody." Then took her mouth in another scorching kiss.

They'd eventually get out and enjoy the real fair rides, but for right now, this moment was everything. They'd survived a lot together. As they battled through the elements, their love burned bright, an unquenched flame in the storm.

Read On For A Preview of Protecting You, A Novella From The Crash Into You Shared Series

Protecting You

Chapter 1

Aiden

"How'd it go last night with that girl?" Stu, whose voice was already a bit slurred, asked after he had slammed their fourth pitcher of beer down onto the table.

"Man, she was *hot*. You always get the good ones," Danny complained.

"Hot but dense," Colin said while refilling his beer stein. He wobbled slightly, and the amber liquid spilled over the rim, forming a puddle on the table, which went unnoticed. Clearly, the guys were headed toward getting completely wasted.

To mark the end of our college years, my buddies and I were out celebrating. In a month, I'd be heading off to bootcamp. This was our last hurrah all together.

"Yeah, so?" Danny asked.

"I may be desperate," he replied, his voice tight, "but I couldn't go there with her."

"Fuck. It's not like you had to commit to her."

"She thought buffalo wings came from actual buffaloes," Colin deadpanned, which sent all of us into a fit of uproarious laughter.

While my buddies argued over the merits of fucking someone dumber than dirt, a commotion snagged my attention. Across the patio, a voice shattered the air like broken glass. "You fucker!"

A girl stood there, unwavering, as she faced a man who loomed over her. Long dark hair pulled up in a messy knot, dark eyes flashing hotter than the string lights overhead. Her tank top hugged her frame, while her denim skirt barely brushed the tops of her thighs. At the moment she didn't look like someone you'd want to cross, despite being maybe five-three on a good day.

And right now, she was ripping into the tall blond guy in front of her like she had a personal vendetta. I shifted my beer to my other hand and leaned against the railing, watching her go.

The man's lips curled into a grin, one that was far from welcoming. "Here comes Ashley's attack dog. Should've known you'd stick your nose in. Relax, Charlie. I was just saying hi to my ex."

Charlie's voice didn't waver as she stepped in front of her friend. "Go inside, Ash. Now." She didn't take her eyes off the guy as Ashley bolted toward the door, clutching her purse. Smart move. Now if only this Charlie chick would do the same.

I set my beer on the table, already shifting my weight forward. Charlie had guts, but this was a big guy, and I'd seen enough nights end ugly when somebody decided to throw their weight around.

Charlie stepped up, folded her arms, and planted her boots. "Somebody has to, Robbie," she snapped, and the flicker of annoyance in the guy's eyes showed he either didn't care for her tone or the childish shortening of his name. "You don't get to stalk her like this."

His smile flattened. "I'm just trying to talk to my girlfriend."

"Does talking usually come with drugging someone's drink?" A wave of gasps rippled through the crowd.

Robbie's grin slipped. His eyes flicked toward the glass then back at Charlie.

"You're imagining things," he said. "Ashley and I are just talking. She needed a little help remembering who she belongs to."

Charlie's voice dropped an octave, edged with steel. "She doesn't *belong* to you. And if you think spiking her drink is going to change her mind, you're not just pathetic, you're about two steps away from a felony."

A muscle twitched in Robbie's jaw. "You've got a big mouth for a bitch who's about to get in over her head."

Charlie didn't move. "I'm not afraid of you, so I'll speak my mind, even if it's loud," she stated, her voice carrying across the area.

The patio had gone quiet; the small crowd of students watched while the tension amped up. "Stay out of it, Charlie," the guy growled, his hands fisting at his side. Not a good sign. I tensed, ready to step in if needed. I wasn't about to stand by and watch a dick with an over-inflated ego hurt a woman.

"Fuck you, Robbie," she snapped, loud enough that even more heads turned. "You cheat on her then act like you're the victim. Ashley deserves better than a lying piece of shit like you." She stepped closer to him, chin tilted up like a general on the battlefield. She was either oblivious to the potential danger or brave as fuck. "I know you liked smacking her around. Never again. You come near her again, and I swear I'll make sure everyone in this town knows what a pathetic and abusive fucking fraud you are."

My buddy Danny whistled low. "Whoa. That chick's got guts, I'll give her that."

"I think I'm in love," Stu slurred.

"She may think she's brave, but she's incredibly stupid," I stated, the words hanging in the air as Robbie's features tightened. "That guy's twice her size."

"Nah," Danny replied. "She's got this."

I didn't answer. Couldn't, really. I was too busy watching the girl. She was fierce. Gorgeous, with dark lashes, high cheekbones, a mouth that looked made for both kissing and telling a guy off. But it was the fire in her that got to me. Most people would have walked away or whispered in the corner. Not her. She stood there, legs planted like she was ready to take on a linebacker. And that's what worried me the most.

"That night was a mistake," he said, as if the words were law.

Charlie rolled her eyes with such theatrical precision that it was visible from one end of the patio to the other. "That's what every cheating, abusive asshole says." She crossed her arms over her chest, which pushed her generous tits up. My gaze lingered, drawn to the elegant lines of her figure. She was stunning. Unfortunately, I wasn't the only one ogling her ample wares. Robbie, the dickhead, gaped, and Charlie's eyes followed his gaze before narrowing dangerously.

It was as if the whole place held its breath, waiting for her next move.

"You are not seriously staring at my tits right now," she spat. "You're more of an asshole than I thought. And believe me, I already thought you were lower than pond scum."

Robbie mirrored Charlie's posture, arms folded, as a smirk crept across his face. He drawled, "I'm a man," his tone dripping with the weight of his ego, as if that single phrase absolved him of his dickish behavior. "Ashley will forgive me. She'll never walk away from me like that." Where this man got his confidence from was beyond me. He drugs a girl's drink and still thinks he's all that? The audacity.

"This guy gives men a bad rep," Danny mused, and I couldn't agree more.

Charlie wasn't having it either. Even with her small frame, she appeared to loom larger as she squared her shoulders and narrowed her eyes. "Maybe that's what you believe, but she's not property. And she sure as hell isn't coming back—especially after this little stunt."

Robbie's grin vanished. He shifted his weight forward, taking one deliberate, heavy step toward her. His shadow loomed over her in the string light's glow. "Someone needs to teach you about respect—"

That was far enough. I stepped out of the shadows and closed the distance in three strides. My hand landed on his shoulder, firm enough to push him back a half-step. "Back off," I said. My voice came out low and even. "You take one more step toward her and you're going to regret it."

He twisted his neck to glare at me, but when he saw I wasn't bluffing, his bravado faltered. The large crowd of onlookers might have had a hand in that as well.

Charlie didn't move. Her arms were still crossed, chin tipped up, eyes fixed on the dickhead. She looked fierce as hell. Fierce and, yeah, beautiful. The kind of beautiful that hit you in the chest before you had time to think about it.

I couldn't let that fierceness get her hurt.

"Go," she told Robbie, voice like a blade. "Before you make tonight worse for yourself."

For a long second he just stood there, glaring between us. Then he spat a curse and stalked off toward the parking lot.

I didn't take my eyes off him until he was gone, then turned to Charlie. "You okay?"

She let out a slow breath, some of the tension draining from her shoulders. "Yeah. Thanks."

I looked her up and down, from her head to her toes, telling myself that I was just assessing her for any potential injuries. A faint bruise along the side of her thigh where the hem of her skirt rode up caught my eye. A roundish mark, not fresh enough to be new, but not old either.

Something in my chest tightened. I didn't know her. I didn't know how she got it. But I hated that it was there.

Charlie shifted, rubbing her upper arm, as if the adrenaline had finally drained out of her. I caught myself taking a step toward her and stopped.

What was I going to do? Introduce myself? Try to make her laugh? I'd be shipping out for the Army in a month. I'd been laser-focused on that for years. No distractions, and definitely no commitments. It wouldn't be fair to start something when I was about to leave.

The patio slowly went back to its usual buzz. I nodded to the table, still littered with remnants of the night's appetizer fest, where my friends and I had spent the past few hours. "Join us for a beer?" I asked, and the hope that bubbled up inside both startled and irritated me, like a sudden itch.

"Sure, why not," she replied. As we made our way to the table, I felt a strong desire to guide her with a hand on her back. I resisted the impulse, heading to the bar and grabbing a couple of empty glasses instead.

"I'm Aiden," I said as I poured a glass of beer from a freshly supplied pitcher, which I assumed one of the guys had refilled, and placed it in front of her. "Figured you deserved this."

"Charlie," she replied eyeing the beer, then me. "Not drugged, is it?"

I grinned. "Not unless you count the hops." That earned a small laugh out of her. The first one I'd heard tonight, and a peculiar flutter seized my chest.

She took a healthy sip. "Thanks. I *did* need that. Usually, I'm not the one breaking up a crime scene at a bar."

"Could've fooled me. You handled that like a pro."

Her eyes sparkled, amused. "You mean like a loudmouth who can't let idiots get away with things?" She lifted her beer in a toast. "Thanks for playing backup. You didn't have to do that."

With a tap of my glass against hers, I accepted her gratitude even though it was unnecessary. "I couldn't just stand there and let him try anything. It kind of goes against my programming."

Her lips quirked. "Programming? You a robot?"

"Future Army," I said, tapping the rim of my glass. "Shipping out in a few weeks. They don't exactly encourage sitting on your hands."

Her brows went up. "Ah, that explains the whole heroic-step-in vibe... and the arms."

I chuckled, glancing at the appendages in question, and couldn't help but flex. The sleeves of my shirt stretched taut as my biceps strained against them. Suddenly, all the hard work I'd put into sculpting my body was worth it. "Not complaining about the compliment."

She smirked. "Just saying. You look like you could bench-press Robbie and still have enough energy to rock climb."

I gave her a look. "I'm just the muscle," I deadpanned with self-deprecating humor. "But you were the fierce one back there. Scary as hell, too."

"Just doing my part to rid the world of assholes, one dickhead at a time," she declared, and sipped again.

I liked the way her confidence sat on her. It was easy and unforced. Dangerous, in the best way. But that could also come back to bite her in the ass, which worried me more than it should.

Ashley came back out just then, calmer now, and Charlie waved her over. Following a private conversation and a warm embrace, Ashley turned her attention to him. "I hope I'm not interrupting," Ashley said, her eyes flicking over the space between Charlie and me that had seemingly shrunk as we'd talked.

"Just making sure your best friend is rewarded for her good deed of the day," I said.

"Another day in the life of Charlie Donahue," Ashley remarked, which made me think the previous drama wasn't a one-time event.

"Hopefully, we can keep her out of trouble tonight," I said, my voice thick with the sudden longing to keep Charlie safe beyond just tonight.

Charlie shot me a side-glance. "Oh, you think you can keep me in line?"

"Pretty sure I'd have my hands full trying."

Ashley laughed and claimed the chair beside Charlie. My buddies wandered over with more beers and joined us. Once introductions were made, the beer flowed freely, and the boisterous laughter of my buddies echoed throughout the entire space. The mood shifted into that warm, slightly tipsy bar-patio vibe.

At one point, Charlie leaned closer to me across the little table, eyes glinting. "So... you always swoop in like that, or was I just lucky tonight?"

I smirked. "I'll call it good timing. But if you want to think of me as your personal bodyguard, I'm not going to argue."

"Careful," she shot back. "A girl could get used to that."

"Boot camp in a few weeks," I reminded her with a crooked smile.

"Ah, yes. That certainly presents a challenge," she retorted with a grin.

That smile stuck with me even as my friends pulled me into a story and the table filled with easy chatter. I laughed in the right places, tossed in a joke or two, but a part of my mind kept circling back to her—the way she'd stood her ground, the quick wit behind the smile.

I could feel it happening. A pull toward her that was too fast and sure to put the brakes on. But underneath it all was the constant reminder I couldn't shake. In a few short weeks, I'd be gone, and boot camp didn't leave room for falling for someone.

I took another sip of my drink, trying to push the thought aside and just enjoy the night. For now, that was enough.

The patio had thinned out, the music inside faded to a muffled thump. Most of my buddies had already called it a night. Ashley had gotten a ride with another friend, leaving Charlie and me lingering near the door.

"Come on," I said, stuffing my hands in my jeans pockets. "I'll walk you to your car."

She raised an eyebrow but didn't argue. "Soldier instinct again?"

"Call it good manners."

The air outside had that dew-covered bite that only showed up after midnight. A single harsh streetlamp illuminated the lot, casting shadows that danced unevenly.

We reached her car, an older hatchback that looked like it had seen one too many road trips. She leaned back against the driver's side door, her arms crossing loosely over her chest. The lot was quiet except for a distant engine on the street.

"Thanks for... you know." Her eyes lifted to mine, serious now. "For stepping in."

I shifted a little closer, hands still in my pockets. "Couldn't have lived with myself if I hadn't. Besides... you were worth stepping in for."

That got a slow smile out of her. Compared to the ones that she had been throwing throughout the night, this one was more intimate. "Careful, Army. That almost sounded like a line."

"Not a line." My voice came out a little rougher than I intended. "Just a fact."

For a second, neither of us moved. She tilted her chin up, and in that moment, I stopped thinking about boot camp, about leaving in a few weeks, about anything except the way she was looking at me.

It would've been easy to lean into it if I weren't already halfway out the door to a whole different life.

I could practically taste her on my lips already. If I just leaned a little closer...

I angled my head to the right, and instead of tasting those luscious lips, I gently kissed her cheek. The look of disappointment beneath her startled expression nearly made me cave.

For tonight, though, I decided I'd let it be what it was—a moment worth remembering.

Nighthawks Search and Rescue

Nadia's Nemesis (Prequel)

Natalie's Nighthawk

Annika's Aurora

Emma's Element

Sutton's Shadow

Hollynn's Horizon

Sophie's Song

Jolene's Justice

Marnee's Mission (Coming Soon)

Condor's Overwatch

Freeing Camila

Freeing Savannah

Freeing Lark (Coming soon)

Freeing Melanie (Coming soon)

Freeing Skylar (Coming soon)

Freeing Kali (Coming soon)

Freeing Haley (Coming soon)

Shared Worlds

One Weekend on Mackinac Island

Protecting You: Crash Into You

Reid: Foxy's Rent-A-Date

Acknowledgements

Dear Reader, Thank you so much for taking this wild ride with me and allowing me to tell this story that means so much to me. I appreciate you taking the time out of your life and offering a piece of yourself to these words and these pages. Your enthusiasm and love for my characters makes this job a joy to do and your support means the world to me.

Did you enjoy Finch and Jolene's story?

People are often hesitant to try new books or new authors. Honest reviews of my books help bring them to the attention of other readers and encourage them to make that leap and give it a try. If you've enjoyed this book, I'd be eternally grateful if you could spend just a few minutes leaving a review on any or all of the following sites to help this story find the readers who would enjoy it. Goodreads, Bookbub, Amazon. Even the short reviews really make an impact.

I would also like to acknowledge the following without who this book would not be possible.

Laetitia Treseng of Little Tweaks and the OG of beta readers, whose advice and prodding have gone a long way to fluff up this story.

Jenni Bara and AJ Ranney, the best beta readers who never hesitate to tell me the truth. I look forward to reading your future books as well.

Beth Lawton, my editor who tirelessly works to clean up my manuscripts. I always thought I was good with the commas. Who knew I was so wrong?

My family, who more often than not, leave me alone long enough so that I can commune with the voices in my head.

About The Author

Amanda Zook has been devouring romance novels since middle school—first cutting her teeth on the old "bodice rippers" but soon finding the kind with slow burns, high stakes, and a healthy dose of danger. Now, after years of letting fictional couples chase each other around her imagination, she's finally giving them a place on the page.

Raised in the Sweetest Place on Earth (Hershey, Pennsylvania), Amanda attended a small liberal arts college where she met the love of her life—no dramatic plot twist necessary. Together, they spent the first twenty years of marriage on the Jersey Shore (the *real* one, not the one with spray tans and club fights), before relocating halfway across the country.

These days, she lives in the southwest corner of the mitten state, right on the shores of Lake Michigan—no sharks, no salt, just sunsets that deserve their own epilogues. She's a proud wife, the slightly overwhelmed mom of teenage twin girls, and a firm believer that true love should come with emotional scars, second chances, and the occasional explosion.

When she's not writing swoony heroes and fearless heroines who fall in love while dodging bullets, Amanda can be found reading her favorite romantic suspense novels, sipping too much Coke (never Pepsi), and wondering why her kids hate both reading *and* pizza.

You can find her at http://www.amandazook.com or email her at amandazook@amandazook.com